The Deathly Network

Aiden Dufort

ISBN: 978-1-62420-876-8

Cover Art: Designs by Ms G
Editor: Sherry Derr-Wille

Chapter One

Swiss biotech multibillionaire and philanthropist Peter Carli's private jet glided through the snowy clouds over Miami. A painting hung on the cabin's wall rattled. Its silver frame reflected a shaft of sunlight from the window, piercing the eyelids of the passenger sitting on a white leather chair. The checkered-patterned cushion slipped from his head as art dealer Alex Hubert opened his eyes, swallowing hard.

I shouldn't have fallen asleep.

He jumped up from the chair. The seatbelt's buckle dropped to the floor with a thud. Alex's eyes landed on the multicolored painting hanging on the wall. It was a piece of contemporary art—a collage of fake Leonardo Da Vinci drawings of human organs. Each organ was painted in sparkling colors, shining like jewels.

This isn't the painting I'm in charge of. I gotta protect S. L. Babel's new digital art.

The airplane sank and shook again. Alex stumbled, crawling to the cabinet along the plane's wall. The forty-inch monitor on the cabinet was playing the movie *Scarface*. As Alex pulled the cabinet door, actor Al Pacino barked, a gunshot erupting from the monitor. Alex's heart raced then calmed when the cabinet door swung open.

A huge briefcase encasing American digital artist S. L. Babel's work, which Alex picked up at Geneva Freeport, lay in the dark corner of the cabinet. The golden 3-dial combination lock glinted. Alex even remembered the position of the tiny specks of dust that had surrounded the briefcase before departure from Geneva, Switzerland. Nobody had touched the case.

"Alex, what are you doing? Do you think someone stole Babel's new work while you were sleeping?"

A hoarse voice reverberated from behind Alex. His eyes traveled over the damask carpet toward another plush armchair near the shower room. Peter Carli put his cappuccino cup on the saucer, staring at him. Alex rubbed his misty eyes. Contemporary art imitating Da Vinci's piece, luxurious interior décor, the roaring engine of the airplane, and S. L. Babel's digital art in the cabinet... The tiny pieces started to come together in Alex's drowsy mind. Alex was in the airplane owned by the Peter Carli Foundation, which aimed to distribute anti-HIV medicines developed by Peter's biotech company to the Global South. By using his philanthropic organization, Peter didn't need to pay property taxes for this plane. Moreover, Peter was actively buying expensive pieces of art in Geneva Freeport—a warehouse in Geneva where the trade of artwork wasn't subject to taxes—and moving them outside Switzerland using this private jet.

Alex jerked his head, looking up at the cabin's ceiling covered with a painting. It was a portrait of Peter's wife, created by a contemporary artist ranked among the top ten on artprice.com. The blond, slim woman with an olive scarf, thirty-seven years younger than Peter, smiled nonchalantly, looking down at Alex. A diamond necklace shone between her collarbones.

Suddenly, a memory of his first meeting with silver-haired Peter Carli in his mansion along Lake Geneva flashed in Alex's mind. They were sitting on black-leathered plush sofas in the drawing room. Through the French windows, Alex could see Peter's wife taking a walk with her Golden Retriever in the garden along Lake Geneva. As her dog dived into the fountain with a Venus statue, Peter started to talk to him.

"*Alex, as you know, Swiss matrimonial law isn't applied to offshore assets held by a trust registered outside Switzerland.*"

Peter's deep voice from three months ago resounded in Alex's mind like hot waves.

"*You know what I mean?*" Peter continued, dropping his voice, his eyes maliciously flashing. "*I want to divorce her. But I don't want to pay for her at all. That's why I want to buy great pieces of art and keep them outside Switzerland. I heard you're the best art dealer in U.S. business. I'm happy to offer you four hundred thousand dollars annually if you help me with this deal.*"

"*Peter, can I ask why you want to divorce her? She's so beautiful,*" Alex asked quietly, eyeing his wife dragging her Golden Retriever out of the fountain.

"*There are only two things that billionaires can't buy on the planet. And neither is love—I bought her love, you know,*" Peter Carli said gruffly, rubbing his chin covered with a silver beard. "*They are health and youth. It's inevitable that I'll die someday. But when I die, my money should be used to fund my unfinished endeavors. I don't wanna bequeath my fortune to my wife, who doesn't understand my noble mission. I wanna pour most of my assets into the Peter Carli Foundation and its scientific research. Is that clear?*"

"*Fair enough,*" said Alex, pretending to be calm. "*What kind of art would you like to collect? I'd recommend classical paintings. They should be stable assets…*"

"*I wanna buy the works of S. L. Babel, the rising and secret American digital artist,*" said Peter enthusiastically.

"*Why?*" Alex was so surprised that he nearly lifted off the sofa.

He thought it would be risky to invest in S. L. Babel's digital artwork, as the prices had skyrocketed in recent auctions at Christie's and Sotheby's in New York and London. Alex thought it was merely a fad.

Peter Carli became silent for a while, his arms crossed. His wife's Golden Retriever rushed toward the French windows of the drawing room, barking at the guest, Alex Hubert. Peter's wife screamed at the dog in French. "*Non, non! Arrête!*" ("*No, no! Stop!*")

"*I like Babel's vision in his art,*" Peter said in a low voice.

Alex sensed Peter didn't want to reveal his real intention to buy Babel's works. Peter continued without a pause. "*Let's talk about the procedure to move artworks from Geneva Freeport to the US. I have a private jet, which is useful for hiding expensive pieces of art.*"

As Alex got to his feet, the soft sound from the fountain in Peter's mansion receded. The cobalt-blue Lake Geneva, stretching beyond the garden, vanished like melted paint. The raucous sound of the airplane's engine filled his ears. He felt the floor shaking and lurching.

"YOU ARE IN MY PRIVATE JET, ALEX!" roared Peter Carli, who was sitting on the armchair in the cabin, stretching his arms as if to show off his own land. "Nobody can steal anything here. And nobody can kill you."

"No, nobody can kill me!" shrieked Alex Hubert, a slight chill rippling down his back.

"You must be careful after landing in Miami, though. All the art dealers who took S. L. Babel's works out of Geneva Freeport died suspiciously," said Peter Carli drily, hitting the Enter key on his MacBook Air on the side table. "Did you read this article?"

The monitor on the cabinet, which had been displaying *Scarface*, switched to an online article from the *New York Times*. The headline read, "THE MYSTERIOUS DEATH OF AN ART DEALER WHO TRADED SECRET DIGITAL ARTIST S. L. BABEL'S WORKS." Three weeks ago, a famous art dealer in New York was found dead. His death was ruled a suicide by overdose.

"I know about this incident. And I knew this art dealer very well," said Alex, passing his tongue over his dry lips. "He was my friend, but a rival in business at the same time. He was a very ambitious dealer who constantly discovered contemporary art pieces at Art Basel in Switzerland and sold them to American billionaires."

"Do you believe he committed suicide?" asked Peter, shifting in his armchair.

"Absolutely not," snapped Alex. "He really loved money, just like me. He was devoting his life to bringing new art from around the world and making money in America. You know, Americans who truly love money and victory never surrender to anything. We never give up. We never commit suicide."

"I agree," said Peter, sipping his cappuccino and straightening his body. "By the way, this art dealer wasn't the only person who suspiciously died. Billionaire investor and collector Hoyt Pence, who bought Babel's work for nine million dollars from this dealer, also died on his yacht. This article says Hoyt crashed his motor yacht into a rugged sea rock lying seven miles off Neptune Memorial Reef in Florida."

"Nobody believes it was an accident," said Alex slyly.

"Have you ever seen the S. L. Babel work Hoyt bought?" asked Peter.

"Not yet," answered Alex blankly.

Peter scrolled down the monitor's screen. A video of Christie's auction house popped up. An auctioneer had hit the gavel. The deceased art collector victoriously raised his hands among the excited crowd, who were gaping at him. The flashlights of cameras shrouded him as he stood in front of S. L. Babel's digital artwork entitled *Your Clone Will Live After Your Death*. In this piece, an AI-integrated camera installed in the artwork recognized a viewer's face, projecting a version of their clone on the screen. Gray-haired Hoyt Pence stepped up to the painting, gawking at it. A sallow, haggard face—the frame and shape were similar to Hoyt's—materialized in the darkness and smiled back at him. Hoyt winced and fell on his buttocks. Laughter tinged with fear erupted among the crowd in the auction house.

"That artwork really became Hoyt Pence's clone, then," said Alex sarcastically. "I mean, he passed away and his clone on screen survived."

"Indeed," said Peter flatly.

Alex squinted at the current time displayed on the monitor. It was 9:11 a.m. Eastern Time. He'd slept for only a couple of hours.

"I've been really looking forward to seeing my friend James again," said Peter, his eyes somewhat glaring at the ocean outside the window. "Hoyt Pence invested a lot in James's company. James looked sad when Hoyt died. But James never stopped collecting S. L. Babel's digital art."

Both Alex and Peter were heading to the mansion of pharmaceutical company CEO and multi-billionaire James Brown on Star Island, Miami. It was the unidentified artist S. L. Babel contacted Swiss-American art dealer Alex Hubert, who could speak English, French, and German and had connections to both New York and European gallerists as well as wealthy art collectors around the world, to hold a private auction in Miami. James Brown accepted the offer to host a private auction in his mansion. As an art dealer, Alex organized small, secret auctions for billionaires several times before. In the art world, art collectors usually didn't fly to see artwork. The most expensive artwork flew to wealthy art collectors around the world.

"I'll do my best to let you win the upcoming auction, no matter what, Peter," said Alex decisively. *I was hired by both art collector Peter Carli and the unidentified digital artist S. L. Babel.* Alex thought, glancing at the briefcase in the cabinet again. Although this new S. L. Babel work was in his private jet now, Peter hadn't managed to purchase it yet. S. L. Babel only allowed Peter Carli to attend the upcoming auction in return for the use of Peter's private jet to bring the new digital art secretly.

"Can you do me a favor, Alex?" said Peter Carli in a silky voice. "Can I see Babel's new work in the briefcase?"

"No, I'm not allowed to do that," replied Alex adamantly. "Babel prohibited me from showing anybody his new painting. I actually don't know the 3-digit PIN to unlock the briefcase. It was already locked when I visited Geneva Freeport. Babel will send me an email to let me unlock the briefcase right before our auction in James Brown's mansion."

Alex took his iPhone out of his jeans pocket. His iPhone was always connected to the fast in-flight Wi-Fi. He refreshed his email inbox. Only advertisement emails from subscribed lists and spam emails popped up.

"Babel hasn't emailed me yet," said Alex disappointedly.

"Have you ever met S. L. Babel?" asked Peter Carli in an undertone.

"Of course not," Alex shrugged. "Nobody on the planet knows who S. L. Babel is. Nobody knows his face. Some say Babel is the most excellent AI scientist who realized selling his invention as artwork is lucrative. Others say Babel doesn't exist, but several Silicon Valley programmers collaborate to sell digital art under a single brand."

"Interesting," said Peter Carli with a French accent, clearing his throat. "The mystery of his identity triggered his popularity, too. Alex, how much should I pay for his new work? Or how much should I NOT pay?"

"I'd recommend you don't offer a bid over twenty million dollars," said Alex decisively.

"I trust you. I think James will bid more money on this work," said Peter, eyeing the briefcase inside the cabinet. "Do you know who'll participate in this private auction?"

"I know only one guest," said Alex, carefully closing the cabinet door. "Her name is Laura Campbell, a journalist for the *Washington Post*. She has been covering the mysterious deaths related to S. L. Babel's works. She received an invitation to the auction at Mr. Brown's mansion from S. L. Babel himself but couldn't believe it was genuinely from Babel. So, she emailed me, asking if the message was real. I told her it was authentic, and I was going to attend the same auction."

"Wait, Alex, you said she's a journalist?" Peter spat, raising his brow. "What's the point in making this auction private then? She'll write about everything she sees during the auction."

"Yeah, but it's probably a good idea to have a journalist there this time," said Alex in an anxious tone. "I mean, a murder is less likely to happen under a journalist's surveillance."

"It makes sense," Peter Carli croaked. "Who else will be invited to the auction?"

"I have no idea. Only S. L. Babel knows," replied Alex with a shrug. "But I assume the wealthiest people on the planet will gather at Mr. Brown's mansion since you and Mr. Brown will be there. There's no point in inviting people who aren't as rich as you."

"I see," said Peter Carli, touching his left stomach and taking a deep breath. His sallow and pale cheeks were trembling.

"Are you sick?" mouthed Alex, squinting his eyes.

"No, not at all."

As Peter mumbled, the pilot's dry voice resounded from the announcement system in the cabin. "We're landing in thirty minutes. Please have a seat and make sure you wear seatbelts."

Alex sank into the white leather chair, glancing out of the small, soybean-shaped window next to his armchair.

The turquoise ocean along snowy Miami Beach was shining under the sun. Alex pressed his forehead against the window, gazing downward.

Among orange surfing boards and huge waves, the shade of a huge shark with two black wings materialized. As the huge waves crashed over the surfers, the shark twisted its body, flew above the sea surface, and engulfed them.

As the airplane tilted its nose down, the cabinet's door swung open. Alex's eyes darted to the cabinet. The briefcase popped out and slid over to his chair. He caught the briefcase between his brown leather shoes.

Once again, Alex glanced at the ocean outside the window. The huge shark with wings had vanished. Instead, the shadow of Peter Carli's private jet was swimming on the water.

Chapter Two

New Entry: Simple Contact Form (ID: #1793)
Name: S. L. Babel
Email: artist@slbabel.com
Subject: Invitation to a Private Auction of My New Digital Art

Comment or Message:

Hi Laura,

This is digital artist S. L. Babel.

If you need confirmation that this message is from me, please contact my art agent, Alex Hubert, at alex@hubertagency.com. He'll verify its authenticity.

To get straight to the point, I'm a huge fan of your work. I listen to your podcast on YouTube every week and thoroughly enjoy your theories about the serial murders connected to my artwork. Your articles in the *Washington Post* have been outstanding as well. Some say my digital artworks are cursed, given the number of dealers and collectors who have been killed. Others suggest that I'm somehow orchestrating these events to gain notoriety. Let me be clear—I'm just as eager as you are to uncover the truth behind these deaths. I have no doubt that you'll solve these mysteries.

Therefore, I'd like to invite you to a private auction of my new digital art, which will be held at James Brown's mansion on Star Island, Miami. As you know, it's common for artworks to attract billionaire collectors worldwide. I'm not suggesting that someone will be killed at the auction, but something significant might happen. I hope you'll find clues that could help solve these crimes.

For further information, please contact Alex Hubert. He'll connect you with Elena Taylor, James Brown's secretary, who will arrange to pick you up at Miami International Airport.

Best,
S. L. Babel

Message sent to journalist.lauracampbell.com

While the American Airlines plane from Washington D.C. was taxiing to a terminal at Miami International Airport, the *Washington Post*'s national arts reporter, Laura Campbell, turned off airplane mode on her phone. She began re-reading the message S. L. Babel had sent to her personal website weeks ago. *Secret digital artist S. L. Babel does exist.* She felt her heart race. *I'll get more clues to the mysteries surrounding him in the upcoming auction.*

The small screen on the back of the seat in front of Laura was showing NBC News, but with her earphones unplugged, no sound came through. A reporter stood in front of Hoyt Pence's Palm Beach mansion, where FBI agents were swarming in and out. She seemed to be discussing the recent revelation about the billionaire's death.

"Do you really think Hoyt Pence died in an accident on a yacht?" asked the Asian-American passenger sitting next to Laura, eyeing the screen. He adjusted his glasses, looking intrigued. "Hoyt Pence was ranked number thirty-eight on *Forbes*'s billionaire list. There must be something behind this, and the FBI is probably hiding some crucial information."

I'll be meeting the multibillionaire ranked number thirty-seven on Forbes *today,* Laura thought with a silent smile. *James Brown, who is hosting a private auction for S. L. Babel's new digital art is worth forty-one billion dollars.*

"Exactly, there must be something behind Pence's death," Laura replied in a sharp voice, turning off her phone screen. "99.9% of highly intellectual, well-planned murders originate from money. They kill people for at least a seven-figure sum, or more. If a multibillionaire was killed, the stakes must be much higher."

"You sound very confident and insightful," said the Asian-American passenger in a jovial tone, glancing at his phone, which showed his transit airplane ticket to the Bahamas. "By any chance, are you an investigative journalist or something?"

"No," Laura lied instantly. "I wish I could be. Journalism is my dream job."

I'll be the first journalist to reveal the biggest crime scheme in America, Laura thought silently, glancing down the plane's aisle. The seat belt signs went off. Passengers stood up and began taking out their baggage. *Arriving at James Brown's mansion, I'll find out who gathers to buy S. L. Babel's new work at the private auction. One of them might be related to the recent serial murders.* Laura got to her feet, opened the overhead storage, and took out her tote bag.

"I feel like I've seen your face on some TV news before," said the Asian-American passenger, retrieving his luggage from the storage. "I could be wrong."

"I've never appeared on TV before," Laura pouted, standing in line with the other passengers in the aisle. "I like to keep a low profile. I hope I'll never appear on TV in the future. Have a safe trip!"

"You too," the passenger said, putting on a blue cap. Laura started to stride down the aisle.

"See you! Have a good day!" a cabin attendant smiled at Laura as she exited the airplane.

Laura didn't reply, clutching her tote bag tightly. *I hope this will be a life-changing day!* As she stepped onto the jet bridge to the airport terminal, she felt the warm, semi-tropical air shrouding her body. Laura undid a button on her apricot blouse with long lace sleeves. Her neck and facial muscles loosened, but she bit her lips, tapping her heart with her fist. *Today, I may be able to get a clue about who is the serial killer behind the trade of S. L. Babel's art.*

While weaving through the crowd grabbing Starbucks coffee in the concourse toward the terminal's exit, Laura pulled a red fedora out of her black tote bag. Trotting down an escalator to the baggage reclaim area, she put the fedora on her wavy brown hair. Laura had emailed James Brown's secretary, Elena Taylor, that she'd be wearing a red fedora today. After she exited the gate, Elena would easily recognize her and take her to the pharmaceutical giant's mansion on Star Island. She tapped her Apple Watch wrapped around her wrist. It was 9:56 a.m. She didn't have much time. A limousine from James Brown's mansion was supposed to pick up all the guests at 10 a.m. at the airport. Her flight from Washington, D.C. had been delayed by half an hour.

"Excuse me!" a raspy female voice caught Laura's attention as she was striding between the rotating baggage carousels.

A pregnant brunette woman wearing a blue scoop-neck lounge dress was perched on the corner of the baggage carousel A7. The monitor hung from the ceiling showed "Airline: American Airlines, Origin: San Francisco, SFO, Flight: AA 369, Status: Last Bag." The brunette looked pale, caressing her swollen stomach. Laura thought she saw the woman's stomach trembling under her blue dress, as if the baby inside was frolicking.

With a sudden beep and rattle, the baggage carousel A7 stopped rotating.

"How can I help you?" said Laura huffily, her eyes still glancing at her Apple Watch.

"My baggage is missing," said the pregnant woman in a miserable tone. "It's a silver suitcase with a pink ribbon on its handle. Can you see if it's still on the carousel? I'm too tired to walk around."

"Sure," said Laura, quickly circling the carousel. There was no baggage left on the conveyor belt. The pregnant woman was following Laura's movement with anxious eyes.

"Unfortunately, there's no baggage left," said Laura as she walked back to the pregnant woman.

"Oh no! My baggage was stolen, then," the woman leapt to her feet, turning on her phone and showing Laura its screen. Her Instagram account was open, displaying a "Story" with a picture of her suitcase and a caption "Trip to Miami :)." More than thirty thousand people viewed her post.

"I posted this picture on my Instagram before boarding in San

Francisco," the pregnant woman sighed, her eyebrows furrowed. "A scumbag must've seen my post and stolen my suitcase."

"I'm sorry about that," said Laura, sneaking a glance at the Instagram icon and the account name @BellaKSaba. Laura let out a short cry, feeling her heart jump to her throat. Eyeing her phone and the woman's face one by one, Laura asked in a shrill voice. "Are you Bella Saba, the popular art blogger?"

"Yes," Bella Saba mischievously smiled. "Do you know me?"

"It's a huge pleasure to see you! I've been following you on Instagram," Laura said, shaking Bella's hand. "I'm Laura. I didn't know you were pregnant."

"I don't want to make my pregnancy public," said Bella in a tremulous voice. "But I've been off my daytime job." Bella worked as a software engineer in Silicon Valley and was also a social media influencer. Her contemporary art blog was famous among art collectors around the world.

"Excuse me, I gotta go, Laura," said Bella hastily, eyeing her watch. "I need to report my missing baggage to the counter—or even to the police—but I don't have time. I must catch a limousine at 10 a.m."

"Which limousine?" asked Laura, widening her eyes.

"It's a limousine that picks up guests for a private art auction. I gotta go now. I'll report the baggage loss later," Bella spluttered and started to shuffle toward the exit of the luggage reclaim area.

Laura followed Bella, stretching out her arm as if she were chasing a pop star avoiding groupies.

"By any chance, are you going to visit James Brown's mansion on Star Island?" said Laura huffily.

"Yes, how do you know that?" snapped Bella, looking surprised.

"I'm invited to his mansion, too!" said Laura delightedly, adjusting her red fedora.

Chapter Three

"You two are the last guests we've been waiting for. All the other guests are in the limousine," said Elena, a tall, blond secretary of James Brown. She ushered Laura Campbell and Bella Saba to the black limousine in the underground garage of Miami International Airport.

"How many people were invited?" asked Laura, squinting at the shaded windows of the limousine.

"Only five, including both of you, according to S. L. Babel's sudden email this morning," said Elena. She then eyed Laura's fedora. "I really like your fedora, Ms. Campbell. It looks gorgeous."

"Thank you," smiled Laura, her eyes still riveted on the shadows of the passengers' heads faintly swaying behind the limousine's windows.

"You look like a pirate starting a treasure hunt, Laura," said Bella playfully, shuffling after the two with her white leather handbag on her shoulder.

Reaching the limousine, Elena tucked the edge of her Italian-wool blazer and knocked on the door six times in a mysterious rhythm. Laura and Bella exchanged glances. *Is there a secret code to open James Brown's limousine?* The door swung open, and a Cuban driver raised his hand to them.

Stepping up several stairs, Laura met the eyes of the other three guests, who sat on black leather seats lining the windows and encircling the aisle. A chubby, gray-haired man in a shaggy purple coat glanced up at her, his brown walrus mustache twitching as he adjusted his black-rimmed glasses. Like a surgeon examining a patient, the man shot an icy look from Laura's white leather loafers to her wavy brown hair under the red fedora. Laura averted her eyes, pulling off her fedora and slouching into a seat by the window. As Bella sat next to her, Laura sneaked a glance at the other two men, who sat across the aisle. A blond businessman, holding a briefcase with a three-dial combination lock tightly on his lap, eyed the new guests, seemingly trying to recognize their identities. Laura recognized his face from Alex Hubert's profile picture on his art agency's website.

"Mr. Hubert?" asked Laura with a smile, standing up. "Thank you so much for replying to my email. If you hadn't, I wouldn't have believed it was an authentic message from S. L. Babel."

Alex Hubert seemed to recognize Laura at the same time. He must've checked her LinkedIn page or personal website beforehand. As Laura ruffled her brown hair, Alex got to his feet, striding toward her and shaking her hand.

"It's a pleasure to meet you, Ms. Campbell," said Alex gently, displaying his white teeth. "I've read almost all your articles about contemporary art in the *Washington Post*. I'm really looking forward to your book on S. L. Babel."

"Are you a journalist for the *Washington Post*, Laura?" asked Bella.

"I hope I can finish writing the book, Mr. Hubert," said Laura sweetly, her eyes smiling at Alex while nodding to Bella. "I hope to learn something new today."

"Absolutely," said Alex, glancing at Bella, who sat near Laura.

"This is my friend Bella," Laura introduced.

"Nice to meet you, sir," smiled Bella, holding out her hand.

"Nice to meet you. I'm Alex."

As Alex shook her hand, the limousine started to move. He trotted back to his seat.

Laura sank into the leather seat, sneaking a glance at Alex's neighbor, an old man rubbing his silver beard. As the limousine trundled through the garage, he coughed, seeming annoyed by the wait. Laura swallowed as she recognized his face. The old man was Swiss biotech multibillionaire Peter Carli, recently in the news for purchasing S. L. Babel's digital artwork for four million dollars. Laura glanced at Bella, who was looking out the window over Peter Carli's shoulder. The limousine pulled out of the underground garage, zooming through streets overhung by palm trees.

"Nice limousine," said Bella nonchalantly, stroking her pregnant stomach. "I wish my baby could see Miami's cityscape, too. Miami is my favorite city in America."

~ * ~

Who is this pregnant woman? What's her relationship to Laura Campbell?

Alex Hubert shot furtive glances at each of the new female guests in the limousine. While his eyes were moving, the rest of his body remained rigid. His sweaty hands gripped the briefcase containing S. L. Babel's new digital art so tightly that its edge marked his skin.

What a weird pair. Two young women—a Washington Post *journalist and a pregnant woman.* Alex silently mused, crossing his legs. *Why were these women invited to the private auction of S. Babel's new work? They don't look rich enough to participate.*

Alex twisted his lips, looking at the briefcase on his lap. His mind dug through memories of wealthy female art collectors. He had memorized the names and faces of around 3,000 billionaires along with their *Forbes* rankings. Laura's and Bella's faces matched none of them. During the auction, the two biotech billionaires, Peter Carli and James Brown, would compete, and the price of Babel's work would likely skyrocket to $10 million. It was meaningless for ordinary art fans to attend. Alex expected more billionaires to join. Or perhaps other wealthy collectors were heading to James Brown's mansion separately? But Brown's secretary Elena said these women were the last guests.

At the back of the limousine, the gray-haired man with black-rimmed glasses, who was surfing the web on his tablet, coughed loudly. He'd introduced himself to Alex and Peter when they boarded the limousine. His name was Terence Miller—if that was his real name—and he was from St. Louis, Missouri. *He doesn't look rich either*, Alex thought, squinting at Terence's tattered coat, a slight, sneaky smile looming on his face. *This won't be a very difficult game for us. I can let Peter win the auction.*

As the limousine trundled through MacArthur Causeway, the

turquoise ocean spread out through the windows. Luxurious yachts floated among pizza-shaped islands, with swimming pools shining under the glaring sunlight. Alex eyed Peter Carli sitting next to him. Peter cast a wary eye on Google Maps on his phone, examining the route the limousine was taking. Alex thought Peter was afraid of being kidnapped—typical for the wealthiest traveling without their bodyguards.

"So beautiful!" Bella exclaimed, taking her iPhone out of her white leather handbag and snapping pictures of the rippling ocean for her Instagram. "If my suitcase wasn't stolen, I could swim in the ocean—I packed my bikinis in the suitcase."

Laura frowned at Bella's stomach, nearly saying, "Can you really swim with that body?" But she realized Bella probably aimed to take a bikini-clad selfie on Miami Beach to boost her Instagram following.

"I hope you find your suitcase soon," said Laura soothingly. "It may not have been stolen. Baggage loss happens often at airports."

"No, it was stolen. I'm sure of it," said Bella hotly. "I've been posting about S. L. Babel's identity on my popular blog. They wanted me to stop and decided to take revenge. Look at this."

Bella opened her Instagram and showed Laura a direct message from an anonymous account. Its profile picture was Babel's digital art piece *Your Clone Will Live After Your Death*, depicting the clone of the late Hoyt Pence.

WED 6:20 AM

Hey Bella,

This is a warning. Stop writing about S. L. Babel on your blog.

Never try to discover his identity. Otherwise, you'll lose something important upon landing in Miami.

"This is terrifying!" Laura shrieked. "You should go to the police, Bella."

"Maybe I should," said Bella darkly. "But I'm in this limousine. I can't miss the auction."

"Can you guess who sent this?" asked Laura, lowering her voice as she noticed Alex's eyes darting toward them. "Is there anyone who doesn't want you to reveal S. L. Babel's identity?"

"I think it's *them*," said Bella sharply. "There must be a secret group that tries to stop anyone from revealing S. L. Babel's identity at all costs. I'm guessing art dealers and collectors have been killed because they got some information about the digital artist."

"Any proof?" asked Laura in a shrill voice.

"Somebody painted graffiti on my car this morning," said Bella grimly, showing Laura a picture on her phone. On the windshield of Bella's Tesla Model X were painted purple letters: "STOP CIRCULATING FAKE NEWS ABOUT BABEL." Bella turned off the screen of her phone and sighed. "Then, someone stole my suitcase at Miami International Airport. There must be people operating together on both coasts."

"Isn't it possible someone stalked you from San Francisco and took the same plane?" said Laura, her anxious eyes darting to the limousine's rear window.

"It's impossible," Bella shrugged, lowering her voice. "I've been very careful. Nobody has stalked me from San Francisco. You also need to be careful, Laura, since you're a journalist. They may try to assassinate you if you write more articles delving into S. L. Babel's identity."

"I know the risks of my job," said Laura drily. "But I've never received threats regarding my investigation into S. L. Babel and his art trade."

"They haven't targeted you yet because you don't know S. L. Babel's real identity," said Bella slyly. After a short pause, she added in a clear and ringing voice, her eyes chasing blue herons flying over the ocean.

"But I know who S. L. Babel is."

All the passengers audibly gasped, their eyes riveted on Bella's face.

Terence dropped his tablet onto the floor, his hands trembling. His panic-stricken feet in disheveled loafers kicked his tablet to the center of the limousine's floor.

Terence's tablet stopped in front of Laura's seat. It displayed the latest article on Bella's contemporary art blog. Laura squinted at the screen. The headline read, "S. L. BABEL IS A SECRET DETECTIVE WHO AIMS TO SOLVE THE BIGGEST CRIME IN AMERICA." Below this headline was a picture of S. L. Babel's artwork, a collage of pictures of dead bodies.

Elena, who sat next to the driver, swiveled around, staring at Bella's face. Her long, purple eyelashes fanned out like blooming flowers, lightning-shaped blood vessels emerged in her cornea. Beads of sweat ran down her cheeks.

Alex Hubert straightened up with a jolt, holding the briefcase containing S. L. Babel's new digital art in his arms. His mouth was agape, sour saliva trickling down his throat.

Peter Carli turned off his phone and placed it in the back pocket of his Calvin Klein pants. His eyes were flashing.

"Ma'am, you said you know who S. L. Babel is?" said Peter sternly. "How do you know? Nobody knows his real identity. We art collectors around the world are desperate to identify him."

"One of S. L. Babel's early works is the key," Bella chuckled mysteriously, pointing to Terence's tablet on the floor and eyeing the shivering man at the back. "I wrote my theory in my latest blog post, which this gentleman was reading on his tablet. Babel created a collage combining pictures of victims murdered by a serial killer in St. Louis, Missouri. The serial killer targeted students and homeless people in a district called Central West End. All the victims lost parts of their bodies; some lost kidneys and hearts."

"Why does that collage make you believe S. L. Babel is a detective?" asked Alex calmly.

"I found a link between the serial murders and art collectors who have purchased Babel's works," said Bella, caressing her pregnant stomach. "Please read my blog if you're interested in the details."

Terence let out a short shout, falling on the floor. As the limousine stopped at a red light, he clutched an armrest, but his trembling legs violently bumped into a side table. The Diet Coke can dropped onto his face, foam covering his nose.

Hearing Bella's words, Peter Carli shuddered, his teeth chattering and breath uneven. A strand of half-blond, half-silver hair fell from his forehead onto his pale nose.

Elena, who was looking back at the guests, gasped, covering her mouth with her trembling hands. Her sapphire ring pressed deeply into her cheeks.

Alex Hubert and Laura Campbell quietly observed the other panic-stricken passengers.

"Terence, you're from St. Louis, right? Do you know about the serial murders?" Alex asked in a throaty voice.

"Ahh," Terence was still shivering, wiping Coke off his face. In twenty seconds, he got to his feet, sitting down shakily. "No, I've never heard of such a lousy crime in my city."

"I actually know about it," Laura interjected. "I once covered the St. Louis serial killings for the *Washington Post* because one of the victim students met with a secretary of a famous politician in D.C. one day before he was killed. That secretary suspiciously died in a car crash after meeting the student in St. Louis too. But the serial killer left his fingerprint—the FBI must still be searching for the killer."

"Where did he leave his fingerprint?" asked Alex hotly.

"The serial killer left his fingerprint on his gun that he dropped at a murder site," replied Bella quickly.

"What you said is interesting, Bella. But, I can't completely believe it. I don't see any connection between the St. Louis serial murders and S. L. Babel," said Alex, placing the briefcase between his back and the backrest. "S. L. Babel must be an excellent programmer. Otherwise, he couldn't make such great pieces of digital art. On the other hand, that serial killer in St. Louis sounds like a fanatic necrophile who loves collecting parts of corpses. Why is S. L. Babel interested in the serial killer?"

"It's up to you whether you believe me or not," Bella smiled impishly. "I detailed my discoveries in my latest blog post. If you read it, you'll change your mind."

"Your website is down now," said Terence in a shaky voice as he picked up his tablet and sat back down. "At least, your latest post isn't available, no matter how many times I refresh the page."

"What?" Bella frowned, turning on her phone and checking her website. "Oh, my website was hacked! A hacker deleted my latest post."

"Awful," said Laura, staring at Bella's phone. The website looked unresponsive. Laura asked in a huffy voice, "Is the hacker the blackmailer who sent you the menacing Instagram message?"

"Probably," said Bella, biting her lip. "They'll do anything to stop me from revealing S. L. Babel's identity."

The limousine stopped. The bridge to Star Island shone ahead. The gate rattled open. Alex's eyes met Laura's for a moment. They instantly averted their gaze and looked out the windows. Their eyes absorbed the palatial mansions and swimming pools near the gate. From the dark shrub of red mangrove around the piers, a green heron flew up, drawing a large loop over the limousine and heading to Brown's mansion on the western side of the island like a scout.

Chapter Four

Trotting through the gate of James Brown's mansion, the guests gasped, their eyes wandering around the sprawling courtyard. The oval swimming pool, surrounded by plush palm trees, reflected the mansion's palatial terrace, ruby-red roofs, and the cloudless sky. The green heron, perched on the terrace, flew across the pool, gliding over the guests' heads and landing on the bow of the sixty-three-foot Lamborghini yacht slowly approaching the pier. The yacht made a graceful tack, its golden gunwale smoothly touching the pier. A thick rope was thrown from the cockpit, and a tall, black-haired man wearing sunglasses jumped from the yacht's edge to the pier, tying the rope around a thick orange pole. He then raised his hand to the guests, taking off his sunglasses and striding toward them.

"Welcome, my friends!" shouted James Brown cheerfully.

"James, great to see you!" said Peter Carli jovially, shaking hands with the pharmaceutical industry tycoon. "How are you doing?"

"I just finished my morning routine. I love sailing under the morning sunlight and breathing fresh air," James replied jubilantly, flicking his chin toward his secretary. "Elena, invite all the guests to the drawing room."

"James, let me introduce my art dealer," said Peter, eyeing Alex Hubert, who stood behind him, looking impressed by the magnificent mansion. "This is Alex, who is in charge of bringing S. L. Babel's work this time."

"It's an honor to meet you," Alex said, holding out his hand to James Brown.

"Great to meet you, Alex. I've heard a lot about the great deals you've struck from my art collector friends," James said brightly, shaking hands with Alex.

The other guests had already reached the entrance door under the porch. As Elena opened the door, Laura and Bella stepped inside first. Their jaws dropped at the sight of the huge atrium, resembling a sumptuous palace. The marble-laden walls were adorned with a luxurious contemporary art collection. Laura moved toward the center of the atrium, illuminated by light from the roof window, rotating her body and casting her eyes over the artwork. Terence, Alex, and Peter followed them inside. Alex whistled in admiration. They all felt their feet rooted to the marble floor, their gazes circling the walls.

"Feel free to admire my art collection, ladies and gentlemen," said James Brown mischievously, his voice echoing in the cool atrium.

Laura shuffled through Jeff Koons's sculptures made of shiny sapphire and ruby balloons on the east wall. Standing on the marble floor reflecting these balloon-made dog and snake sculptures, she tiptoed and stared at a Jean-Michel Basquiat painting hung on the wall. The Picasso-styled human skull with asymmetrical yellow eyes floated in the sky, glowering back at Laura. Alex Hubert, stepping behind Laura, observed the same painting over her shoulder. He knew the value of the Basquiat painting. James Brown bought it for twenty-three million dollars at a Christie's auction last year.

"This is so funny, Ms. Campbell," said Alex with a tinkling laugh, pointing to another painting next to the Basquiat. "It's so satirical, isn't it?"

Laura's eyes followed his pointing finger. It was a cartoon-like painting depicting a famous politician she'd once covered in the *Washington Post*—Senator Susanne Caldwell from Missouri. The painting represented Caldwell as a marionette, manipulated by strings tied to her head, nose, fingers, legs, and feet. The background was a dark stage of a puppet play. Under a spotlight that illuminated her varnished brown hair, puppet Susanne Caldwell curtsied to the viewer, her glass-like eyes flashing maliciously.

"Indeed," said Laura snidely, her lips curving with unsuppressed laughter. "It's interesting that James Brown owns this painting. Susanne Caldwell is an influential politician who makes important policy decisions on national health. Who made this painting?"

"I have no idea," said Alex, reading the label indicating the artist's name. "I've never heard of this artist. I think this is an amateur's work, but Brown bought it for fun."

"I see," said Laura.

"Laura, Laura, come here!" Bella's high-pitched voice made Laura turn around.

Bella stood on the west side of the atrium, pointing at a piece of artwork hung between Tracey Emin's paintings, which depicted naked women drowning in poems written like foggy graffiti.

"Oh, I know this work," said Laura enthusiastically. "It's one of S. L. Babel's 'Transplant' series, isn't it?"

As Laura stood in front of Babel's digital art, a red triangular light in the camera attached to the digital art started to blink. Gray ripples whirled across the screen. Then, golden fire exploded. Laura swallowed. From the bottom of the darkness on the screen, a thin cyborg with a thick metallic chest shuffled toward Laura. The cyborg had Laura's face, smiling wanly at her. Its robotic hands caressed its swollen stomach, kicked and swayed by a small creature inside—Bella's pregnant stomach. Laura's eyes slipped toward the cyborg's legs. They were James Brown's long legs in blue jeans.

The white label attached to the artwork read:

S. K. Babel (born ???)
Fusion, 2023
Artificial Intelligence on monitor
In this work, Babel shows a future human being incorporating robotic technology based on the bodies of viewers. The cyborg has the face of the most recent person who stood in front of this work, as well as the stomach and legs of the second and third most recent viewers.

DO NOT TOUCH THE ARTWORK

"This digital art is so creepy," said Laura shakily, retreating from the painting. "I feel like it infringes on my privacy."

"There's something I noticed," Bella whispered in Laura's ear, gripping her wrist and sneaking a glance at the others.

"Alex and Peter, shall we prepare for our auction?" James Brown said, motioning them to the drawing room across the atrium.

"Sure, I just got an email from S. L. Babel," said Alex, his breath uneven, eyeing the heavy briefcase in his right hand. "He sent me the 3-digit PIN for this briefcase. I can finally open it."

Terence, who seemed uninterested in the artwork and stood near the entrance door, scratched his potbelly, and followed them to the drawing room.

"James, I'll bring some drinks for the guests," said Elena, disappearing into the corridor leading to the dining room in the opposite direction.

Only Laura and Bella remained in the atrium.

"This digital art is fake," whispered Bella indignantly.

"What?" Laura's eyes widened.

"This can't be S. L. Babel's work. I know all of his pieces and have written articles about each one on my art blog," said Bella, lowering her voice. "Babel's real *Fusion* also mixes the faces of the three most recent viewers. Making such a counterfeit is an insult to a genius like S. L. Babel."

"But I know James Brown bought Babel's work for an eight-figure sum at Christie's auction," rasped Laura. "I read it in the *New York Times*."

"James Brown must have replaced the real work with this counterfeit. I don't know why," said Bella conspiratorially. "Maybe he wanted to hide the real artwork because it reveals something that shouldn't be public. This piece probably serves as a security camera."

"Security camera?" Laura looked up at the atrium's ceiling. There was no camera in sight, except for the mysterious one welded to Babel's *Fusion*. "Indeed, there's no security camera here, even though there are dozens of expensive contemporary art pieces."

"If we touch one of the works in this atrium, that fake digital art will send signals, and the security team will storm in," said Bella in a low voice.

"But why does James Brown want to hide the original piece?"

asked Laura.

"I have no clue," Bella shrugged. "Billionaires often do this. They show off fake luxurious items to watch people drool over them. But there's always a hidden scheme behind these art deals."

As Laura and Bella walked toward the drawing room, Alex's shrill voice echoed from inside.

"Is this really art?" shrieked Terence, sitting in an armchair by the emerald-felt billiard table.

After opening the locked briefcase, Alex placed S. L. Babel's new work on the blond-wood dining table. Both James Brown and Peter Carli stood up, knocking over their chairs as they stared at Babel's new work with their mouths agape.

Artist a.k.a. S. L. Babel

"This is totally unexpected, Peter," said James in an undertone. "We might be witnessing a completely new definition of digital art."

"Indeed. This could be cutting-edge, revolutionary digital art," Peter nodded, his eyes fixed on the painting.

"You guys are delusional! It's just a QR code printed on a white canvas!" snarled Terence behind them. "I'd be surprised if you smart billionaires decide to pay millions for such a crappy piece of contemporary art."

"Shut up, Terence!" Alex barked. "You know nothing about art. Salvador Dali, Andy Warhol, Damien Hirst... Those who create new concepts become victorious in contemporary art. S. L. Babel is the greatest digital artist on the planet right now."

Terence is right. This work is garbage. But I can't fail to sell it.

Alex closed his eyes for a moment, wiping sweat off his eyebrows. *S. L. Babel promised to pay me half the profits from selling this.*

"Do you still believe this QR code is worth at least ten million dollars, Alex?" asked Peter huffily.

"Of course, no doubt about it," answered Alex vigorously. "Think about Marcel Duchamp's *Fountain*, the greatest readymade sculpture in history. That simple urinal signed by the artist became the most remarkable milestone in that genre."

"Hahahahaha," Terence guffawed, scratching his bulbous nose mockingly, his eyeglasses flashing.

Elena entered the drawing room with a tray filled with cups of coffee, glasses of red wine, Coke, and Sprite. Eying her pale boss and upset guests, she looked confused, standing stiffly in front of the door. Terence picked up a glass of Coke, slurping it as he approached the dining table. Putting the glass down loudly, he growled, "Contemporary art is a scam! You billionaires need to realize it."

"No, contemporary art is the best investment in the world," Alex, standing between the two multibillionaires, replied curtly. "I have no doubt that the price of this piece will triple in two years."

"I have a question, Mr. Hubert," asked Laura.

"Call me Alex," said Alex sulkily.

"Okay, Alex. Why did S. L. Babel invite us and aim to sell his work in this small auction?" Laura asked, looking at his face squarely. "I mean, I obviously can't pay millions for this artwork. But I came here to report on his new work as a journalist"—*and to uncover the serial killings and crime deals behind S. L. Babel's works*, she thought to herself, swiveling to face Terence. "But why were you invited, and why did you accept it if you're not interested in contemporary art, Terence? What made you fly from St. Louis to Miami?"

"I just wanted to see his new work, too," said Terence uncomfortably. His voice was uneven. "I can brag about my experience later. At a local bar in my hometown, I can talk about my visit to James Brown's mansion and seeing the trendy digital artist's new work before anybody else."

"Excuse me, let me scan the QR code!" Bella squeezed between

Peter and Alex, aiming her smartphone at the huge QR code in the painting. In a few seconds, her default Internet browser automatically opened, and a website popped up.

"What's this!?" Bella let out a short cry.

Laura also scanned the QR code and swallowed. A mysterious network showed up on her phone's screen.

The Deathly Network
Mortal virus will be circulating around like this...

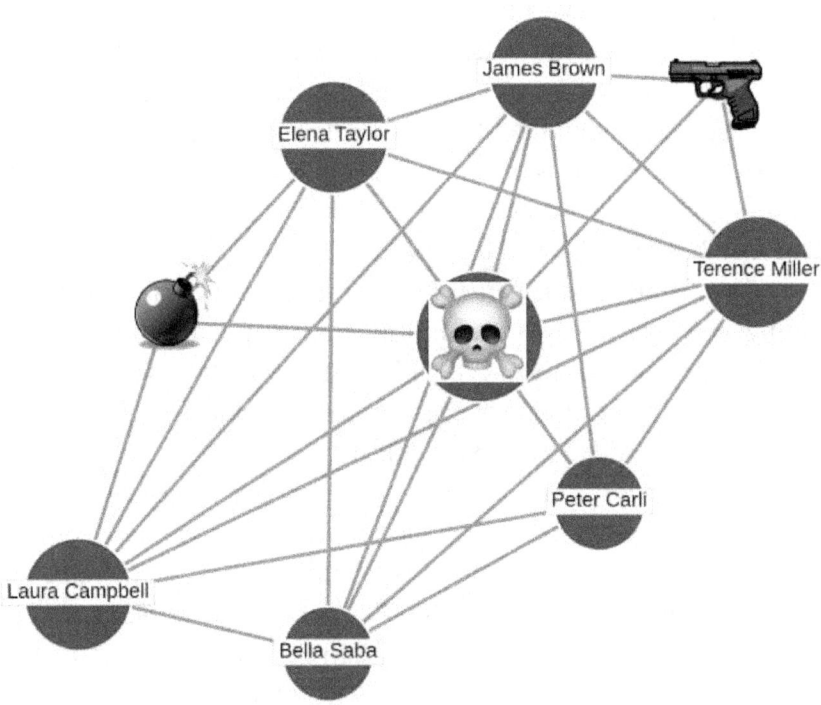

Everyone in the drawing room scanned the QR code with their phones, their eyes absorbed in the screens. They froze as they saw their names in the nodes—except for art dealer Alex Hubert, whose name was missing in this network—dancing and glinting in an ominous purple color.

Suddenly, the node named "James Brown" shone like bloody magma. This ominous burgundy light transmitted through the edges to the next nodes, "Terence Miller" and "Peter Carli," enveloping them in whirling flames. In ten seconds, the fire subsided, and cartoonish puppets, whose faces resembled James, Terence, and Peter, materialized in each node. Gunshots pierced the puppets of James and Terence, causing them to tumble down. The puppet resembling Peter transformed into a bronze huc, disintegrating as if infected with a deadly virus. Subsequently, the bloody light ran across the nodes named "Elena Taylor," "Laura Campbell," and "Bella Saba," with snaky flames wrapping around them. As the flame vanished, three puppets resembling each of them appeared in their respective nodes. A bomb fell onto Elena's puppet, exploding her body. Another bomb flew toward the chest of the puppet resembling Laura, erupting. The puppet resembling Bella took a helicopter, soaring into the sky and exploding in snaky flames.

Macabre letters appeared under the blackened network:

This is how human body traffickers will be punished.

Laura's scream rent the cool air in the drawing room. She dropped her phone onto Bella's sneaker. On the other hand, Bella bit her lips, glowering at her phone's screen.

James Brown fell on his buttocks, crashing his wine glass on the floor and shivering. His lips were shaking.

"Boss!"

Elena, who also looked pale, shouted between her shaking teeth, crouching near James. They exchanged fearful glances. They attempted to speak to each other but couldn't utter a single word from their trembling mouths.

Peter, whose face was white, clasped his hands tightly to collect himself. His shoulder was rocking as if to dissipate poisonous smoke filling his lungs.

"What a crazy prank. This is an insult!" Terence mouthed apprehensively, swiping the screen of his phone and leveling his horror-struck gaze at the QR code printed on the white canvas on the table.

What's going on? Alex, the only person who didn't appear in the network, stared at his phone's screen with his dark eyes. *Human body traffickers? Are these folks invited to this auction criminals? Are there any connections between them as indicated in this network?*

"Alex, you didn't appear in the network," said Peter in a shaky voice, holding up his phone.

Now, the network in the URL linked to the QR code showed the original network before the "Deathly Virus" circulated through the edges.

"Good for me," said Alex tartly. "Probably, this predicts I won't be killed like the other art dealers who sold S. L. Babel's works."

"Let's start the auction as instructed by S. L. Babel, Alex," said James through his trembling lips, getting to his feet with his secretary Elena's support.

"How much is the reserve price?" asked Peter breathlessly.

"Five million dollars—that's the minimum S. L. Babel wants," replied Alex.

"That's nuts!" Terence's sarcastic laughter echoed in the room.

The two multibillionaires, Peter and James, cast silent and menacing eyes at Terence as if they possessed information that could ruin him. Suddenly, the laughter vanished from Terence's face.

"Hmm, it's actually great if either of you buys this piece and hides it from the public's eye," said Terence, scratching his jaw sunk in his chubby neck.

"I'll buy this for six million dollars," said James firmly.

"I'll pay seven million!" Peter roared instantly.

James eyed his billionaire friend and whistled, meeting Peter's aggressive gaze.

"Peter, I can't concede this time. This painting is mine—I'll pay ten million dollars."

Elena, who stood beside her boss, swallowed, looking stunned.

"I don't mind paying fifteen million dollars," Peter smiled maliciously. "I know the value of S. L. Babel's works will skyrocket in a few years."

Alex was on the verge of saying "Peter, that's too much," but he strangled the words almost running out of his throat. A million-dollar payday was materializing in front of him.

"It's still too cheap given S. L. Babel's recent trade," said Alex, pretending to be calm and convincing. "I'd like to remind you that S. L.

Babel is the fourth most Googled person this year."

"Twenty million!" growled James impatiently.

"Twenty-one million," said Peter within a second.

"Then, thirty million! I'll pay thirty million for this painting!" James barked.

Bella, who was looking at each multibillionaire in turn, whistled loudly.

"Well then," Peter mouthed, sneaking a glance at Alex's victorious face. "I'll step aside. This QR code is yours."

Laura, who was secretly recording their conversation with a tiny bug embedded in her necklace, swallowed, sneaking a glance at Alex's face. While Alex tightly closed his mouth to conceal his feelings, she could see sneaky laughter blooming in his eyes.

"Then, sold!"

As if to hit a gavel, Alex tapped the dining table with the edge of an empty wine glass.

James Brown's face was a mix of victory and regret. He picked up his phone from the back pocket of his jeans and turned on his Coinbase app.

"I'll send thirty million-dollar Bitcoins to S. L. Babel right now," said James Brown drily. "This is how he wants to receive money, right?"

As Alex nodded, a victorious smile spilling over his face, James Brown sent the Bitcoins to S. L. Babel with one click and then flicked his chin at Elena. Without a word, Elena seemed to understand James's order. She shrouded S. L. Babel's thirty million-dollar QR code, printed on a white canvas, in a blanket, and brought it out of the drawing room. All the auction invitees named in the network watched the painting in her arms until Elena stepped out of the drawing room.

James Brown strode toward the exit after Elena and suddenly turned back to the guests.

"I want to see S. L. Babel's painting alone in my serene room. Why don't you guys take a cruise on my Lamborghini yacht? Alex, I heard you have a license to sail a yacht."

Chapter Five

James Brown's Lamborghini yacht sailed counterclockwise through the calm waters between Star Island and Hibiscus Island. As the yacht trundled along Palm Island, Laura stood on the bow, peering over the handrails and scanning the beachside mansions with their swimming pools. Suddenly, she heard a dog barking in the wind, followed by a small boy crying. Laura's eyes swept over the colonial-style mansions on northern Palm Island but couldn't find the source of the noise. Averting her eyes from the dazzling swimming pools, Laura turned to look at the mansions on Hibiscus Island. A small boy wearing a blue cap was pulling a leash as his dog ran onto the wharf, barking at James's yacht. The dog suddenly calmed down and turned sideways. The boy waved to Laura and the other passengers. As Laura trotted to the starboard side, she met the eyes of Alex, who was gripping the steering wheel in the cockpit.

"Nice sailing," said Laura cheerfully.

"No problem," Alex replied nonchalantly, sipping a Sprite he'd taken from the refrigerator.

"Bella should've come, too. This is wonderful," said Laura, thinking of the art blogger who needed to rest at Brown's mansion due to her pregnancy.

Turning to go to the cabin for a drink, Laura noticed Terence looking at her. Terence, sitting on a white sofa in the air-conditioned cabin, averted his eyes instantly. Laura knew his emotionless gaze was monitoring her and Alex like a jailor's. Meanwhile, Peter sat in an armchair by the floor-to-ceiling windows, always looking toward Star Island as if eager to return to James's mansion.

The Lamborghini yacht made a smooth tack in the channel, its bow now facing Star Island. As the yacht sailed forward, they could see the swimming pool of James Brown's mansion reflecting the blazing sun climbing above the magnificent palm trees. Alex stopped the engine and dropped the anchor with a long rattle. The wind died down, and total calmness reigned on the yacht.

Standing on the gunwale, Peter threw a green floating mat out onto the ocean.

"I'm too old to enjoy this," said Peter in a throaty voice. "But you should enjoy your youth, Alex."

"Are you serious?" Alex responded in a high-pitched voice.

"No worries. If you fall into the sea, I'll throw you a floating ring," said Peter, lowering his voice and tapping Alex's shoulder. "That girl has been watching you constantly, Alex."

"She's a journalist, Peter," Alex said, dropping his voice a notch. "It's her tactic to seduce men to glean information."

"This is so nice!" said Laura jovially, trotting down the boat ladder at the stern and jumping onto the floating mat. Ripples circled around the mat, seawater crawling up onto the edges. As Laura smoothly moved to its center, the mat stabilized. "I made it! Why don't you join me, Alex?" Laura shouted, raising her arm invitingly.

After rolling up the hem of his pants to avoid getting wet, Alex nervously planted his feet on the floating mat and took a breath. A bluish-yellow veil floated up to the surface near the mat. Through the turquoise water, Alex saw a queen angelfish dance and kiss the surface. As he clapped his hands, the fish vanished like a ghost. Alex thumped down onto the mat. Laura stepped back to keep it balanced. They simultaneously sat down at opposite ends, smiling at each other. The queen angelfish swam beneath the mat, surfacing on the opposite side with bubbles. As Laura stared at its ethereal yellow scales and blue wrinkles, the fish started to look like floating jewelry. She stretched out her hand, tapping the water. The fish darted away into the deep ocean.

A long buzzing engine noise of a jet ski heading toward their yacht echoed in the air. The rider, a blond man resembling Alex, adjusted his black sunglasses and smiled at them through the water spray. He uplifted the handles, sending the jet ski flying upward.

"This is the first cruise I've taken since I went to Ellis Island two years ago. By the way, are you from New York, Alex?" asked Laura, shielding her eyes from the sun with her hands.

"Yes. I was born in Geneva and grew up in New York," said Alex, eyeing Laura's face. "I'm half-Swiss and half-American, Laura."

"Cool! I have a question," said Laura impatiently. "Why did you decide to undertake this mission to bring Babel's work from Geneva Freeport to James Brown's mansion? Some art dealers involved in Babel's works were killed."

"I won't be killed," said Alex indignantly. "My name didn't appear in the network. You must be careful, though. Your name appeared in S. L. Babel's latest work."

"I don't understand why S. L. Babel included my name in that ominous network at all," replied Laura firmly.

As the jet ski thundered past the Lamborghini yacht, huge waves rushed toward the floating mat. Laura and Alex swallowed, moving to the same edge to maintain balance. When the floating mat climbed and descended the waves, the splash soaked their faces.

Laura gripped Alex's arm.

"You know some shady deals behind the trade of S. L. Babel's works, don't you?" said Laura, puffing out her chest. "Do you know why other dealers and collectors were killed?"

"I have no idea, but if I did," said Alex sarcastically, "I wouldn't tell you. You're a journalist for the *Washington Post*, right? Keeping clients' secrets is very important to art dealers."

"So, Alex, you know what those billionaires are up to!" Laura stood up on the floating mat, looking at Alex earnestly. "I won't write what you know in an article, but I'd appreciate any information that'll help me uncover the crime behind S. L. Babel's works."

Alex turned back and sneaked a glance at Brown's yacht. Peter Carli was standing on the starboard, gripping the handrails and looking pale. Peter's nervous eyes were scanning the coast of Star Island, searching for James Brown's mansion.

"What makes you believe there's a crime ring behind the trade of S. L. Babel's works in the first place?" asked Alex, lowering his voice.

"Ultra-wealthy people are eager to buy Babel's works, and some of them were killed," said Laura fervently. "If huge money is behind the murders, there must be something big."

"Laura, the only thing I know is," Alex whispered, "Peter Carli wants to buy expensive art pieces to divorce his wife."

"What do you mean?" Laura frowned.

"I can't say anymore," said Alex mischievously.

"Tell me more, please! We can collaborate from now on," said Laura passionately.

"How can we collaborate?" Alex asked in a low voice.

"I've researched the serial killings revolving around Babel's works and found interesting things," said Laura crisply. "We can exchange information if you want to continue dealing with Babel's works."

"Tell me what you know first, then," said Alex, unperturbed. "Otherwise, it's not fair."

"Okay, I'll tell you what I discovered," said Laura, lowering her voice. "The real reason James Brown became a multibillionaire is…"

A gunshot erupted from the coast, shaking the air around them.

Both Laura and Alex gasped, turning around. The gunshot seemed to come from the direction of James Brown's mansion on Star Island.

Five seconds later, two more gunshots reverberated. Screams, shattering windows, and the roar of an engine followed.

The green heron, which had been perched on the terrace, flew into the sky, drawing a heart shape in the air. Soon, a stringy contrail of an airplane flying in Miami's sky pierced the heart.

Both Peter and Terence stood on the deck, staring at Brown's mansion anxiously.

"Get on the yacht right now!" Peter roared at Laura and Alex, throwing a rope at them.

Laura caught the tip of the rope, and Alex gripped it. The floating mat slowly moved toward the yacht's stern. Laura climbed up the boat ladder to the deck. As Alex jumped to the ladder, Terence, who didn't know how to sail, kick-started the engine. The yacht started to move before Alex reached the deck. Clutching the last rung of the ladder, Alex heard Peter on the deck say in a throaty voice.

"Somebody must've been killed in James's mansion."

Chapter Six

As Alex, Laura, and the others entered the atrium of Brown's mansion, Bella and Elena, their eyes still dilated with horror, turned back and recoiled against the nearby wall. Bella, unconsciously leaning her trembling body against Jeff Koons's two-million-dollar blue balloon dog, let out a cry, pointing to the dead body in front of S. L. Babel's new digital artwork, the QR code painting, hanging on the wall. Elena covered her face with her shivering hands, her tears trickling down through her fingers and over her sapphire ring.

"He's dead," said Elena in a trembling voice.

It was James Brown. He lay supine, his face unnaturally turned sideways, as if his vengeful soul had made him turn back to see the face of the killer who had shot him from behind. James's bloodshot eyes were still open. Alex crouched down, feeling as if the killer's face might still be reflected in his blue irises. Instead, James's eyes reflected an ax thrown onto Tracey Emin's painting nearby, piercing a naked woman depicted in creamy fogs. Alex thought to himself, examining the position of James's right hand thrown upward, the ax embedded in Emin's painting, and S. L. Babel's QR code above James's head.

"James tried to break Babel's new digital art he bought for 30 million dollars with an ax," said Alex firmly. "Why did he want to break the QR code?"

"Look at the footprints!" Peter blurted out, jerking his head toward the broken window near Tracey Emin's painting. On the ground, where lush palm trees grew, a straight line of giant, jagged footprints— longer than thirteen inches—led to the paved driveway and gate of the mansion.

"So, the footprints prove neither of these two ladies is the killer," said Terence contemptuously, eyeing Elena's enamel high heels and

Bella's small sneakers.

"Do you suspect me?" rasped Elena and Bella furiously.

"Calm down! We need your help now," said Peter edgily. "Did you see the killer? What happened?"

"I helped James bring Babel's new work to this atrium. Then, he asked me to leave him alone," said Elena shrilly. "I went to the drawing room, reading emails and checking his meeting schedule for the next week. After this, I went to the restroom. Then, suddenly, gunshots erupted in the atrium."

"Did you hear anyone open the entrance door?" asked Peter.

"Yes, I did," replied Elena instantly. "But I didn't pay attention to it—I thought one of his employees visited. We're on one of the safest and most luxurious islands in the world."

"So, the killer entered through the main entrance door," said Peter, gazing furiously at the huge door of the atrium.

"What about you, Bella?" asked Laura in a tremulous voice. "Did you see the killer?"

"Yes, I saw the killer from the terrace," said Bella breathlessly, still leaning against Jeff Koons's balloon dog, as if her pregnant stomach was too heavy to support by herself.

Everybody in the room swallowed, looking at her.

"But I only saw his back," spluttered Bella. "When I heard the gunshots, I hid in a dark corner of the terrace and called 911. I only thought I couldn't die for my baby." Her trembling hand drew circles on her stomach. "When the killer broke the window, I stood up a little and gazed at the driveway. S. L. Babel, the lanky killer wearing a dark suit, jumped on a bike and thundered toward the north wharf. Then, I saw him ride a jet ski, speeding away in the ocean."

"You said the man who killed James is S. L. Babel," said Alex in a strained voice. "Why do you think so?"

"Because S. L. Babel predicted the murder of James Brown in the network. What I said in the limousine was wrong," said Bella shrilly. "The digital artist S. L. Babel isn't a detective. He is a serial killer."

"That doesn't sound convincing to me," said Alex in a shaky voice, eyeing Babel's new work on the wall. "Why would he kill one of his most generous patrons who paid thirty million dollars for this crappy QR code painting?" Alex quickly covered his mouth with his hand after uttering the word "crappy."

"Look at this!" barked Terence, who turned on his phone.

The network shown in the URL embedded in Babel's QR code had slightly changed its shape. A gunshot pierced the head of the puppet resembling James Brown in his node. Blood gradually trickled down the edges to different nodes, including those named Terence and Peter. Alex also turned on his iPhone, watching the same network. Soon, macabre letters materialized above the network.

First, the deadly virus killed the apparent leader of human organ stealers.

The sentence quickly disappeared, and another blood-colored line appeared.

But the virus won't stop until it kills the most clandestine evils.

Alex's eyes traveled over all the trembling faces in the atrium. Now, nobody seemed to object to Bella's opinion.

"Did you notice this, everyone?" said Laura in a high-pitched voice, pointing to a piece of digital artwork hung twenty-five feet away from S. L. Babel's QR code painting.

It was S. L. Babel's *Fusion*, displaying a cyborg using body parts of viewers. Alex squinted at the work. The AI-operated camera welded to the edge of the digital art was shattered, its debris scattered on the floor. A bullet hole marked the wall, suggesting a bullet was buried within. The electronic panels showing the cyborg's face were completely shattered, but other parts of the screen were intact. Alex read the metallic label on the wall: "The cyborg has the face of the most recent person who stood in front of this work, as well as the stomach and legs of the second and third most recent viewers." The cyborg in the broken digital art had James's chubby stomach in his white T-shirt and Laura's slim, long legs in a skirt. What about its face? Alex gasped. This digital art should've shown the serial killer's face—possibly, if Bella's hypothesis was true, the unidentified digital artist S. L. Babel's face. To hide his face shown in this digital art, the killer must have shot the cyborg's face and camera.

"S. L. Babel was here," said Bella darkly. "His face was captured in this digital art—or this secret surveillance camera."

"It's disgusting that part of my body is used in this painting," shrilled Laura. "My legs and James's stomach were combined with the scoundrel's creepy face."

Suddenly, the sirens of police cars reverberated through the shattered windows.

"Hey, we need to act quickly," shouted Alex, looking pale. "We have to hide the new S. L. Babel work from the police."

"Why?" asked Laura, raising her eyebrow.

"The police will confiscate this digital art for their investigation," said Alex breathlessly. Ruffling his blond hair around the forehead, Alex silently thought for a moment. *I haven't received my commission from S. L. Babel yet. If the police start investigating and suspect S. L. Babel, he may refuse to pay me.* Alex continued eloquently, "Also, if the police learn James won the auction for this expensive painting, they'll suspect you guys, who lost in the private auction."

"I don't want the police to know about that ominous network accessed through the QR code," Peter said stiffly. "This work is defamation against us. I have nothing to do with the 'human body traffickers.' If news of James Brown's murder gets out along with this egregious aspersion, the media will tarnish our reputation."

"Let's move this painting to the drawing room and hide it in your briefcase," Terence suggested. "Since James paid via bitcoin, nobody except for James and S. L. Babel knows the payment was finalized. So, we can argue that James was shot to death before he purchased this, and the artwork still belongs to you, Alex."

Alex and Terence stripped the QR code-printed canvas off the wall and quickly walked toward the drawing room.

Through the shattered windows, they could see the red burning lights of police cars approaching the driveway.

When they placed the painting in the briefcase, the bell at the main entrance rang.

Chapter Seven

An African-American FBI agent stood at the main entrance, his huge hand resting on his gun holster.

"I'm Sampson Castor from the FBI," he announced in a deep voice, striding briskly toward the end of the atrium with a cadre of uniformed officers. "Was James Brown killed?"

Why has the FBI arrived before the local police? Laura wondered silently. *This agent must be involved in other important missions in the area and keeping tabs on James Brown's mansion.*

"The killer's face was shown on this screen," said Bella shrilly, pointing to Babel's broken artwork titled *Fusion*.

"It may be worth checking the camera, though there seems to be little hope the video record is intact," said Sampson, eyeing the cyborg's bullet-riddled face. He seemed familiar with the digital art's mechanisms. "Everyone, please leave the mansion and wait in the courtyard. We need to preserve the murder scene."

"Mr. Hubert?" Sampson addressed Alex, keeping him in the drawing room as the guests moved to the courtyard.

"Yes?" Alex answered with a suspicious look. "Do you know me, sir?"

"Yes, it's a pleasure to meet you, Mr. Hubert. I've been investigating serial murders related to the trade of S. L. Babel's works," said Sampson, handing him a business card. "You're one of the most important art dealers in New York. We feared you might be next. It's our job to protect you—don't hesitate to call me."

"Thank you," said Alex, his voice trembling, fear stabbing his heart. "But why are you here in Miami?"

Alex glanced at the cadre of FBI agents behind Sampson. There were fifteen agents, indicating a significant operation. *Am I the next target?* Alex wondered. *If this agent is investigating the murders, why is he in Miami? Did someone tip off the FBI about the private auction of Babel's work at Brown's mansion?*

"One of S. L. Babel's works will be exhibited at Art Basel Miami Beach tomorrow," snapped Sampson. "We came to Miami expecting another murder. Unfortunately, our hypothesis was correct." Sampson's dark eyes fell on James Brown's body, surrounded by forensic officers. "Is there any other S. L. Babel work in this mansion, Mr. Hubert?"

"No, I don't think so," lied Alex instantly.

"Do you know who S. L. Babel is?" Sampson asked, staring squarely into Alex's eyes.

"No, I have no idea," replied Alex curtly. "But I wouldn't be surprised if he's the one who killed James."

Sampson squinted at Alex's brown leather shoes. "Can you take off your shoes?"

"Pardon?" Alex frowned.

"Take off your shoes now," Sampson demanded haughtily.

As Alex removed his shoes, an FBI officer picked them up and passed them to another officer standing by the shattered windows. The officer compared the shoes to the footprints on the ground and shook his head. "No, they don't match!"

"Do you suspect me?" Alex said resentfully, flushing. "I was sailing Brown's yacht with Peter, Laura, and Terence when James Brown was killed."

"It's our job to suspect everyone," growled Sampson. "At least, the footprints at the scene don't match yours. You're probably innocent, assuming the murder was committed by one person."

"What do you mean?" Alex asked scathingly.

"It's strange that all the guests disappeared into the ocean, leaving only his secretary and a pregnant guest," Sampson said, his eyes glinting. "You might have sailed Brown's yacht to take the other guests away, creating the perfect opportunity for the murderer to strike."

"Are you serious?" Alex snorted. "Why would I kill James Brown?"

"I don't know. But we'll find out who stands to gain millions by killing him," said Sampson coldly. "Why were all the guests invited?"

Alex hesitated, debating whether to tell the truth. S. L. Babel had asked him to keep the auction private. However, lying to Sampson would only raise suspicion. Looking around, he saw the other guests outside. Sampson's colleagues were likely questioning them. Someone might reveal the true reason for their gathering. Alex met Sampson's sharp, dark eyes, realizing he had no choice.

"My client asked me to bring a new artwork for a private auction here," Alex said stiffly. "The other guests were invited to bid."

"Interesting," Sampson whistled. "Did James Brown win the auction?"

"Yes," Alex admitted after a brief silence. He couldn't lie anymore.

"How much did he pay?" Sampson asked gruffly.

"I can't disclose that," Alex said evasively.

"Where is the artwork now?" Sampson snapped.

Alex bit his lip, feeling his insides go cold. Despite selling Babel's latest work for thirty million dollars, the buyer was dead, and the FBI was about to confiscate the painting. Would Babel still pay his commission? Probably not. But he had no choice but to show the FBI agents the artwork.

"It should be in the drawing room," Alex said begrudgingly, pointing to the door and leading the way.

"It sounds mysterious," said Sampson sarcastically as he followed Alex. "So, James Brown hadn't moved the new artwork from the drawing room to the atrium where he was killed. It's unusual if he paid a substantial amount of money for the new work to outbid other competitors in the auction. Don't you agree, Mr. Hubert? If I were him, I would have kept that work with me, especially while other auction invitees were still present." Sampson's icy voice reverberated in the atrium. "I can't shake the suspicion that someone might've moved the artwork to conceal its connection to the murder."

Sampson's words felt like needles jabbing at Alex's chest. Alex never replied. As he crossed the threshold of the drawing room, a new terror gripped him. He let out an ear-splitting cry.

There was nothing left on the blond-wood dining table.

The painting was gone.

Alex's panicked eyes searched the empty room for the briefcase containing Babel's thirty-million-dollar QR code painting.

"Where is the painting!?" Alex shouted, running out of the mansion.

FBI agents and police officers turned toward him, alarmed.

Terence's chubby face and sinister eyes under his glasses flashed in Alex's mind.

Stepping down from the porch, Alex blurted out, "Where's Terence? Has anyone seen him?"

"No, Terence isn't here," Peter, who was talking with a cop, looked around. "I haven't seen him for a while."

"What happened, Alex?" Laura asked, worried.

"Terence stole the QR code work and ran away," Alex said bitterly.

Peter and Laura froze.

"I saw James's limousine crossing the MacArthur Causeway bridge a minute ago," Elena's voice called from the terrace. She was speaking with FBI officers. Through the French window behind her, Alex could see Bella resting in an armchair. Elena shouted, "Terence must've stolen the limousine and escaped with the thirty-million-dollar painting."

Alex's iPhone beeped in his back pocket. An email had popped up.

From: S. L. Babel
Subject: Your New Mission
Date: June 15th, 2024 12:58 PM
To: Alex Hubert

Hi Alex,

Wherever I am and you are, I know everything that happens to my artworks—they are like my children, and I can feel them breathe anytime.

If you retrieve my stolen painting and return it to Geneva Freeport, I'll give you the entire thirty million dollars I got from James Brown.

Don't forget to bookmark the URL embedded in my QR code painting. Regularly check the network from your phone because it'll update and help you find Terence and my work.

Good luck!

Best,
S. L. Babel

Chapter Eight

"James and I were planning to play golf today in Miami Beach."

Peter Carli said to Alex with a sad sigh the day after James Brown's murder. They were squeezing through the crowd on the first floor of the Miami Beach Convention Center, where Art Basel Miami Beach was being held. Peter looked sick, constantly massaging his stomach while gazing at the hundreds of art collectors, gallerists, and critics meandering among the pieces of contemporary art.

"Alex, do you think all of these people truly understand art?" Peter asked scornfully. "Art was democratized and thus became vulgar and ugly."

"No, they don't understand anything. Ugly contemporary art generates loads of ugly money," Alex replied ironically. "There's only one way forward for us today. You've got to keep making money, or you'll be a loser. If contemporary art makes money, it makes sense. You're a clear winner, Peter, and I admire all the billionaire art collectors around the world because you're all modern aristocrats who fund art, which keeps tricking people for centuries and lasts longer than life."

Having spluttered enthusiastically, Alex spread the map of Art Basel Miami Beach and circled the location of S. L. Babel's digital art with a pen. It was exhibited in the east wing, across from the booth for Jackson Pollock and other works of abstract expressionism. Somehow, he had a hunch that watching another work of Babel might give him a clue to find the stolen digital artwork. The stolen QR code kept floating in his mind. *I'll get thirty million dollars if I retrieve the digital art. But where is Terence Miller, that lousy rat?* Since Alex didn't want to reveal he was dealing with S. L. Babel's work, he couldn't tell the FBI about what Terence stole. *Terence might have left the USA and never come back. But it'll be difficult to sell that QR code painting since the world hasn't known of Babel's latest work yet.*

"Hey, what's going on there?" Peter's deep voice jolted Alex back to reality. "What a huge crowd—is that a fashion show?"

Alex followed Peter's gaze. Blue searchlights were circulating around a makeshift catwalk. Upbeat pop songs were playing, and the blue letters displayed on the huge LED screen on the wall read, "WELCOME TO APOLLO BARTON'S BIO-LINGERIE FASHION SHOW."

"Apollo Barton!? Holy cow!" said Peter, looking surprised. "Isn't Apollo your client?"

"Yeah, but I didn't know his bio-bra fashion show was gonna take place here at Art Basel Miami Beach," snapped Alex, equally surprised. Apollo Barton was one of the richest contemporary artists and Alex's most important client, known for his BioArt works that combined bio-engineering with art. "I called Apollo a week ago. He told me a luxurious apparel brand would organize a fashion show for the bio-bras he created."

"What's a bio-bra, Alex?" Peter asked excitedly.

"Look at her bra," replied Alex, pointing at a skinny Latina model who had just appeared on stage from behind black curtains. The spectators' ear-splitting roar and applause swirled around the floor. Peter and Alex edged forward, squeezing between male art collectors who were passionately trying to take pictures of the model. The Latina model stopped at the end of the catwalk, shaking her hips and raising her arms skyward. As she smiled at the captivated crowd, her breasts lolled in her pink, leafy bra. Squinting at her skimpy pink bra and V-strip panty, Peter gasped.

"Is her lingerie made of pink lettuce?" panted Peter, rooted next to Alex.

"That's what bio-artist Apollo Barton likes to do," said Alex huffily. "Maybe he and his scientist team genetically modified lettuce's color for this."

"Interesting," said Peter, his eyes shining in awe.

"Gentlemen," a familiar female voice echoed from behind Alex. "Both of you look so enthralled by half-naked women," said Laura impishly, clearing her throat.

"Oh Laura, good to see you," Alex swiveled around, looking

awkward. "I never thought you'd visit Art Basel Miami Beach. Are you interested in contemporary art?"

"Yes, a little bit," said Laura casually, tiptoeing to see over other spectators' shoulders to the catwalk. "But I came here to see our friend appear in this fashion show."

"*Our* friend?" said Peter, his silver hair at the top of his head standing up.

"Yes, look at the next model," said Laura, pointing at the catwalk. "She looks like an angel. She asked me to take some pictures for her Instagram posts."

A shadow of a pregnant woman with angelic, golden feathers appeared on the wavy curtains at the back of the stage, dancing toward the center of the catwalk. The woman wore a navy, backless halter-neck dress with a large cut-out, revealing her pregnant stomach. As she twisted her waist, she placed her sinewy hand on her ample chest, sending a flirtatious gaze at the spectators. Alex swallowed. It was Bella Saba. As she stepped to the foremost edge of the catwalk, the five blue searchlights welded to the ceiling concentrated on Bella, illuminating her body. Bella's halter-neck dress, embedded with bioluminescent cells, shone like an ocean filled with glowing jellyfish. "She looked awesome," Laura cried out, stopping her phone's video as Bella's back vanished behind the curtains.

"I knew she was a contemporary art blogger and programmer," said Alex, looking bewildered. "But I didn't know she was a fashion model."

"I didn't know either," Laura admitted.

"Shall we go see S. L. Babel's work, Alex?" Peter asked from behind them.

"Sure," said Alex.

"I'm curious about that, too!" chirped Laura, following as the two began walking toward the east wing where S. L. Babel's work was exhibited.

"By the way, Laura," Alex whispered when they turned a corner and Peter shuffled slower, out of earshot. "What kind of information do you have about the serial killings connected to the dealings of S. L.

Babel's digital art? Is the *Washington Post* close to uncovering the truth?"

"We need to talk alone, very urgently," replied Laura in a strained voice. "Let's chat at a coffee shop nearby after seeing Babel's work at this art fair. You've got to leave the US right now, at least by tonight."

"What?" Alex frowned.

"I'll explain later," said Laura stiffly.

S. L. Babel's digital art piece, *A Bloody Dormitory*, was exhibited in a vacant room. Surprisingly, there were no visitors when the three stepped inside. The painting depicted a male college student's room in a dormitory, with a rectangular screen embedded in the canvas. A puddle of blood spread over the tattered sheets on the sunken twin bed, reaching the hem of the green college flag hung on the wall. A male hand, white and lifeless, was thrown out toward the headboard, clutching a duvet. The student lay supine, his chest bleeding heavily. A shaft of sunlight through the window illuminated his beautiful white face turned sideways. His eyes were half-closed, but one could see a grayish-blue glint through his long lashes, slightly wet with tears, his left finger pointed to a whiteboard near the bed, as if leaving a dying message.

Alex's eyes darted toward what the murdered student was pointing at.

The whiteboard depicted on the upper-left side of S. L. Babel's painting was made of a digital touchscreen. Suddenly, as Alex took a step closer, purple, quaky letters appeared.

Welcome to Josh Stevenson's room.

"Josh Stevenson... I feel like I've heard this name before," said Laura pensively.

The letters vanished like ripples.

Tell me your name. This is a touchscreen. I can only reveal the truth of my death to the brave people I've been waiting for.

"Who wants to write?" said Alex, looking at Peter and Laura.

"Go ahead, Laura," said Peter quickly.

Laura widened her eyes.

"I agree," Alex said. "Since you've been investigating the murders related to S. L. Babel's works and got an invitation to the private auction from Babel himself, this AI-chat system will probably favor you."

"Okay," said Laura snappishly, printing her full name, Laura Campbell, with her sweaty finger.

As she withdrew her hand from the touch panel, the letters disappeared like melted sugar and other letters materialized.

I was waiting for you to visit me, Laura.

They swallowed and winced.

Three years ago, I was killed by the scumbag who stole S. L. Babel's new work in James Brown's mansion yesterday. It is Terence Miller who killed me.

Laura let out a cry. Alex froze, his eyes slightly bulging with fear. Peter folded his arms, staring at the whiteboard.

Laura quickly jotted down a sentence as Josh Stevenson's purple words disappeared from the whiteboard.

Why did Terence kill you, Josh?

Laura's letters drew a whirlpool and disappeared. In five seconds, new letters popped up.

Terence Miller was a surgeon and biomedical researcher at the time. At the medical center where Terence oversaw the preservation of donated human corpses, I worked for him as a research assistant. One day, I discovered his serious crime, and it was just the tip of the iceberg. He was part of a huge, organized crime network across America.

Alex, Laura, and Peter, all standing rooted to the spot, felt dread running through their bodies.

"Terence Miller, a surgeon at a medical center…" Laura said in a low voice. "When I met him in the limousine at the airport, I thought I heard his name somewhere before during my investigation into the serial murders in St. Louis."

While Laura was speaking, Alex quickly wrote a question on the touchscreen as Josh Stevenson's message vanished.

What is Terence's crime?

Instantly, Josh Stevenson replied.

I can't tell you. You have to find it out on your own. But I can share his whereabouts with you.

Alex exchanged fearful glances with Laura and Peter. Josh continued.

Go visit my tomb in the Catholic Cemeteries near Mackenzie Hills Park, St. Louis. Terence is heading there to hide S. L. Babel's QR code painting in my tomb. Also, you'll find another clue to uncover his crime.

Laura wrote another message, rubbing her finger on the touchscreen.

Tell me more, please.

Josh shortly replied.

No, I can't tell you anymore, Laura. Go find the stolen artwork and the truth.

The touch screen embedded in the whiteboard inside the painting went blank. Laura wrote "PLEASE," but no more letters appeared no matter what she wrote.

The three left the exhibition room as other visitors came in.

Chapter Nine

After walking the catwalk, Bella Saba returned to the dressing room through the black curtains on the stage. Even as the spectators' voices and their heat faded, she maintained her stride and smile, still imagining their gazes on her back. Surrounded by the chatter of other fashion models, Bella let out a sigh of relief and sat on a stool in front of a vanity mirror. Picking up her phone from beside a curling iron on the table, she smiled at her own made-up face in the mirror and took a selfie for her Instagram story. As she added the hashtags #ArtBaselMiami, #BioBra, #ApolloBarton, and #Fashion to her post, a text message from Laura popped up: "You looked so stunning!" Laura had also sent some pictures she'd taken of Bella. Bella saved the pictures and replied with a simple "Thanks!"

In the fashion show, Laura was with art dealer Alex Hubert and Swiss billionaire Peter Carli. As she removed the golden feathers from her halter-neck dress, Bella thought of them. When she stood at the end of the catwalk, Laura, Alex, and Peter had all looked astounded, as if they never knew a pregnant woman could be so beautiful and powerful. *You guys will never know where I am heading.* Bella smiled at the mirror, imagining their faces in the empty space of the reflection. *I'm the only person who knows the real identity of S. L. Babel on the planet. And I'm the only person who knows what S. L. Babel is aiming to achieve.*

Bella stood up from the stool, staring at her reflection. She put her hands on her cold, swelling stomach, which the cut-out of the halter-neck dress revealed. The bioluminescent cells in the dress began to shine navy under the dressing room light, encircling her stomach like jewelry. Bella closed her eyes, imagining the small creature breathing and pulsing beneath her fingers.

Laura, perhaps, either of us has to die first, Bella thought darkly.

Babel's Deathly Virus Network shows our nodes clustering closer, indicating we will be killed separately, but at a short interval. I can't die because I'll bring another life into the world someday.

"Great performance, Bella!" The Latina model wearing the bra made of pink lettuce passed behind Bella, speaking to her. Bella opened her eyes and met the model's gaze in the vanity mirror.

"How old is your baby?" asked the model, her eyes riveted on Bella's exposed stomach in the mirror.

"Six months," snapped Bella.

"Boy or girl?" asked the Latina model in a raspy voice.

"It's a secret," said Bella after a moment of silence.

"I see," said the model, still smiling casually. "I wish you the best, Bella. You might be a real Bio Art piece."

As the Latina model left, Bella smiled at herself in the mirror.

Yes, I'm Bio Art myself. But all art is fake. The greatest works in art are those that deceive people into believing in their value.

Bella stripped off her Bio Art halter-neck dress. As she touched the surface, the bioluminescent cells turned red as if sending her a warning for the future.

Chapter Ten

"Good luck, Peter."

Outside the exit of the Miami Beach Convention Center, Alex shook hands with Peter as he got into a taxi.

"It was a pleasure to meet you, Mr. Carli. Take care!" Laura said to Peter, who was weakly smiling through the half-open shaded window.

"Good luck with your further journey, both," Peter said in a throaty voice as the taxi pulled out onto Washington Avenue. "Alex, call me whenever you need my assistance to find the stolen S. L. Babel work—not just for us, but for James."

The black taxi started to trundle down the sunlit avenue while Alex and Laura waved at the rear windshield.

"I didn't know Peter had a serious illness," said Alex with a sigh.

When they had left Art Basel Miami Beach, Peter revealed that he would be going to a hospital for surgery, which might have been another reason for his trip to the USA.

"He never said what kind of illness he has," replied Laura reassuringly. "It might not be serious."

"Billionaires don't reveal their sickness because their health affects their stock prices," said Alex sarcastically. "He never said where he's going, either. I'm worried about him. According to S. L. Babel's network, Peter will die next."

"I don't trust the network, Alex," said Laura skeptically. "I think the network is irrelevant to the murder of James Brown. S. L. Babel just elaborated on a prank. If the network is a prediction of the future," Laura twisted her lips nervously. "I may be killed, too."

"No worries, Laura," snapped Alex. "I agree. The network must be a prank. We've left James Brown's mansion and are moving apart. Some folks featured in the network, like the scumbag Terence, must be out of town. It's impossible for the serial killer to track everyone now."

Alex drove his rental Toyota RAV4, taking Laura to a coffee shop in Wynwood. They found a vacant table in the shop's corner, where they could chat out of other customers' earshot. The TV hanging from the ceiling was showing Fox News. They ordered two cappuccinos.

"You said I need to leave the USA right away, Laura?" said Alex in an undertone, staring squarely at Laura's eyes. "Why?"

"Because you're in a very dangerous situation," replied Laura, looking around to see if other customers in the coffee shop were overhearing or overseeing them. A mid-forties, tourist-looking, black-haired guy clad in an aloha shirt came in after them and sat four seats away, his sharp eyes riveted on Fox News featuring the launch of SpaceX's latest space shuttle.

Laura took out her iPad from her tote bag and handed wireless earbuds to Alex while the erupting noise of the space shuttle engines reverberated from the TV.

"I set a bug under the dining table in the drawing room of James Brown's mansion," Laura whispered.

Alex raised his eyebrows.

"As a journalist, I wanted to hear James's conversations with his guests because it would be the most effective way to uncover his criminal dealings," said Laura firmly.

"What criminal dealings?" said Alex, his nose slightly wrinkling.

"I'll tell you about it later," said Laura, tapping the desk gently. "I never imagined James would be killed. The bug accidentally caught FBI agent Sampson's voice before they discovered and took it away. Put the earbuds in and hear what he said, Alex."

As Alex put on the earbuds with his clumsy hands, Laura turned on a secret application on her iPad, playing Sampson's recorded voice. Alex closed his eyes, straining his ears.

"*We've got to arrest Alex Hubert as soon as possible. There's a flight risk since he has dual citizenship in Switzerland,*" Sampson Castor's gruff voice resounded in the darkness under Alex's eyelids. "*Hubert's accounts are all contradictory. While Hubert never revealed it was S. L. Babel's work that was auctioned, Elena Taylor and Bella Saba* told us Hubert brought Babel's new digital work. Nonetheless, I have no doubt that digital artist S. L. Babel doesn't exist. In fact, S. L. Babel, the serial killer operating behind the contemporary market, is Alex Hubert. I believe so because Hubert is the one who organized the private auction in Brown's mansion. Hubert was never willing to tell me the real reason behind this gathering. But Brown's secretary, Elena Taylor, told me the truth. I'm guessing Hubert created a new Babel work to lure James Brown to invite him along with the artwork. During the investigation, Hubert ran out to the courtyard and claimed Terence stole the artwork. I believe this behavior was staged."

"How do you account for the footprints on the ground? They didn't match Hubert's footprints," said another FBI agent.

"The footprints are camouflage," said Sampson stoutly. "He could change shoes whenever he wanted. He probably threw out the shoes in the ocean."

"What about his alibi? Hubert was sailing Brown's yacht when Brown was killed," said the other agent.

"We shouldn't trust what all the others allegedly sailing on the yacht—Swiss billionaire Peter Carli, surgeon Terence Miller, and journalist Laura Campbell—said. We found psychedelic, hallucinatory drugs in the drinks in the refrigerator on the yacht. Alex Hubert must've mixed the drugs. I found Hubert's fingerprints on the knob of the refrigerator," said Sampson in a low voice. "A boy living in a mansion on Hibiscus Island witnessed Brown's Lamborghini yacht, which he always admired, at that time. He testified that he'd seen a gray-haired man with a long mustache sailing the yacht in the cockpit—it must've been Terence Miller. The boy also said he saw a blond guy resembling Alex Hubert driving a jet ski around the yacht. My hypothesis is Hubert boarded the yacht, mixed the psychedelic drug into the drinks to manipulate the passengers' minds, then drove the jet ski from the yacht to the mansion, killing James Brown and stealing the artwork he'd purchased."

"What!?" Alex mouthed, opening his eyes and looking at Laura.

"Since Hubert is S. L. Babel himself, he managed to steal thirty million dollars from James Brown, as well as the artwork he'd sold," added Sampson passionately.

"*It indeed explains everything, Sampson,*" said the other agent approvingly. "*After killing James Brown, Hubert must've returned to his yacht on the jet ski. Then, he sailed the yacht back to the mansion. We can't trust what the other passengers heard was a gunshot. They were all drugged by Hubert.*"

"*Exactly,*" said Sampson in a deep voice. "*Above all, Brown's secretary, Elena Taylor, who was in a restroom close to the drawing room, heard James Brown's voice when he was killed. According to Elena, Brown shouted, 'STOP, ALEX, I CAN GIVE YOU ANYTHING YOU WANT. STOP, ALEX, PLEASE!!!' before the gunshots.*"

Alex froze, feeling a cold chill running down his spine.

"*I see,*" the other agent whistled. "*We gotta find a way to arrest serial killer Alex Hubert, then. We must find evidence now.*"

The recording ended there.

Alex Hubert stripped the earbuds off his ears and threw them onto the table.

"Ridiculous!" Alex said indignantly. "They're trying to frame me!"

"But the outlook is very bad for you," Laura replied calmly. "Elena testified that James shouted your name before being killed."

"That's hogwash!" Alex snapped, his face contorting. "Elena is lying. But I don't know why she's trying to frame me. Do you also think I killed James Brown?"

"No," said Laura, her voice clear. "We were on the same yacht when the gunshots echoed from James Brown's mansion. And I wasn't drugged. But the variety of witnesses and circumstances don't favor you. The FBI is likely to arrest you wrongly—you might spend your life in prison, or worse, be executed. We're in Florida. The death penalty exists."

"I'm not leaving the US until I retrieve the thirty-million-dollar S. L. Babel work," Alex said stubbornly. "And I need to visit Josh Stevenson's tomb in St. Louis."

"Are you serious?" Laura said, raising her brow. "Do you risk your life to get that QR code? Isn't it crap? Your enemy is the FBI—you can't escape them in this country."

"Aren't you interested in the message that popped up in Babel's work at Art Basel Miami Beach?" Alex asked, his voice tense.

"Do you trust the message?" Laura rasped. "It might be a trap."

"Terence is from St. Louis," Alex said. "It's not surprising that he went back there to hide the QR code art."

"Okay," Laura sank into the leather chair, exhaling slowly. "I'm not going to stop you, then. It's your choice. I'm also interested in Josh Stevenson's tomb. I feel like I've heard that name while covering murder cases in St. Louis. Anyway, I believe we can find a clue to uncover the biggest organized crime operation in America that I've been investigating for years."

"Don't be cryptic," Alex said in a deep voice. "What is the organized crime you've been investigating?"

Suddenly, Laura's face froze, her eyes riveted on the TV.

The letters "BREAKING NEWS" appeared on the screen.

"The mystery of the multibillionaire's death in Miami will be resolved very soon once this man is arrested," the Fox News anchor said in a ringing voice. "Just now, the FBI announced art dealer Alex Hubert as a wanted suspect."

Alex's Facebook profile picture was displayed. It was a selfie taken on a yacht sailing in Lake Geneva. Behind Alex, who smiled at the camera, the Jet d'Eau Fountain shot toward the sky, a veil of rainbow dancing around the splash.

"Alex Hubert, who allegedly murdered pharmaceutical mogul James Brown in his Star Island mansion, is currently on the run," the Fox News anchor continued. "If you have any information about his whereabouts, please call the following number. If you provide crucial information, the FBI will award you up to a one hundred-thousand-dollar bounty."

There was an abysmal, petrified silence between Alex and Laura, during which they exchanged frozen gazes.

"Would you like a check?" the waitress's voice broke the silence, making them look up at her.

"Oh, yes," mouthed Alex.

The waitress roamed across the floor to the cashier.

"We must run away from this coffeeshop right now," whispered Laura, glancing at the tourist-looking man in the aloha shirt at the corner. "He's an FBI agent. I recognized him just now."

"What!?" Alex's chin shot up.

"I remember his face even though he's wearing a strange wig. He was one of Sampson's team officers who visited James Brown's mansion. He must've been following us from the Miami Beach Convention Center," Laura whispered into Alex's ear. "I saw him type a message on his phone under the table. The police will be here to arrest you any minute. Also, the officer likely has a gun. I saw the left side of his pants bulging."

"Well then, Laura," said Alex in a clear voice. The buzzing sirens of police cars suddenly became audible outside the windows. "Do you remember where I parked my rental car?"

"Yes," replied Laura firmly.

"I'll count to three. Let's run out, okay?" Alex's eyes traveled around the coffee shop. The waitress was striding to their table with a check. "One, two ...three!!!"

Both Alex and Laura jumped up from their seats and ran toward the exit. Laura's shoulder bumped into the waitress, causing her to slip and scream.

As Alex and Laura reached the sliding doors of the exit, they saw the glass door reflecting the FBI agent in the aloha shirt who had jumped on a table and aimed his gun at them. They rushed out without looking back, crouching under the wall. A gunshot roared, shattering the glass door inches away from Alex's arm, and its fragments cut his forearm. Alex and Laura jumped into the Toyota RAV4. When the FBI agent emerged and aimed his gun at Alex, Laura stretched her body over Alex.

"I'm not a wanted criminal! You can't injure me!" Laura shouted at the agent.

"Great job, Laura!" Alex kickstarted the engine, and the SUV thundered out of the driveway.

Four police cars were heading to the coffee shop, seemingly unaware that Alex was driving the Toyota.

"Stop that fucking car! Alex Hubert is driving the car!" the aloha-clad FBI agent barked behind them.

Alex's car swerved through the fleet of police cars and turned the corner at Wynwood Walls. A group of tourists pouring out of the museum looked abashed at the rushing car.

"Where are we going, Alex?" shrieked Laura.

"To the airport, of course," said Alex, crossing a junction with a red traffic light. The cars that tried to avoid Alex's car crashed into each other with a bang. While putting his foot on the accelerator, Alex phoned Peter Carli. His Swiss multibillionaire client answered in three seconds.

"Peter! Peter!" Alex shouted. "I need your help. Where are you now?"

"I'm at Miami International Airport," Peter's throaty voice replied. "I'm on my jet. What's happening, Alex?"

"Can you wait for me, please?" said Alex earnestly, turning the steering wheel to enter NW 12th Avenue. "Laura and I must fly out of Miami right away."

"Probably out of the USA, forever," said Laura darkly from the passenger seat.

"Okay, I'll tell my pilot to wait for you," Peter replied drily. "But where do you want to fly? I'm heading to St. Louis, Missouri."

Alex and Laura looked at each other.

"Us too," replied Alex, out of breath.

Chapter Eleven

The New Wave of Digital Art: Bella Saba's Art Blog

The Theft of S. L. Babel's New $30-Million Digital Art

The Murder of James Brown

Multi-billionaire pharmaceutical giant and art collector James Brown was murdered in his mansion on Star Island, Miami. Is this surprising? Not really. Many art collectors and dealers involved in S. L. Babel's digital art have been mysteriously killed. Notably, James Brown was keen to discover Babel's identity. Once, he posted on X:

@Real_James_Brown
3.7 million followers
I'll pay 5 million dollars to anyone who reveals S. L. Babel's identity.
2:34 pm 8/13/24 From Earth **1.2M** Views
6.5K Reposts **1.2K** Quotes
1.1M Likes **3.3K** Bookmarks

His post resulted in thousands of false leads about S. L. Babel. The mainstream media never attempts to report the truth, but all the people who were killed were not just involved in Babel's works; they tried to reveal Babel's identity.

Who Killed James Brown and Why?

Following the FBI's announcement, the media started to suggest that Swiss-American art dealer Alex Hubert, the FBI's prime suspect, killed James Brown. Many speculate that Hubert couldn't strike an ideal deal with Brown, which led him to murder. I hardly believe this theory. I've never trusted the corporate media's narrative. Why would Alex Hubert need to kill one of his wealthiest clients?

I firmly believe S. L. Babel, or someone hired by Babel, killed James Brown. Babel's new digital artwork, which was secretly brought to Brown's mansion on that day, predicted Brown's death. Babel's new painting, which only depicted a QR code, has an embedded URL leading to a website showing a network entitled *The Deathly Network*.

However, Babel's new QR code painting was stolen. I WITNESSED THIS PAINTING BEING STOLEN FROM BROWN'S MANSION. The FBI and media never report this news. Why? Because they're all corrupt and try to protect the person who stole the painting.

We must acknowledge Babel's intelligence. Although the painting itself was stolen, its extended part of the artwork always exists online. The network ominously predicts that a deadly virus will kill Brown's billionaire friend Peter Carli, another collector of Babel's digital art. At the end of the network, the virus is predicted to take the life of either me or Laura Campbell, a journalist for the *Washington Post* investigating the serial murders surrounding Babel's works. What do the people named in this network have in common? We are all trying to unmask S. L. Babel.

Should I stop writing this blog post? No, I won't stop investigating. True art aficionados are not afraid of death, because art is more precious than life.

Be Careful of Counterfeits of Babel's New Work

It seems that S. L. Babel is already aware of the theft of his work. Babel quickly reported this to the Art Loss Register. I confirmed that Babel's QR code painting was already registered on their website last night.

We expect to see a surge of counterfeits masquerading as S. L. Babel's works in the dark market, as it is easy to create a similar QR code painting. The most effective way to distinguish the real painting is to examine Babel's signature at the bottom. See <u>my previous post</u> for the details.

Who is S. L. Babel?

Harvard art historian Thomas Field published an interesting article about S. L. Babel's identity in *Computational Art Studies.* Dr. Field analyzed the relationship between artists' psychological characteristics and their works through enormous amounts of data, arguing that the angle of people's faces in paintings offers clues to their creators' personalities. According to Dr. Field, S. L. Babel, who mostly painted smiling women from the left angles (85% of women in his digital art are smiling, 94% are depicted from the left angles, and 100% have eyeshadows), must be a vengeful, cold-blooded person who lacks empathy due to a deeply grave incident, such as the loss of a lover or family member. Do you buy into this theory?

I don't. It's a silly idea that one can infer an artist's personality based on their works. S. L. Babel's artwork reflects the supremacy of algorithms over human creation. What we can safely say is that S. L. Babel is a highly intelligent programmer and engineer capable of producing sophisticated digital art. Additionally, Babel might be a calculated killer playing a complex game.

Arguably, the FBI has S. L. Babel's fingerprints. Although they have never released this information, someone's fingerprints were found on Babel's recent digital art *Your Clone Will Live After Your Death*. These fingerprints weren't from auctioneers or dealers. We want to know if the FBI found the same fingerprints at the murder scene in James Brown's mansion.

What Are the Current Prices of Babel's Works?

All these murders have driven the prices of Babel's works up. Before his death, James Brown bought Babel's QR code painting for thirty million dollars. How much is it worth now? In the past, the price of S. L. Babel's works skyrocketed by 70 to 120% after the deaths of affluent art collectors who had purchased them. The QR code painting should be worth at least fifty million dollars now.

No comments:
COMMENTS HAVE BEEN CLOSED due to an enormous amount of spam and blackmail.
Subscribe to Bella Saba's email list

Closing the web browser window for her own website and putting her MacBook Air into sleep mode, Bella Saba heaved a long sigh and raised her gaze to the crowd around the oval swimming pool. She sat at a table in a bar near Miami Beach. As the DJ started a new song, some of the crowd, wearing swimsuits and sunglasses, jumped into the swimming pool, dancing to the cadence of Electropop.

"Your laptop looks so cool, baby," said a tall Caucasian man in his mid-twenties with blond undercut hair and a long beard, wearing only swim trunks. He stood in front of Bella's table, tapping it with his tattooed hand, and smiled. "I'm looking for a new friend at this party. Did you get a drink? I can treat you."

"No, thank you. I can't drink anything," said Bella, leaning back in her chair and putting her hand on her swollen stomach.

The blond man's face twisted as he realized his mistake. *This girl is pregnant.* He grabbed his sunglasses and put them on to hide his expression. Feeling his desire shrink, he glanced at Bella's fingers. There was no wedding ring.

"I see," said the blond man in a slightly irritated voice. "Take care!"

As he turned to walk back to the swimming pool, he bumped into a stout African American man in a black suit, striding toward Bella's table with two glasses of lemonade in his hand. A small amount of lemonade spilled over the glasses and splattered on the floor.

"I'm sorry, man," said the blond man evasively, jumping into the wave of the party crowd as the African American man glowered at him.

"How are you, Bella?" smiled FBI agent Sampson Castor, placing the two glasses of lemonade on the table.

"Good, and you?" replied Bella curtly, taking one of the glasses and sipping it.

"Great! We'll arrest Alex Hubert very soon in Miami. I'm very excited about this," said Sampson, his eyes glinting. "We've been following Hubert since the murder of James Brown. We'll catch him quickly."

"I don't believe Alex killed James Brown," said Bella, lowering her voice a notch. "I know the FBI wants to arrest him for another purpose."

Sampson Castor raised his brow, looking around to see if anyone was overhearing their conversation. The high-pitched Electropop reverberated around them, drowning out their voices.

"I read your latest blog post, Bella," said Sampson in a thick voice, placing the glass of Diet Coke on the table. "I suggest you seriously consider deleting your post. The public shouldn't know about the existence of Babel's stolen new work. It will hinder our investigation."

"It's too late, sir," said Bella slyly. "Millions of people actively view my blog and social media every day. The news has already circulated online, no matter how you guys in the FBI try to censor the mainstream media. I'm an American citizen. WE HAVE THE RIGHT TO FREEDOM OF INFORMATION."

With his arms crossed, Sampson fell silent, his gaze on the table. Bella could see the pulse in Sampson's temple beating violently.

"So, are you meeting with me to chastise me, Mr. Castor?" asked Bella impishly. "When you called me, didn't you say you wanted to discuss something?"

"I did," said Sampson, clearing his throat, turning on his phone, and showing Bella a picture of a glass. "Do you remember who used this Sprite glass left in the cabin of Brown's Lamborghini yacht?"

"I need time to remember," said Bella after carefully observing the picture for ten seconds. "It seems there is a fingerprint on this. Did you attempt to compare it to S. L. Babel's fingerprint left on *Your Clone Will Live After Your Death?*"

Is this bitch reading my mind? Sampson, who didn't immediately reply to Bella's question, felt a bead of sweat running down his back.

The blond man who had approached Bella before walked to the bar in front of their table with a brown-skinned girl, casting a scornful look at them.

"I can't answer your question as there is a risk you'll write what I say on your blog," said Sampson sharply. "But I gotta ask this. Who drank Sprite using this glass on the Lamborghini yacht on the day James Brown was killed?"

"It's Alex, if I remember correctly," said Bella.

"Thanks," said Sampson, a victorious smile flashing on his face for a moment.

"Was there S. L. Babel's fingerprint on the Sprite glass?" asked Bella huffily.

"I can't say," replied Sampson tartly.

"It could be a fingerprint of someone else who was on the yacht," said Bella indignantly, pointing to the picture of the glass shown on the screen of Sampson's phone. "Terence might've touched the glass. In the first place, Terence stole the QR code painting. You gotta arrest Terence right away instead of Alex."

"We just wanted to confirm who might've touched the glass containing Sprite in the cabin of the Lamborghini yacht," said Sampson in a thick voice.

"Alex touched the glass for sure. But others might have touched it," said Bella firmly, glowering at Sampson. "Did his fingerprints match S. L. Babel's fingerprints?"

"Again, I can't answer, Bella," said Sampson in a deep voice. "Did you see anyone else touch the glass during the sail?"

"I saw Terence touch the glass on the table in the cabin to make room for his own glass," said Bella furiously. "Honestly, this is BS! Why aren't you guys chasing the lousy surgeon Terence, who stole the painting and ran away?"

"It's Alex Hubert who lied to us during our investigation," shrugged Sampson. "Your recent blog post gave us crucial information. Using the pretext of customer privacy, Hubert never tried to reveal the details of the artwork he brought to the private auction at James Brown's mansion. In your blog, you described the artwork auctioned there as S. L. Babel's work, which merely depicted a QR code. Is that true? Are there any other signs that reveal some secrets?"

"I won't answer your question, either," snapped Bella, getting to her feet stiffly. "I'll never cooperate with you guys. You're trying to frame an innocent citizen and hide the real murderer. Alex isn't S. L. Babel."

"Answer my question!" Sampson roared, also standing up and glowering at Bella. "We're interested in Babel's new work because it must convey some messages and clues."

"No, I'll never help you again," Bella shouted back, her lemonade glass dropping onto the floor and shattering. "Remember, I don't need the FBI to reveal who S. L. Babel is."

The bartender, waitstaff, and other guests cast frightened looks at them. They could see Sampson wearing a holstered gun on his waist.

"Have a good day!" said Bella with an impish smile, turning back to the exit. "I'm sure you guys will fail to arrest Alex Hubert."

As Sampson gritted his teeth, his phone on the table rang. It was his fellow FBI agent who was following Alex Hubert from the Miami Beach Convention Center.

"Sorry, boss," shouted the agent's panic-stricken voice. "Alex Hubert escaped us and ran away."

Sampson fell silent for a moment and answered, "I have another issue I need to deal with quickly now. Never allow Hubert to leave the USA, okay?"

"Yes, sir. I'll report to you when I find out where Hubert is heading," the agent spluttered, sounding a little surprised that his boss wasn't so angry, and hung up the phone.

Sampson looked around. Nobody was observing him. The wave of electropop music from the swimming pool engulfed his body. Sampson squinted at the screen of his phone and found the phone number registered as "VIP contact." It was senator Susanne Caldwell's phone number. He called her. In seven seconds, Caldwell picked up the phone.

"Did you get any new information about S. L. Babel?" asked

Caldwell's silky voice.

"No, congresswoman, unfortunately," said Sampson in an unctuous tone. "I'm calling you because I have a question. There was a fingerprint on a glass in the cabin of James Brown's mansion. The fingerprint didn't match Alex Hubert's fingerprint, which we had already obtained from the desktop PC in his New York office. But it matched the fingerprint of the serial killer in St. Louis. A surgeon named Terence Miller was likely the one to touch the glass."

Susanne Caldwell at the other end of the line was breathing slowly.

"Congresswoman is Terence Miller on *our* side?" asked Sampson in a deep voice.

"Yes," answered Caldwell firmly. "Terence Miller is part of us and in charge of our mission. The FBI must protect him."

Chapter Twelve

As Peter's private jet angled upward, Alex glanced at the grasslands of the Everglades stretching out beneath the cabin window, drawing a breath of slight relief. He took off the black mask and Laura's red fedora, which he'd borrowed to hide his face in the airport.

"So, the FBI wants to arrest you for the murder of James Brown?" Peter Carli said in a throaty voice, sitting in a leather armchair across the aisle. "That's ridiculous!"

"Indeed," Laura, who sat next to Alex, said indignantly. "We were on the same yacht when the gunshots echoed."

"Mademoiselle, you said the FBI agent thinks we were drugged on the yacht, right?" said Peter scathingly. "It's nonsense. We weren't drugged. It may be Sampson who mixed psychedelic drugs into the drinks on the yacht to nullify our testimony and frame Alex."

"It's possible. But for what?" said Laura in a tremulous voice.

"I don't get it either," said Alex crossly. "Why does Sampson Castor want to arrest me?"

"Maybe, if they manage to arrest you on some charge," said Peter pensively, "they'll finally find out who S. L. Babel is. You've been communicating with S. L. Babel by email, right? The FBI might be able to track his IP address if they get your phone and PC."

"I disagree, Peter," said Alex, his voice cracking with anxiety. "If they wanted to arrest me as a lead to solving S. L. Babel's mystery, the FBI wouldn't have publicly announced I am wanted as a suspect for James's murder. Sampson Castor and his FBI team are trying to frame me to cover up the real reason why James Brown was killed, and probably James's crime," said Alex grimly, eyeing Laura's pale face. "Laura, you said you know something about James Brown's crime, right? Can you tell me what you know about the organized crime associated with James now?"

"Okay," sighed Laura, her anxious gaze floating in the air. "James Brown built his massive fortune by human trafficking and illegal trade of human organs and dead bodies across America."

"What!?" said Alex, looking bewildered.

Peter remained silent, sitting deeply in his armchair with his arms crossed.

"One day, an anonymous letter was delivered to my office at the *Washington Post*," said Laura in a slightly trembling voice. "Enclosed in the letter was a picture of a truck loaded with dozens of dead bodies donated for scientific research purposes and undocumented immigrants— mostly children from Central and South American countries. The printed-out letter argued that the truck delivered those cadavers and illegal immigrants to one of James Brown's pharmaceutical company branches in St. Louis."

Laura took out her iPad, logging into her OneDrive account via high-speed inflight Wi-Fi. Opening a Word document of her ongoing book draft, tentatively titled *Stolen Organs: Billion-Dollar Human Body Trade of the Pharmaceutical Titan*, she found the picture sent to her desk and showed it to Alex. Taking a glance at the picture, Alex recoiled in horror. The picture must've been taken by one of the immigrant children packed in the back of the truck. A pale, haggard Mexican boy with hollow cheeks opened the edge of one of the sealed coffins, illuminated by another child's phone. The face of an embalmed, white middle-aged man appeared. The children gathered around the cadaver, gawking at the thyroid-hormone injected, sallow face of the dead man. The children's muddy faces were fraught with awe and fear. The dead body somehow looked sacred to them, but at the same time, it was a terrifying mirror reflecting their future.

"This is horrifying," sputtered Alex, feeling his skin crawl. "So, James Brown was illegally using bodies donated for scientific purposes and engaging in human trafficking to support his pharmaceutical business?"

"Possibly. And these kids were probably forced to sell their kidneys," said Laura darkly. "I've been investigating this for more than a year. While I was reviewing my notes for my upcoming book, I finally remembered who Josh Stevenson, the murdered college student depicted in S. L. Babel's work, was."

From her OneDrive account, she pulled up a PDF article from the *St. Louis Riverfront Times* that her journalist friend wrote. The headline read "MYSTERIOUS DEATH OF A COLLEGE STUDENT AT A DORMITORY." Medical school student Josh Stevenson was killed in his dormitory years ago. The killer stabbed him, leaving him sprawled on his bed. His PC, flash drive, and a printed-out picture on the whiteboard were missing.

According to the dormitory's printer log, the title of the stolen picture's JPEG file was "Truck_corpses_kidnapped_children.jpeg" However, the local police couldn't locate the data of the picture.

"I googled the name Terence Miller last night," said Laura, a note of fury in her voice. "That lousy scumbag is a professional surgeon and director of a medical center in St. Louis. He must be part of James Brown's operation."

"You've worked hard to get closer to the truth, Laura," said Peter sharply. "But I guess there's more to this than human trafficking. You both saw the enormous collection of art in the atrium of his mansion. According to *Forbes*, he didn't sell the shares of his company, which make up most of his multibillion-dollar assets. How did James Brown get the enormous amount of cash to purchase artwork? On top of organ trading, there must be a more elaborate scheme generating billions."

"I couldn't agree more, Peter," said Alex hotly. "Why doesn't the FBI investigate this human trafficking and organ trade instead of framing me?"

"It's because James Brown donated a lot of money to powerful politicians," snapped Laura. "I'll reveal the connections between Congress and James Brown's company in my book. He hasn't just donated money, but organs to politicians and wealthy people. Anyone is willing to wield political power or pay millions of dollars to save their own lives. Death comes to anyone, no matter how powerful or wealthy."

"Indeed," said Peter grimly, heaving a deep sigh.

"I think S. L. Babel invited me to the private auction in Brown's mansion because S. L. Babel wants me to uncover all the crimes behind James Brown," said Laura passionately. "Now I feel like James Brown deserved his fate. The digital artist S. L. Babel may be punishing them."

"In any case, S. L. Babel is nuts, honestly," Alex mumbled. "Think about the network that predicted James Brown's death. Babel is a cold-blooded killer, no matter what."

Alex turned on his phone connected to in-flight Wi-Fi and opened the bookmarked URL embedded in Babel's QR code artwork. He froze.

"What's going on in this network?" Alex squealed, showing Laura his phone's screen.

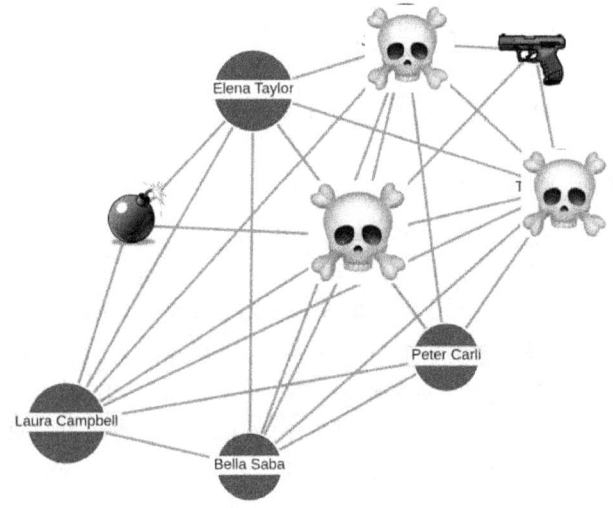

A gunshot pierced the puppet in Terence's node. The puppet vanished like a bubble. Then, a skull on crossbones appeared on Terence's node just like James Brown's node.

Ominous letters appeared at the top of the network:

The Deathly Virus executed the second criminal.

The red light that had shrouded Terence's node trickled down to the next node, named Peter Carli.

"Peter, be careful," said Laura in a shaky voice. "You might be next."

"Where's the evidence that proves Terence was killed?" said Peter sulkily. "I believe this network is a prank."

Alex gazed at the monitor hung from the ceiling. Peter Carli's jet was flying over Georgia. They would land in St. Louis in an hour.

"I'm taking a rest now," said Alex weakly. "It's a waste of time to wonder if the network's prediction will be correct or not. But I don't think anyone can come here to kill us on this private jet. Let's rest, everyone."

"Yeah," nodded Peter.

"Good idea," replied Laura.

Placing his head on the headrest, Alex closed his eyes and breathed slowly. Fatigue and coldness suddenly shrouded his body, a soft, black veil enveloping his vision.

The roaring sound of Peter Carli's jet gradually receded. Instead, the idling engine of James Brown's Lamborghini yacht whined behind Alex. There was nobody on the deck. Alex was on a green floating board in the turquoise ocean, and Laura crouched down next to him. They were alone. No other boat was in sight. Laura watched James Brown's mansion and its swimming pool on the island with an anxious eye. Suddenly, gunshots erupted from the mansion on the coast. They sounded like the plummeting of Alex's destiny down a staircase.

"I can't go back to the time before the gunshots erupted and killed James Brown," said Alex shakily.

Cool winds whistled around them, ruffling their hair. Both Alex and Laura remained still. Calm waves gently rocked the floating board.

"The gunshots and Brown's mansion are a dream," said Laura in a soothing voice, shaking Alex's hand. "We're on the side of reality."

"What reality?" snapped Alex in despair, screwing up his face. "If we go back to the coast, the FBI will chase me to the ends of the earth. Reality is hell."

A queen angelfish appeared near the surface of the water, dancing in the waves. Alex approached it, trying to touch the fish. The water felt like ice. The queen angelfish evaded his hand, sinking deep.

"Money, art, power, and fame... All of these are mirages," said Laura, clutching Alex's hand, soaked with seawater. Soon, the warmth of her hand reached Alex, who grasped it tightly.

"But we're the reality," said Laura passionately. "And the world around us will return to reality once we solve the mystery of the murders behind S. L. Babel's artworks."

~ * ~

Over five hundred miles away from Peter Carli's jet, Terence Miller thudded onto the tombstone bearing Josh Stevenson's name. When he heard gunshots and felt the scorching bullets pierce his stomach, he never felt pain. Before another bullet shot through his head, Terence had thought his own blood spreading on the tombstone was somebody else's. As a professional surgeon, he never felt fear at the sight of blood, which made him react slower. When Terence fell to the ground, his gnarled hand dropped the unlocked briefcase containing S. L. Babel's QR code work beside him. A petal from the white rose placed on the tombstone floated in the air and slowly landed on the briefcase.

The bell of a nearby Catholic church tolled, its magnificent melodies echoing in the air.

Lowering her gun, Elena Taylor stepped toward Terence, who lay motionless on the tombstone, and squinted at the pulse in his neck. Confirming Terence's death, Elena smiled maliciously, her eyes roving over his body. The image of a secret research center owned by her former boss, James Brown, flashed in her mind. The room was filled with tanks preserving frozen cadavers, into which thyroid hormone was injected. She remembered roaming the center with James Brown, her eyes wet with awe. "All of these bodies will be used for research to design artificial organs and life-extending technology. We'll build the most lucrative biotech business," James Brown's thick voice echoed in her mind. *Death makes money*, Elena thought. *Death creates new lives and forms of biotechnology. We don't apologize when we kill worthless people to achieve our goal. Our mission will be far more noble than any human life.* She tucked up the hem of her blouse, caressing the shark tattoo on her stomach. Her fingers traced the sharp teeth of the shark.

Licking the tip of her lips, Elena picked up the briefcase containing Babel's QR code painting beside Terence's body and briskly walked toward her black sedan. It didn't have a number plate. As she revved up the engine, a sudden wind blew through the cemetery, lifting the white rose back onto the tombstone:

Joshua Stevenson
19 December 1999
11 March 2023
Here lies the body of the kindest adolescent who hoped to save sick people around the world. Death can't steal his heart. His soul remains eternal.

Chapter Thirteen

"Where's my mom?"

When she was seven, Laura asked her father this question while they were in a hot air balloon rising into the sky over Forest Park in St. Louis. Her father, Steve Campbell, was an internal medicine doctor at a local hospital and a professional hot air balloon pilot. On weekends, they often drove to Forest Park to ride in a hot air balloon. Steve practiced diligently to win the annual Great Forest Park Balloon Race.

Another orange-colored hot air balloon floated above theirs. Laura's gaze wandered upward toward the balloon, where a girl around her age waved at her.

"Dad, where's my mom?" Laura asked again. The wave of hot air streaming from the burner in the cabin shook her brown hair. "Why don't I have a mom?"

Steve didn't reply immediately, his eyes reading the direction of the wind. Pulling a rope downward, he opened the parachute valve. The hot air balloon slightly descended, catching a downward draft. Their balloon drifted away from the orange one.

"Your mom was the most selfless, generous woman on the planet," Steve said in a deep voice. As the balloon descended toward the snaky river running through Forest Park, breezy spring winds ruffled his unkempt black hair. "You were born from a brain-dead woman, Laura. Your mom donated her organs to save other lives."

Laura felt her insides turn glacial. *I was born from a brain-dead woman. What does brain-dead mean?* In a few seconds, she found herself collapsing onto a stool near the burner. Her father was gazing at fountains in the lake, which splashed towering water into the sky. Steve closed the parachute valve, turning up the burner. The balloon soared back into the cloudless sky.

"She had a stroke, Laura." Steve hugged his daughter from bchind. "You don't need to worry about yourself. You're perfectly healthy. And I'm blessed to have you in my life."

Laura started to cry. Due to the heated air pouring out of the burner, she felt her tears simmcring. Laura touched her hands, face, chest, waist, hips, and legs. Suddenly, she felt her body didn't belong to her. *I was born from death.* A freezing chill crawled up from her stomach to her throat. Steve caressed her back. Laura closed her eyes. She imagined her mother flying down from the shiny sky, landing behind her. Her mother's warm and soft hands stroked Laura's back.

As Laura woke up in Peter Carli's private jet twenty years later, her eyes captured hundreds of hot air balloons swirling over Forest Park through the cabin windows. That day, the Great Forest Park Balloon Race was taking place. Just like jellyfish underwater, the multicolored hot air balloons floated and sank, inching toward the finish line.

"Alex, I must tell you something," Laura said in a muffled voice. Alex, who wore her fedora and sunglasses to hide his face, turned to her. "I grew up in St. Louis. This is my hometown."

As Alex widened his eyes, the seatbelt signs lit up above their heads. Peter Carli, who sat in his armchair behind them, was silently observing the landscape outside the windows.

The private jet began its descent to St. Louis Lambert Airport.

Fifty minutes later, Alex and Laura arrived at the cemetery near Mackenzie Hills Park in a Kia Soul they had rented under Laura's name. This was the place S. L. Babel's digital art at Art Basel Miami Beach had recommended they visit, through Josh Stevenson's voice. Peter didn't accompany them. He'd said goodbye to them at the airport and left for a hospital for an upcoming surgery. As Alex and Laura stepped through the cemetery gate, hundreds of white tombstones spread around huge, lush oak trees came into view.

"It's difficult to find Josh Stevenson's tomb here," said Alex nervously, slightly sliding off his sunglasses to look around.

"We should walk around and check all the tombstones," said Laura sharply. "We're bound to find it."

"You wanna check the names on the tombstones one by one?" said Alex, screwing up his face. "That's not feasible."

All of a sudden, a scream reverberated from the direction of a small, red-roofed chapel adjacent to the cemetery.

Alex and Laura darted their eyes to the grass field. A priest wearing a black cassock stood in front of a tombstone shining under the sunlight. As they briskly approached, they saw a bloody corpse lying in front of the tomb. The tombstone bore the name Josh Stevenson.

The Caucasian, red-haired priest was trembling, crossing himself and praying with his eyes closed.

"This is Terence Miller," said Alex, his horror-struck eyes scanning the body. There was no briefcase containing Babel's work around Terence's body. "Somebody killed Terence and might have stolen Babel's QR code work."

"The prediction of the digital art we saw at Art Basel Miami Beach was right," said Laura shakily. "Terence came to Josh Stevenson's tomb, and he was killed as predicted by *The Deathly Network*. How can S. L. Babel predict these murders?"

"Babel must be pulling the strings," said Alex jerkily, rubbing his chin with a shaky hand. "But how could Babel or Babel's digital art track Terence and know he'd come to this cemetery? It's all insane."

Laura's eyes rested on the ground covered with grass. Under her feet, the body of young medical student Josh Stevenson, who had seized the decisive clue to the huge, organized crime with which James Brown and Terence Miller were associated, was rotting. His beautiful face must have been eaten by vermin, and his crystal, ambitious eyes must have collapsed inwardly under the air pressure. The words and stories he wanted to convey must be silently echoing in the language of dead people in the coffin.

"Excuse me, sir," said Alex calmly. "Are you the first person who found his body? Did you see anyone else around here?"

"I heard gunshots thirty minutes ago but hid in the chapel for a while. My lord, I never imagined this day would finally come!" said the priest in a trembling voice. "Forgive me, my god, but I can't help feeling happy to see the evilest man in the city murdered like this. A godsend killer took revenge on the lousy corpse stealer Terence Miller for my beloved friend Josh Stevenson."

"Did you know both Terence and Josh?" asked Laura hotly.

"Oh, yes," the priest replied, getting to his feet.

"Did you call the police?" asked Alex quickly, hoping he hadn't.

If the police were approaching, Alex would need to hide immediately.

"No, I didn't. And don't call the corrupt police now!" said the priest. "The local police are bribed by a hidden criminal group. They'll cover this up."

"Could you tell us anything you know about Terence Miller and Josh Stevenson, please?" asked Laura softly. "We are journalists from the *Washington Post*."

Alex darted a surprised look at Laura's face.

"Jesus, finally mainstream media is investigating this hideous crime ring!" the priest cried, crossing himself again. "I'm happy to talk with you both. Why don't you come to my church?"

Chapter Fourteen

Priest Robert Porter invited them to a small meeting room in the vacant church next to the cemetery. Alex and Laura sat on rickety chairs, which creaked on the gray, broadloom carpet. Bumping her elbow into Alex's, Laura blinked at the painting hung on the wall. It depicted the deceased pharmaceutical mogul and multibillionaire James Brown. James Brown, in a pinstriped gray suit, sat on a posh, burgundy armchair in his office. He stretched out his right hand to the viewer of the painting, holding a throbbing human heart entangled with purple arteries. A monitor, hung on the wall behind him, displayed a bar graph of his net worth for each year along with his ranking on *Forbes*. This painting stood out among the crucifixes, rosaries, and other classical paintings depicting Jesus Christ hung on the walls.

Squinting at the white plate attached to the corner of the painting, Alex swallowed.

Josh Stevenson (born 1999)
Billion-Dollar Human Body Dealer, 2023.

"Did you know Josh Stevenson?" Alex asked the priest.

"I did," replied Robert Porter darkly. "Josh was my best friend. He exhibited this work at the Saint Louis Art Museum. After that, he gave me this painting. Did you know him, too?"

"We came across Josh Stevenson's name during our investigation of the serial murders in St. Louis," said Laura edgily, eyeing the painting hung on the wall. "The person in the painting looks like James Brown."

"Josh told me it's James Brown himself," said Robert crisply. "I was very surprised to hear he was killed in Miami yesterday. God bless him."

Alex's insides froze. He nervously stared at Robert, relieved that the priest didn't recognize him as the FBI's suspect in James Brown's murder.

"Can you tell us about your relationship with Josh Stevenson?" Laura asked, gripping a pen and a bound memo book.

"Sure. Josh grew up in a very religious family. His family often came to this church on Sundays. He used to sit on the chair you are sitting on," said Robert, his voice deeply wounded, tears brimming in his eyes. "I also conducted his funeral here. Josh Stevenson was a kind, benevolent, and ambitious medical school student. If he hadn't been killed, he would be the best doctor in the city now."

"Do you know why Josh Stevenson was killed in the dormitory?" asked Laura quietly.

"I do," replied Robert breathlessly.

Laura and Alex gasped, staring at each other.

"Josh Stevenson once came to my church to make a solemn confession," said Robert hotly. "He told me he couldn't withstand the paradox between his beliefs in Christianity and medical science. At first, it was hard for me to understand him, but Josh explained step by step. At the medical center where he worked as a research assistant, he was forced to sign a non-disclosure agreement for what he was involved in. If he breached it, he would have to pay million-dollar fines. That's why he confessed here," Robert swallowed, caressing his own chest, and continued. "I can't let you know what Josh confessed to me, however. I must protect their secrets, no matter what."

"Josh said he saw illegal trades of human corpses and organs, didn't he?" asked Laura sharply, staring squarely at Robert's face. "I'm guessing Terence and others traded cadavers donated for scientific research at college."

Robert Porter shuddered, rubbing his rosary with green beads. His tear-soaked eyes fell onto the table, avoiding Laura's gaze.

"Again, I can't say anything that Josh confessed to me," Robert said breathlessly. "But as a priest who manages the cemetery, I can share an important piece of information with you, Ms. Campbell. And this is somewhat related to what Josh told me, I believe."

Laura and Alex exchanged glances, swallowing hard. Laura gripped her pen tightly.

"There were crooked embalmers and funeral directors who stole human organs from the dead bodies buried in our cemetery," said Robert furiously, clenching his fists. "I once opened Josh's coffin buried under the tombstone. His leg was stuffed with some hard substance." Robert Porter trembled, his rosary with green beads rattling around his neck. Taking a long breath, he plowed on. "Somebody hired those lousy embalmers. Who? I don't know. But I can tell you this. Terence Miller was the director of the medical center where Josh Stevenson worked, and malicious surgeons collect human corpses and organs in this city. Josh was a diligent, excellent student. Terence tried to manipulate him, but Josh refused to obey. I believe Josh made the painting to convey some messages to us."

Robert pointed to Josh Stevenson's painting, which satirically depicted James Brown, hung on the wall. "Terence's medical center is tied to James Brown's pharmaceutical company, you know."

"So, Josh discovered illegal organ trade deals at Terence's medical center," said Alex darkly. "He might've taken some evidence out of the laboratory. Then, Terence noticed this and killed him."

"Or Terence might've hired a hitman to kill Josh," added Laura in a low voice.

"It's one of the most plausible interpretations," mouthed Robert, ruffling his red hair with his trembling hand.

Cold silence hung in the room. Alex's eyes rested on Josh Stevenson's painting hung on the wall.

"When we found Terence Miller's body, you said the local police are corrupt," said Laura slowly. "Did they cover up the theft of human bodies by the embalmers, too?"

"Yes, they swept everything under the rug," said Robert, infuriated. "Terence and James Brown's company are the biggest donors to the police department."

"Why didn't you publicly reveal the truth about Josh Stevenson?" asked Alex coldly. Laura gazed at him reproachfully.

"Oh, it's because," said Robert hysterically. "I'll be killed next if

I reveal it."

What this priest said sounds weird to me, Alex silently thought. *He must've managed the cemetery for a long time. Why didn't he realize any shady deals in the embalmment until recently?*

"By the way, Mr. Porter," said Alex in a throaty voice. "Did you see anything belonging to Terence around his body—something like a briefcase?"

"No, I only saw the killers' footprints around his body," said Robert huffily. "I'm guessing Terence had an appointment to meet somebody at the tomb. Through my chapel's windows, I saw him checking his watch impatiently around Josh Stevenson's tomb before the gunshots echoed. I never thought it was Terence Miller at that time."

"Did you see the killer?" asked Laura.

"No," said the priest quickly. "But I heard the killer's car driving away. I was hiding in the chapel for a while to protect myself. Excuse me, I'll bring cups of tea for you."

Robert Porter stood up on wobbly legs, smoothing the hem of his cassock and walking away through the creaky door to the kitchen.

Dusk had fallen. The pendulum wall clock indicated 7:10 p.m. Through the lead-framed window, the crescent moon shone in the sky.

As Robert's footsteps grew fainter in the corridor, Alex got to his feet and stood in front of Josh Stevenson's painting. Examining the bottom right of the painting closely, Alex said in a low voice.

"Laura, this is not Josh Stevenson's work. This is S. L. Babel's work."

"Really?" said Laura, sounding surprised. "How can you tell?"

"Look at the autograph," said Alex, pointing to the thick signature painted in different colors at the bottom right.

Artist a.k.a. S. L. B.

"This is S. L. Babel's autograph he always uses for his artwork," said Alex firmly. "The same autograph was at the edge of his QR code work, too."

"This means," said Laura shakily, squarely looking at Alex's face,

"S. L. Babel is actually Josh Stevenson?"

"If so, it explains why S. L. Babel's digital art exhibited at Art Basel Miami Beach recounted the truth of Josh's death," said Alex, ruffling his brown hair with his fingers. "But Josh Stevenson was killed. His body is supposed to be under the tomb."

"He may not have been killed," said Laura sharply. "He still lives like a ghost. The dead body that Robert saw might be a fake."

"Is that possible?" said Alex, his voice uneven. "But if Josh Stevenson is S. L. Babel, everything makes sense. He's trying to kill everyone involved in organ trades."

"Or Josh was indeed killed and his ghost became S. L. Babel, taking revenge on criminals," said Laura mysteriously.

"Ghosts don't exist, Laura," said Alex snidely, turning on his phone to see the network in the URL embedded in S. L. Babel's QR code work. Alex let out a shriek. The structure of the network had changed; the nodes of James Brown, Terence Miller, and Peter Carli were covered with death symbols—skulls and crossbones.

As Alex scrolled up the screen, a puppet resembling Peter Carli, which appeared in his node, turned blue as if infected by a deadly virus, crumbling like a shattered doll.

"Peter was killed," said Alex in a shaky voice, looking pale.

"We don't know for sure," replied Laura in a trembling voice, glancing at Alex's phone.

Suddenly, a notification of an email popped up on his phone.

From: S. L. Babel
Subject: Location of My Stolen QR Code
Date: June 16th, 2024, 3:52 PM
To: Alex Hubert

Hi Alex,

An artist is a sort of God in relation to their artwork. Their creation oftentimes lasts longer than their life. My life will decay, but my artworks live forever. And I wanted to track where my split soul roams on the earth.

The QR code painting you brought from Geneva Freeport had a mini-GPS tracker embedded inside the canvas. You can tell where my stolen painting is from **this link**. The thirty-million-dollar award is almost in your hands.

All the best,
S. L. Babel

"The QR code painting had a GPS tracker in it!" said Alex, staggered. "That's how S. L. Babel has been tracking me until I arrived at James Brown's mansion."

"A very smart artist," Laura said, widening her eyes. "Probably, Babel's other digital artworks have similar GPS trackers or perhaps bugs. It's worth investigating them later. For now, show me the location of the QR code painting, Alex."

With his trembling finger, Alex touched the hyperlink in S. L. Babel's email. Google Maps popped up. The screen automatically enlarged the map of the USA, only showing Midtown St. Louis, Missouri. A blue light, indicating the location of Babel's stolen work, was glinting in Brentwood, a western inner-ring suburb of St. Louis. Scrolling the screen, Alex enlarged the district. The blue light was perched on a building named "St. Louis Innovative Medical Center."

"It's the medical center directed by Terence Miller," gasped Laura.

"Probably, some insider at the medical center, who had access to the building, murdered Terence and brought S. L. Babel's QR code painting there," said Alex in a strained voice. "We don't know how to enter the building, though. There must be strict security measures."

"Alex, didn't you hear a child's voice just now?" said Laura shakily.

"What? Child's voice?" said Alex blankly.

"From that painting!" snapped Laura, pointing to the painting *Billion-Dollar Human Body Dealer*, which depicted James Brown, hung on the wall.

As Alex gazed at the painting, a pounding noise came from behind it, shaking the painting. He strained his ears.

Help me!

A child's vibrant voice seeped through the wall and painting.
"Is there anyone?" barked Alex, frowning at the painting.

Yes, I need your help.

The same child's voice echoed. But James Brown's face with a vicious smile in the painting didn't change at all.

Stepping forward, Alex touched the edge of the painting falsely attributed to Josh Stevenson but actually signed by S. L. Babel.

Laura anxiously turned back and slightly opened the door at the back of the meeting room, craning her neck to the dark corridor. Closing the door, Laura said in a low voice, "Mr. Porter is so slow to prepare coffee. He hasn't come back yet."

The next moment, Alex took the painting off the hook. A secret, circular door appeared. The child kept pounding.

Open the door, please! We've been held underground for a couple of days.

"You said *we*? Are there other people, too?" asked Alex, raising his brow.

Yes, we're all starving. We haven't seen sunshine for a while. We've been packed in a truck, circulated all over America like slaves.

The child's sobbing voice replied.

Alex looked at Laura. Laura nodded to him, grabbing the door's knob. Alex also put his hand on the knob. The two silently pulled the knob, opening the door.

A black-haired Mexican teenage boy in a red Adidas T-shirt stood on the last rung of the hidden staircase.

"Thank you, sir," said the boy with a heavy Spanish accent, blinking his dazzled eyes to get accustomed to the light. "I'm Pablo. What's your name?"

"I'm Bill," lied Alex. "What arc you doing hcrc, Pablo? This is a church, right?"

"Oh, am I in a church?" said Pablo shrilly, looking around the meeting room filled with chalices, crucifixes, and classical paintings depicting Jesus Christ. "Bill, are you a visitor to this church? You're not part of the dealers?"

"What do you mean by dealers?" asked Laura, her eyebrow furrowed.

"American dealers who buy kidnapped children from Mexican mafias and sell them throughout the USA," said Pablo in a clipped voice. "My family lives in a small town close to the border with the US, just twenty miles away from San Diego. Four days ago, I was delivering tacos ordered on Uber Eats with my brother to a hotel in Tijuana. It was 11 p.m. When we stopped our bike at a dark junction, Mexican gangs menaced us with their guns and forced us into a van. They let me out later at a gas station. I read a traffic sign that showed Phoenix, Arizona. There, they made us ride on a truck loaded with other Mexican kids. Where am I now?"

"You're in St. Louis, Missouri, Pablo," said Alex.

"Wow, I finally came to the Midwest?" Pablo shrieked. "I want to go back to Mexico."

"Are there any other kids, too?" said Laura shrilly.

"Yes, the truck and kids are downstairs," replied Pablo, ruffling his unkempt hair. "There is a TV and a Nintendo Switch that the dealers provided. They're playing video games now. The poor kids don't understand the situation and they're enjoying being kidnapped."

"What's the traffickers' objective?" asked Alex, gazing at the dark staircase through the hidden door. He heard other children's voices echoing from downstairs.

"They try to sell us to a medical center, Bill," said Pablo, showing his yellow teeth. "When they locked us up in the underground room, a priest wearing a rosary with green beads told us he'll pay five thousand dollars for each of us and liberate us after we participate in a scientific experiment that puts us under anesthesia. Other kids looked delighted, but I'm older than them and won't be tricked by that priest. Unfortunately, my brother was taken away to a medical center."

Pablo bit his lips, his eyes looking watery.

"Hey, Pablo," said Alex shakily, feeling fear stab his heart. "Was the priest you saw a Caucasian, red-haired guy?"

"Exactly," replied Pablo shortly.

Alex and Laura exchanged frightened looks.

"We're in serious trouble, then," said Laura, trembling.

"Yeah," spat Alex.

The hinge of the meeting room door creaked behind them. Alex and Laura turned back. Robert Porter was locking the door from the corridor. Through the small window embedded in the door, they saw a malicious smile blooming over Robert's face. As Alex started to run toward the door, the metallic lock resounded in the room. Alex pounded on the door. Robert's back became smaller and smaller in the corridor, his vicious laughter echoing.

"Today's the greatest day that God gave me!" Robert's voice echoed through the door. "The scumbag Terence was killed! I stole human organs from the dead bodies and sold them to him for years. But lousy Terence tricked me and never paid the money in full! Then, Alex Hubert, wanted by the FBI, came to visit my church! Oh Jesus! Our real boss will reward me soon. Hubert and Campbell, James Brown isn't the guy who controls our group. You guys will never know who is directing us!"

Suddenly, the siren of police cars reverberated outside the windows. Waves of red beacons from police cars were flashing, rushing toward them from the end of the street.

"Are the police coming to save us?" said Pablo in a delighted tone.

"They're coming, but not to save you," said Alex gloomily.

"Alex, that fucking priest recognized you as a wanted suspect and must've called the corrupt police," said Laura, looking pale.

"Who is Alex?" asked Pablo in a clear voice.

"Pablo, you said there's a truck in the basement?" asked Alex without replying to Pablo's question.

"Yes, that's the truck they used to bring us here," said Pablo flatly. "And I know how to open the garage's roller shutter."

"Really?" said Alex and Laura simultaneously.

"One of the kids who was once brought to this meeting room saw the priest, who was wasted on pot that day, open the garage's roller shutter from this room," said Pablo crisply. "That kid was sent to a medical center later and never came back. But he told me to lift up Mary's picture, the third painting from the left corner."

Alex and Laura looked at the painting depicting Mary with a halo, embracing baby Jesus. They took the painting off the wall, revealing a box buried inside. As Laura pressed a button in the corner, its door swung open, revealing a green lever switch glinting inside.

"Pablo, can you do me a favor?" said Laura sharply. "Once we descend to the garage and get on the truck, can you pull this lever switch?"

"Sure," said Pablo, a smile emerging on his face. "I'll get all the kids out of the underground garage too."

"We need the truck key, Laura," said Alex, sweat trickling down his forehead.

"No worries," said Pablo, rummaging through his distressed jeans pocket and pulling out a key. "I stole this from the priest when he brought our meals to the garage at noon."

"Nice!" shrilled Laura, taking the key from Pablo.

"Excellent, Pablo," said Alex excitedly. "Let's go downstairs. The cops might have already surrounded this church. We'll all leave through the garage."

Alex and Laura descended the secret staircase to the underground garage. As they stepped down each rung, the lamps became brighter, and the Spanish voices of children playing video games grew louder. When they reached the bottom, all the children, apparently from Mexico, looked back at them. On the TV monitor, Super Mario was jumping on the roof of a huge castle. Suddenly, dazzling sunlight cascaded into the garage as the shutter door slowly rattled open.

"It's too early to open the shutter, Pablo," mumbled Alex, getting into the White Box Truck with Laura.

"I'll drive this time!" said Laura, inserting the key and starting the engine.

"*¡Vinieron a salvarnos a todos!* (*They came to save us, everyone!*)" roared Pablo, running down the staircase to the garage. "*¡Sal de aquí, ahora!* (*Get out of here, now!*)"

The haggard children in shabby T-shirts looked at each other, leaving their Nintendo Switches on the floor. As the garage's shutter door opened completely, the crescent moon floated over the sparse buildings across the church. The kidnapped children opened their mouths in awe, their eyes absorbed in the beautiful night sky filled with stars.

"*¡Ahora!* (*Now!*)" Pablo jumped onto the garage floor and barked again.

As Laura slammed on the gas pedal, Alex, who sat next to her, saw the kidnapped children start to burst out of the garage in the side mirror.

The doors of two police cars, parked in front of the church's main entrance, swung open. The cops shouted, pointing at the garage's roller shutter as it opened. Another police car approached, its headlights illuminating Laura and Alex's faces in the truck. The cops ran toward the garage with their guns aimed in the air.

"Stop shooting!"

One of the cops shouted as the truck thundered out of the garage. Dozens of children poured out into the street, preventing the cops from shooting at the truck's driver.

"HELP US, WE WERE KIDNAPPED BY THE FUCKING PRIEST!" Pablo shrieked at the cops, diverting their attention from the truck.

Laura turned the steering wheel, escaping in the opposite direction from the police cars. Alex turned on his phone, checking the location of the stolen S. L. Babel artwork. The blue light was still glinting in the facility named "St. Louis Innovative Medical Center" in Brentwood. Turning on the automatic navigation, Alex placed his phone on the dashboard so Laura could see it.

"The cops haven't followed us yet," Alex said, jerking his head out of the window to look back at the dark street behind them.

"Alex, you've got to hide your face!" shrieked Laura as she drove at breakneck speed westward.

"You're right!" Alex pushed her red fedora onto his head and put on sunglasses. "Pablo might've held the police."

"He saved us," said Laura breathlessly. "I don't need the navigator. I grew up in this city, so I know all the routes."

After their truck sped through numerous streets and over the bridge at Deer Creek, the prison-like medical center became visible at the end of a boulevard in Brentwood. Compared to the areas filled with Walgreens and banks across the boulevard, the center looked bleak and impenetrable. Laura slowed down and pulled up the truck outside a garage with a closed metallic door lit by streetlights.

"I don't see any entrances to this building," said Alex nervously.

"There's a camera. Hide your face," said Laura in a hushed voice, eyeing a camera welded to the tip of a robotic arm at the garage entrance.

"Laura, read that signboard," said Alex, lowering the tip of his red fedora. He pointed at the silver signboard illuminated by the lamp. "That camera isn't meant to capture our faces."

STOP YOUR VEHICLE TWO FEET BEFORE THE CAMERA
THIS AI CAMERA SCANS YOUR NUMBER PLATE
ONLY PRE AUTHORIZED VEHICLES ARE ALLOWED TO ENTER
MAKE SURE YOUR NUMBER PLATE IS VISIBLE

They watched the robotic arm for several seconds. Just like a living worm, the robotic arm stretched out and snaked as if inviting them to step forward.

"Since this truck was used to sell kidnapped children to this medical center, its number plate is likely registered in the system," said Alex, squinting at the robotic arm. "Shall we try?"

"It's worth trying," replied Laura, gently stepping on the gas pedal and inching the truck forward. The robotic arm lowered its camera, which stopped midair right in front of the number plate. Both Laura and Alex swallowed nervously. With a creaking noise, the robotic arm retracted to the edge of the driveway, glinting green. The gray metallic door rattled open.

"We were so lucky," whistled Laura, driving the truck into the garage of the medical center.

"Yeah," said Alex, gazing at his phone. "S. L. Babel's stolen work is surely inside this building, but it's currently moving west."

"The killer who murdered Terence is walking with Babel's QR code inside this facility, then," said Laura, parking the truck inside the vacant garage.

"I'm worried about Peter," said Alex anxiously. "The network shown in Babel's URL indicates he's dead."

When Alex and Laura arrived at St. Louis Lambert International Airport in Peter's private jet, Peter, who looked sick, told them he was heading to a hospital for surgery.

"Focus on what you can do now, Alex," said Laura. "What you need to do is to retrieve S. L. Babel's stolen work and flee from the USA, right?"

"I wish the real serial killer would be arrested, and the public would know I'm innocent," Alex shrugged.

"I'll reveal who S. L. Babel is, who killed James Brown and Terence Miller, and what crimes these people were committing," said Laura fervently. "You can stay outside the USA until I discover everything."

"You're the greatest journalist on the planet, Laura," said Alex, shaking her hand. "Be careful. Your name was on the network too. You may be the next person to be killed. This medical center might be dangerous."

"I know," said Laura weakly.

"Let me ask, Laura," said Alex in a strained voice. "So, you don't buy the FBI's narrative that I'm actually S. L. Babel and murdered James Brown? You won't report my location to the FBI for the one hundred-thousand-dollar bounty? Do you still want to risk helping me when the whole world is hunting me?"

There was a ten-second silence as they looked into each other's eyes. They never averted their gaze, feeling the silence warm up between them.

"No, I don't buy into that bullshit," said Laura sharply, eyeing Alex's phone showing the location of the stolen work. "All we need to do now is search for the killer who stole Babel's work. I'm sure it will lead us to uncover the entire crime scheme."

"Alright," mouthed Alex.

Laura turned off the engine, flung open the door, and jumped out of the truck. Alex followed her.

They briskly walked toward the elevator with green lamps. The garage was empty. No other cars were parked. It was almost 8 p.m. The employees of the medical center must've gone home.

The metallic garage door shut behind them.

There was no way back. The only way was forward.

"I must confess, Alex. The reason I decided to enter this building with you is also personal," said Laura shakily. "My father was killed two weeks ago. His laboratory is inside this building. He must've left some messages in his lab."

Alex gasped, silently looking at Laura's face.

"I have a hunch that S. L. Babel's stolen painting is in my dad's laboratory," said Laura nervously. "The GPS location doesn't tell us which floor the digital art is on, but it's currently on the western end of the building. My dad's laboratory is also on the western end, on the seventh floor."

Chapter Fifteen

"I was in this corridor before," said sixteen-year-old Laura to her father, Steve Campbell, as the elevator doors rattled open. They stepped into the corridor on the seventh floor of the St. Louis Innovative Medical Center. It was eleven years before she would enter this medical center with Alex in the truck.

"Dad, I feel like I remember the day I was born," said Laura in a mysterious tone, squinting at Steve's laboratory at the end of the corridor. On a dark winter evening, Laura was born to her brain-dead mother in this center.

"That's impossible, Laura," Steve said firmly. "Nobody can remember what they saw when they were born."

"I kept seeing this corridor in my dreams for years," said Laura insistently. "Someone held me in her arms, walking through this corridor and taking me to a basin. When warm water surrounded me, I felt warmth shrouding my body for the first time." Laura closed her eyes for a moment. *You're a miracle...* A nurse Laura had seen in her dream had passionately whispered while she lathered Laura in the basin. *Even with her dead brain, your mom's body gave birth to you.*

"You were actually born on this floor, Laura," said Steve hoarsely. "It was indeed a miracle that you were born so healthily."

"What do you want to show me in your laboratory today, Dad?" asked Laura in a husky voice.

"If something happens to me in the future, come to this laboratory as soon as you can," Steve said as he unlocked the door to his laboratory with his fingerprint.

Without Steve's intention, the gray, thick door slightly opened with a beep. The lights inside the laboratory automatically lit up. Freezing air from the inside seeped out, chilling Laura's skin. Before Steve could stop the half-open door, Laura peeped inside. Cylindrical glass tanks were lined up, illuminated by ominous navy lights. She gasped. Dead, sallow bodies were floating in these tanks, moving their limbs as if to welcome her. As she rubbed her eyes, Steve instantly closed the door. The heavy clicking noise of the lock echoed in the bleak corridor.

"You don't enter my laboratory today, Laura," said Steve stiffly. "I brought you here to register your fingerprint for the biometric scanner on this door. If I die someday, there will be only two people who can open this door—you and me."

Steve grabbed Laura's finger, pressing it on the biometric detector near the doorknob. After pushing her finger hard on the detector five times, Steve freed her hand. The biometric lock beeped again, and the words "Registration Completed" appeared on the screen.

"Remember, Laura," said Steve, looking her squarely in the eyes. "If something happens to me, come to this laboratory as soon as you can."

"What's inside?" asked Laura, widening her eyes.

"I can't say now," replied Steve tartly. "You'll find out what I want you to see in this laboratory in the future."

"But I can't enter this medical center without you," said Laura doubtfully. "Without your ID, I couldn't have entered today."

"You're right," said Steve, scratching his head and mulling over her question. "But I think you'll find a way to enter anyway. As you get older, you'll get smarter."

Steve turned around, motioning Laura toward the elevator at the end of the corridor.

"All set, Laura. Let's go," said Steve, his eyes wandering to the distant future.

~ * ~

Eleven years later, Laura sank into the armchair in her office at the *Washington Post*'s headquarters in One Franklin Square, Washington D.C., closing her eyes. Her entire body trembled. Deep hatred and shame swirled in her chest, beads of sweat running from her forehead as if to suppress her emotions. The bleak corridor on the seventh floor of the St.

Louis Innovative Medical Center materialized in the darkness under her eyelids. The end of the corridor was shrouded by ominous navy lights from her father's laboratory. Laura felt his sinister laughter reverberate through the locked door. Her father, Steve, must be part of the illegal human organ trade that multibillionaire James Brown was secretly organizing. Laura remembered the tanks containing dead bodies she'd seen through the slightly open door of Steve's laboratory. Hatred for her father crawled up her throat like a sticky lump.

Heaving a long sigh, Laura opened her eyes and clicked her mouse to open a Word docx file saved on her PC. It was a draft of her book, *Stolen Organs: Billion-Dollar Human Body Trade of the Pharmaceutical Titan*. Chapter four would cover the St. Louis Innovative Medical Center and reveal her father's involvement with the secret organ trade network. *Am I really entitled to write this book? Will the public believe what I'm writing?* With her shivering hands, she scrolled down the document to the ongoing chapter. *How will I introduce myself if I manage to publish this book? I was born from a brain-dead woman. I went to New York University to obtain a bachelor's degree in journalism and media studies. But what if I received all my education thanks to the dirty money my father got from his illegal business?*

Through her investigation, Laura discovered that the pharmaceutical giant James Brown funded the St. Louis Innovative Medical Center, where her father worked. After receiving the anonymous letter and the attached picture showing a truck loaded with dozens of dead bodies and illegal immigrants, Laura even asked a secret satellite surveillance company to analyze any vehicles regularly entering the medical center's facility. The truck, identical to the one in the picture, entered the high-security garage of the St. Louis Innovative Medical Center twice a week. She never doubted the link between Brown's organ trade and the company her father worked for. The glimpse of Steve's laboratory she caught ten years ago—dead bodies swimming in liquid nitrogen in the tanks—flashed often at the corner of her vision.

Did my mother's brain really die from a stroke before bearing me? Laura gripped her fists tightly, knocking on the table. She'd never contacted her father since her discovery. She'd never taken his phone calls. When she received a text message from him on her birthday, she finally replied with only one emoji.

As she started to advance the chapter, she realized that writing the book was programming her to hate her father and herself. *If this book is non-fiction, I mustn't fictionalize my hatred. I must hate my father and myself. This is the only way to finish my book.*

Laura covered her eyes with her hands. Tears trickled down. *No, I have a meeting in the afternoon. I don't want to reapply eyeshadow.* She bit the edge of her lip until she tasted blood. Turning on her phone's camera, she saw her face on the screen. The black tears from her melted mascara drew a bow on her left cheek.

At that time, Laura didn't know her father, Steve, would be killed.

~ * ~

Twelve years after her first visit to the St. Louis Innovative Medical Center with her father, Laura was back in the same elevator with Alex Hubert, heading to the seventh floor. This time, she knew she would never walk this corridor with her father again. Steve had been killed two weeks ago.

"I'm sorry for your loss," said Alex gravely as they stepped into the elevator from the underground garage.

"The medical examiners ruled that my dad committed suicide by overdosing on a psychedelic drug at home," said Laura, gnashing her teeth furiously. Her voice shook with anger. "I don't believe it. My dad never used any illegal drugs—he used to tell me not to use any. He wasn't the kind of coward who would commit suicide. There was no reason for him to do it. No will was found in his house. They also found acetaminophen in his body, but the police ignored that."

"It's clear the police and FBI are desperate to hide some murders connected to S. L. Babel's works and James Brown's circle," said Alex scathingly, clutching the elevator's banister. "Do you think S. L. Babel killed your father? James Brown may not have been the first victim. The serial killings might have started before the network that the QR code shows."

"I don't know," snapped Laura, banging her fist on the wall. "No matter what, I'll never forgive the killer, and I'll never stop investigating until I discover the whole truth."

Alex's nervous eyes tracked the elevator's monitor as it moved between the sixth and seventh floors. He felt as if he were in a labyrinth without an exit.

"The answer to why my dad was killed should be inside his laboratory," said Laura firmly. "My dad set up the most robust security system for his lab. Even the director of this medical center can't enter without him unless they blow up the door with a bomb."

"So why can we enter his lab, Laura?" asked Alex doubtfully.

"My fingerprint is registered. I can open the door with my finger," Laura replied sharply.

The elevator beeped as they arrived at the seventh floor. The door slid open.

The corridor was dark, illuminated only by a few green emergency exit signs. Offices, surgery rooms, and CT and MRI rooms along the corridor were all quiet, with no lights on.

I've been in this corridor before, Laura thought as she stepped out of the elevator. *The place where I was born. Both my mom and dad used to be here.* She closed her eyes for a moment, straining to hear anything. The footsteps of her and Alex disappeared into silence. Suddenly, a baby's cry reverberated—her own cry that Laura had often heard in her dreams. Laura claimed she remembered her mother's breath and warm arms wrapping her at the moment she was born, a story her late father never believed. As she opened her eyes, Laura took a deep breath. Her mother used to breathe here.

When they reached the locked door of Steve's laboratory at the end of the corridor, Alex spoke darkly.

"Laura, Babel's stolen painting is probably not inside this lab. The GPS location of the painting is moving westward. It's outside the building now."

Alex held out his phone to Laura. The blue light indicated the painting was leaving the medical center.

"We need to go back down," said Alex in a low voice. "We might be able to see who is taking the stolen Babel work."

"I can't leave now, Alex," replied Laura, pressing her finger on the biometric scanner by the doorknob. "I finally managed to get in here. You can go if you want, but I have to enter my dad's lab to get his message."

Alex glanced back at the end of the corridor. The green light of the elevator's button went out as it descended toward the first floor with a rattle.

With a sharp click, the laboratory's door unlocked. Laura wrenched the door open.

She stepped inside, and seconds later, Alex followed her. The door shut automatically behind them. Cold air enveloped them, making them cringe.

Laura and Alex stood still, their eyes darting around her father's laboratory.

The lab was partitioned into several rooms. In the first room, a dozen silver, cylindrical tanks were placed against the walls like pillars. Tubes snaked between the tanks, echoing the sound of pumping liquids. Ghostly reflections from the navy lamps on the ceiling danced on the silver tanks. Under the rotating blades of ceiling fans, the lamps seemed to float between the tanks. As Laura and Alex walked to the room's center, the acrid smell of chemicals grew denser, twisting their noses. Laura, tiptoeing between the tanks, tapped Alex's arm and pointed to the top of a tank. A small glass window was set into the top. Gazing at it, Alex swallowed hard. A frozen, middle-aged woman's face with half-closed eyes looked down at them.

Hello, how are you? Alex felt the dead woman's thoughts reach their mind.

The pipe connected to the tank emitted a long, steam-whistle noise. The dead woman in the tank appeared to shift her face, smiling at them. Her lips moved slightly as if speaking to the visitors. Alex stepped closer to the tank.

Suddenly, the hand of the meter on the tank swung to the right, beeping noisily. The cascading liquid nitrogen running through the pipes between the tanks deafened Laura and Alex. The woman's body sank to the bottom of the tank, disappearing from view.

Laura stepped toward the next tank and let out a cry.

"I know this guy," shrieked Laura, her eyes riveted on the frozen man's face through the window of the tank.

The tanned man in his mid-forties, with a thick, brown beard, appeared to be smirking, his eyes glinting through nearly closed eyelids.

"He's billionaire investor Hoyt Pence, who bought S. L. Babel's digital art *Your Clone Will Live After Your Death* for $9 million. He mysteriously died on his yacht in Florida several days later," said Laura, her quaky voice echoing in the laboratory.

"Yeah, I recognize Pence's face. Why is his body here?" asked Alex nervously.

"I read an article about his death. He left a weird will," said Laura, lowering her voice. "Hoyt Pence believed in eternal life. He made a million-dollar contract with a medical institution to freeze his body so future technology could revive him."

"I see," said Alex in a shaky voice. "It's wise he made that contract before buying Babel's works."

As liquid nitrogen splashed over Pence's face, Alex and Laura saw the dead billionaire's mouth move, as if trying to speak.

"Did you really die in an accident on the yacht?" asked Alex to Hoyt Pence's frozen body in a low voice. "Or were you killed like the others who purchased S. L. Babel's works?"

"Alex," said Laura, nudging him with her elbow, "the dead man can't say anything."

In the swirling liquid nitrogen, Pence sluggishly smiled. Both Alex and Laura strained their ears. But no voice came out of the frozen, dead billionaire's mouth.

Hoyt Pence closed his eyes and mouth tightly, and his body sank to the bottom as the pipe connected to the tank made a deep noise like a long steam whistle.

As Laura and Alex turned back, the dead body of a Caucasian boy floated toward the top of another tank, smiling through the tiny rectangular window. He looked like Pablo, whom they met in the church.

"Are you Pablo's brother?" Laura shrieked.

The dead boy didn't reply immediately.

The liquid nitrogen inside the tank flowed down toward his face, moving his lips. But no voice came out.

The boy's body frolicked in the tank's tidal wave, then sank downward and vanished from sight.

Alex spun around and slipped. He clutched Laura's shoulder. A blood-soaked sterile drape lay on the floor. As Alex lifted his leather shoe from the drape, a scalpel glinted on the floor. He noticed a piece of paper stuck to the bottom of his shoe. It was a fragment of a sticky note. Pinching it up, Alex brought it under the navy light. They silently read it.

February 7th, 2024. A perfect kidney from a healthy boy.

A conflict between the cardiothoracic team and abdominal team. One surgeon in the abdominal team was fired by Terence.

Not sure if this body voluntarily donated his organs. I decided to preserve his body until his family reaches out to us.

"These are my dad's letters," said Laura, her voice uneven.

Alex and Laura squinted at the floor. There were long, bloody footprints from the same sandals, leading from where they stood to the large aisle between the tanks containing embalmed bodies. They followed the footprints to the end of the partitioned room and stopped in front of the door to the next room, where the bloody footprints ended. Another scalpel glinted on the floor nearby.

"These footprints aren't new, Laura," said Alex, gripping the knob to the next room. "There should be nobody here."

Laura tiptoed, peeping into the dark room through the small window in the door. She could see something resembling an operating table surrounded by numerous side tables in the center of the room.

"I agree," said Laura in a trembling voice. "Probably, my dad brought donated bodies here to harvest organs. Let's go inside."

As they opened the door and stepped inside, the room lamps

automatically lit up.

A huge calendar hung on the left wall. A picture of the Grand Canyon shone inside the calendar, the colors slightly reflecting on the desk with a desktop PC, binder files, and picture frames placed against the opposite wall. One picture frame on the desk reflected the VR gaming chair in the center of the room.

"This is a VR gaming chair. Why is this here?" said Alex, striding toward a cushioned emperor chair.

What Laura thought was an operating table was actually a cushioned emperor chair with six LED screens attached to its scorpion-like back. The bloody footprints ended right in front of its footrest, suggesting the person who made them had slumped into the chair, immersing himself in the VR world. Alex planted his foot on the footrest, craning his head to look at the LED screens. All the screens were blank.

Meanwhile, Laura's eyes were riveted on a picture on the white desk against the wall. A picture frame stood there, showing her mother, Linda, in a bridal wedding dress. Her father, Steve, in a black suit, was smiling at her as he held her hand. They were standing in a grassy park with the St. Louis Gateway Arch shining behind them like a wedding ring. Linda's right hand was stretched out, about to throw her bouquet to the guests.

Laura's eyes followed the imagined trajectory of her mother's bouquet. Her gaze landed on a ring binder file left open on the desk. The open page showed a picture of seven-year-old Laura blowing out candles on a birthday cake at their home in St. Louis. Laura still remembered that day. Steve had given her a heart-shaped pendant. Next to her picture were Steve's notes.

Laura reached age seven. Height: 48 inches. Weight: 72 pounds. A little chubby, but very healthy. Normal blood pressure. Blood was taken yesterday. Normal hemoglobin, glucose, and calcium levels.

With trembling hands, Laura turned the pages of the file. They were filled with pictures of her MRI and CT scans, displaying the condition of her organs along with Steve's detailed annotations. She flipped to the beginning page and found another person's notes.

Laura Campbell is the first child born from a dead mother we treated using our innovative method. We must record her health and life as much as we can.

Terence Miller

They treated my mom in their innovative way. Laura gasped, feeling her pulse quicken. *And I was the first child born that way.*

"I have no idea why a VR gaming chair is necessary in this laboratory," said Alex nonchalantly behind her. He turned to Laura, noticing her chest heaving. "What did you find, Laura?"

"I've been the object of their scientific research," Laura said in a trembling voice. "My whole life was recorded by my dad and Terence."

Alex squinted at the binder file clutched in Laura's shivering hands. "What do you mean, Laura?"

As Alex spoke, a sudden thudding noise reverberated from the door at the back of the room. There was another door leading to the next room.

"There's somebody!" Laura shrieked.

Both Laura and Alex jumped back, holding their breath and casting frightened gazes at the door.

A shadow of a tall man loomed in the frosted glass of the door.

Chapter Sixteen

The door swung open.

Peter Carli's sallow face appeared in the darkness. He smiled weakly at Alex and Laura, clutching the doorframe with his gnarled hand.

"Peter, why are you here? Are you okay?" Alex asked, looking bewildered.

"We were worried about you because S. L. Babel's network showed…" Laura said in a strained voice. Peter collapsed against the doorframe, accidentally tapping a button in the room he'd just exited. The lamp in that room lit up, revealing a surgery room with an operating table and a ventilator illuminated by overhead surgical lights.

"Are you okay?" Laura asked, crouching to help Peter stand up.

"No worries," Peter mumbled, coughing up blood and pressing his hand to his stomach.

"Peter, what happened?" Alex spluttered, looking frightened. "We need to call an ambulance—or take you to an ER right now!"

"Don't do that, Alex. I know my life is over," Peter said, blood trickling from his mouth. "James Brown tricked me."

"What do you mean?" Alex asked in a trembling voice.

"Even billionaires can't skip other patients waiting for donated organs," Peter spat. "James Brown was selling organs to wealthy people around the world illegally. I bought a kidney from his company and had a secret surgery in this building last year. However, the surgeon employed by James implanted an imperfect artificial kidney in me instead. It's failing, and now my life is ending."

Alex and Laura froze in shock, feeling their bodies go cold.

"I had an appointment with a surgeon named Steve, who graciously let me know I got an imperfect organ. He was supposed to conduct another transplant for me," Peter mumbled, his face twisting in pain. "Steve registered my fingerprint for the biometric scanner on the door to give me access to this lab. But he hasn't shown up yet."

"Is the surgeon named Steve? If it's my father, he was killed two weeks ago," Laura said grimly.

Peter didn't look surprised.

"I thought he might've been killed," Peter said hoarsely, his chest heaving. "Steve was the only surgeon in this medical center with a normal human heart and empathy."

"Did you kill James Brown?" Alex asked sharply.

Laura cast a horrified look at both Alex and Peter.

"Did you mix psychedelic drugs in the drinks on the yacht?" Alex asked passionately. "I sailed the yacht, and you were on board. Is everything I remember an illusion? Did you kill James Brown while we were hallucinating?"

"No, you weren't drugged. But I was planning to kill that bastard James Brown, Alex. That's why I visited his mansion—I had no interest in buying S. L. Babel's digital art," Peter said, his eyes glinting fiercely. "I had an appointment with him to drink at night. I was going to poison him. But I was surprised when somebody killed him while we were on the yacht. I felt like somebody stole my pleasure of murdering that rogue."

"Who mixed drugs in the drinks on the yacht, then?" Laura asked in a high-pitched voice.

"The FBI, probably," Peter said, his lips shaking. His breath was weak. "They were all corrupt, bought by James Brown and someone powerful in the US government. What Brown, the FBI, and the bribed politician desperately aimed to find out is S. L. Babel's identity. It's because S. L. Babel knows their secret, which will overturn the US government if revealed. Who killed James Brown? I have no doubt that S. L. Babel murdered him, based on the prediction of *The Deathly Network*. But Alex and Laura, I want to ask you to save S. L. Babel."

"Save S. L. Babel?" Alex and Laura said simultaneously, sounding surprised.

"Yes," Peter said, out of breath. "S. L. Babel is both an executioner and a victim. That's why Babel tries to assassinate all the people involved in illegal organ and human trafficking. Laura, I didn't know you're Steve's daughter."

Peter stopped speaking, coughing up a lump of blood.

Laura shrieked, putting her trembling hand to her mouth. The Swiss multibillionaire philanthropist was dying in front of her.

"Take this if you're Steve's daughter," Peter said, taking out a flash drive from the chest pocket of his shirt and handing it to Laura with his trembling hand. "Insert this flash drive into the VR emperor chair in this room."

Laura and Alex strained to hear Peter's last words. No more came. In twenty seconds, they noticed no breath seeping through his emaciated throat. Peter's eyes were half-open, slight tears trickling down his face with a sparse, snowy beard.

Chapter Seventeen

With her shivering fingers, Laura inserted Peter's black flash drive into the USB port in the corner of the VR emperor chair. As she sank into the chair, Laura looked at Alex, who stood in the corner of the laboratory. Alex was anxiously gazing at her, as if Laura was going to enter a completely different world and become another person. Taking a deep breath, Laura turned on the armrest switch and put on the VR headset. With rattling mechanical sounds, the scorpion-like back of the chair stretched out the LED screens, imprisoning her. She felt the chair sway like waves. The sounds of the room faded. Darkness enveloped her. The next moment, her body was floating in the air like a ghost. Laura let out a shriek, but she couldn't even hear her own voice. She felt her back touch the ceiling.

Peter stood on the VR chair, stretching out his hands to the acrylic cover on the room light. His silver hair was shining. He wore a white hospital gown, its hem swirling around his body in the breeze from the AC.

Laura's eyes met Peter's dark eyes.

"Peter! Are you alive?" Laura shouted.

Peter didn't seem to hear her voice. His eyes were nervously following the rotation of the acrylic cover. Once he finished putting the cover on, he jumped off the chair, taking off the blue vinyl gloves. He took out his phone and turned on an application. Laura, whose body was floating above Peter's head, squinted at his phone's screen and swallowed. *Peter placed a hidden 360-degree camera inside the room light in my dad's lab*, Laura thought. *This VR video on his flash drive shows me what he secretly recorded.* Laura darted her eyes to the calendar on the wall. The page for March 2022 was open, showing a picture of the dazzling sun rising over the ocean in Hawaii.

Suddenly, the door to the next surgery room opened. Steve, in blue scrubs, appeared. Laura's heart raced.

"I bought this VR chair for surgical simulations," said Steve nonchalantly. "Before every important surgery, I practiced with this VR simulator."

"Did you practice for me, Steve?" said Peter in a tremulous voice.

"Of course, Peter," said Steve reassuringly, tapping Peter's shoulder. "I've never failed any organ implants in my life."

"The surgery room is ready, Steve!" another surgeon's voice reverberated from the room.

All of a sudden, Laura's eyesight became hazy. A thick fog formed around her, enveloping Steve, Peter, and everything in the room. Laura's body started to swirl in a whirlpool, a chill running through her spine. She closed her eyes, forgetting to breathe for a moment. As a hot wave of air snaked around her, she opened her eyes. Her body was hovering once more in the same laboratory. The room was dark, with some lights turned off. The calendar now read July 2022.

Steve, his face covered with tears, was sobbing and flipping through the pages of a binder file containing Laura's pictures.

"So, you broke the law to save your wife and daughter," said Peter calmly, standing in the corner of the room. He looked like he'd undergone some medical examinations.

"Yes, I sold my soul to the devil to save my angels," said Steve, his intermittent sobs interrupting his breath. "I really want to quit my job at this medical center now. But Terence won't allow it. He and his boss will send goons to assassinate me."

"*What do you mean, Dad?*" shouted Laura, whose body was floating above their heads. "*Did you sell your soul to save your angels? Who are the devil and angels? Terence has a boss? Is there an even bigger secret institution that controls Terence?*"

Steve and Peter didn't hear her voice. Both looked downward at the floor.

"Now I understand you're the only surgeon I can trust in this medical center, Steve," said Peter in a throaty voice, stepping toward Steve's desk. Peter's eye was fixed on the picture frame, which showed

Steve and Linda in bridal attire, both standing behind the St. Louis Gateway Arch. "Other surgeons work for money here. But you seem to be an exception. You started working here to save your wife and daughter."

"That was the only possible option for me," said Steve in an unsteady voice. "Terence told me if I worked for him, he would give my wife a donated kidney. I couldn't save her life anyway—her brain died due to a stroke before giving birth to Laura. It was a miracle of the century that Laura was born healthy."

"*My mom wasn't just brain-dead? Did she undergo a kidney transplant during pregnancy?*" Laura spluttered, stretching out her arms to swoop down to the floor. But her body wasn't moving away from the ceiling.

"I respected Linda's wishes," said Steve nervously. "Her organs were donated to this medical institution. By implanting her heart, we saved a young girl's life. The girl was almost the same age as my daughter. She may not live like a normal child, but Linda's heart will allow her to live for at least two more decades."

"If I were you, I would do the same thing," said Peter compassionately. "I'd break any laws to save someone I truly love."

"You'll never understand me, Peter," Steve replied, his voice filled with distress. "My daughter believes I'm a surgeon involved in illegal activities. She became an investigative journalist at a major newspaper, trying to uncover everything we're doing. But I'll never let her know the truth about her own birth. If she learns she was born and saved illegally, she would be ashamed of herself for her entire life."

Laura felt as though her entire body was being torn apart and sinking into deep, icy water.

"Terence showed a huge interest in my daughter, who was miraculously born," said Steve scathingly. "Laura was the subject of scientific research until she turned five. Fortunately, he has forgotten about her since then."

"Is your daughter well now?" Peter asked, staring at him.

"Yes, she lives in Washington D.C. now," replied Steve quickly. "She is perfectly healthy."

"Great! By the way, I have to ask one question," said Peter, gazing up at the hidden 360-degree camera in the lamp. Laura's eyes met Peter's, but she knew he couldn't see her. "Why did James Brown establish the network to harvest and trade organs?"

"To sell them to wealthy clients like you," said Laura's father, clearing his throat. "Even the wealthiest people sometimes can't buy life. Famously, Steve Jobs, the legendary founder of Apple, couldn't find a donor organ to prolong his life."

"Don't fool me, Steve," Peter sighed. "Selling organs can't be the only thing James Brown was doing. He owns one of the biggest pharmaceutical companies in the world. You must know what research the harvested organs were used for."

Steve averted his eyes from Peter, then looked around the room as if checking for eavesdroppers. Crossing his arms, he spoke in a strained voice.

"James Brown aims to develop artificial organs that resemble real human organs. He believes we can achieve immortality."

Suddenly, a mist loomed in the room. Laura's body was absorbed in turbulent, cold air. She felt a jerk behind her head, and the two men beneath her vanished. After her body rotated in a swirl of lights and colors, the same laboratory materialized in front of her eyes again. Her dizzy eyes read the calendar on the wall. It showed May 2024, along with a picture of Niagara Falls. A rainbow arched over the water.

"Peter! Peter!" Steve barked into the dark room, roaming around with his phone glued to his ear. There was nobody else.

"How are you, Steve?" Peter's French-accented voice reverberated from Steve's phone.

"Where are you now?" Steve said in a high-pitched voice.

"I'm in Geneva, as usual," Peter replied.

"You must come to St. Louis right now!" Steve roared. "You need another transplant operation as soon as possible!"

"Why?" Peter asked, his voice deep with concern.

"I secretly logged into a folder that Terence manages to record organ trading," Steve said, lowering his voice. His anxious eyes scanned the room, ensuring no one was overhearing. "James Brown tricked me.

Before the last surgery, he ordered an employee to replace your healthy kidney with a corrupt one to kill you."

"What!?" Peter exclaimed, his voice indignant.

"James Brown never liked your influence as a philanthropist on global health," Steve spluttered.

Suddenly, a loud knock echoed from the wall.

"I gotta go now, Peter. Text me when you arrive in the U.S," said Steve hastily, hanging up the phone.

The knocking resounded again.

Laura, floating near the ceiling, looked at the door. It wasn't shaking at all. She couldn't tell where the noise was coming from.

"Open the door!" a female voice roared.

Steve, looking pale, bolted toward the huge calendar on the wall. As he peeled it off, a small lid appeared with numerous locks, including two-barrel bolt locks and chains. With trembling fingers, he unlocked each one. The small door swung open, revealing a secret lift. A blond female head emerged. Laura swallowed. It was Elena Taylor, James Brown's secretary.

"What are these fucking locks?" Elena said scornfully. "I should always be allowed to come here from Anthony's place."

Who is Anthony? Laura wondered. *The lift is connected to someone's place?*

"This is just a precaution," Steve mumbled.

"Remember, Steve, I have information that can ruin you and make you work for us," Elena said viciously. "You have to follow my orders."

"OK," Steve said, pretending to be calm. "How can I help you today, Ms. Taylor?"

"Do you know who S. L. Babel is?" Elena asked aggressively, raising her chin.

"Who?" said Steve, raising his brow.

"Don't lie! You must know who the crooked digital artist is," Elena barked, unholstering her gun and aiming it at Steve's forehead.

Laura, floating above their heads, let out a scream. But neither Elena nor Steve heard her. Laura tried to jump down on Elena's head to protect her father, but her body wouldn't move. No matter how she wriggled, her back remained glued to the ceiling.

"I'll pull the trigger if you lie," Elena said maliciously. "Tell me again. Do you know who S. L. Babel is?"

"The only thing I know about S. L. Babel," Steve said sharply, staring squarely at Elena, "is that he's your boss James Brown's favorite artist."

There was a moment's silence as Elena's finger tapped her gun's trigger and Steve's trembling feet winced.

Then, Elena lowered her gun. Her long, mirthless laughter echoed in the room.

"Do you think my boss is James Brown, the stupidest billionaire on the planet?" Elena said scornfully. "James Brown isn't the real boss of our organ trade network. My partner Anthony took it over. I'll love Anthony until I die. Nobody knows he's a billionaire. From the early 2010s, Anthony discovered the power of blockchain technology and kept investing in cryptocurrency. He created a dark web where illegal commodities were traded anonymously in crypto. Nobody knows he's been controlling the US government and the biggest pharmaceutical company in the world. I can't forget the day I met Anthony in the drawing room of James's mansion on Star Island." Elena took a long breath, closing her eyes as if she were in a dream. Then, she continued. "James Brown, the thirty-seventh richest person on the planet, looked like crap in front of shrewd, cold-blooded Anthony, who talked about organ trade schemes and future industry of life-prolonging technology. I decided to work for Anthony the moment I saw the fierce shine in his eyes. Remember, Steve, James Brown is now our puppet. Do you even know the real reason why James buys contemporary art?"

Steve recoiled several inches, shaking his head.

"James is only in charge of our money laundering," Elena said, raising her gun toward the ceiling. "He buys contemporary art in Geneva Freeport to launder the profits we gain through organ trades."

Laura swallowed, her heart drumming.

"So why does James Brown buy S. L. Babel's works?" Steve asked jerkily.

"Okay, it seems you really don't know who the crooked digital artist is," Elena spat, clearing her throat. "S. L. Babel, our biggest enemy right now, somehow knows about our business and started blackmailing James. That's why James keeps paying millions for Babel's crappy works. If James keeps paying to protect his pharmaceutical company, we must kill him."

Laura gasped, clenching her fists. *So, it was Elena who killed James Brown*, she thought, remembering the day he was killed. Elena wasn't on the Lamborghini yacht with Alex, Laura, and the others. She was in Brown's mansion when he was shot to death.

"Someone in this medical center must've leaked our business to the digital artist," Elena said indignantly. "Steve, you must keep harvesting organs and helping our business. Otherwise, you'll be next."

Again, a thick mist materialized in the laboratory.

"*Dad!*" Laura shouted as the hazy mist shrouded Steve's head, sinking him into the whirlpool of smoke. Laura's body floated upward. A violent howl of wind enveloped her. She felt as though her ears were being torn off. When her body was caught in the stream of frigid air, her feet slammed onto the ceiling. The mist below her dissipated. The same laboratory was beneath her. The calendar showed June 2024, the present day. Inside the picture of the Grand Canyon, a long, lightning-shaped blue river shimmered, disappearing into the rugged red rocks like a concealed pathway to heaven.

The calendar suddenly dropped to the floor. The hidden lid to the secret lift swung open, and Elena's head appeared. She tossed the briefcase containing S. L. Babel's work into the room. *It was also Elena who killed Terence and stole Babel's thirty-million-dollar QR code painting*. Laura bit her lip, glowering at Elena.

"Steve Campbell lied before. He must've known who S. L. Babel is!" Elena muttered, striding towards Steve's desktop PC. Laura squinted at Elena's ear, noticing a black wireless earbud nestled among her wavy blond hair. Elena was talking to someone. "Anthony, we hacked Steve's Apple note from his iPhone. If what he noted was true, we can log into this desktop PC via —"

Having turned on the PC, Elena ignored the prompt to enter passwords and clicked a tiny circular icon in the corner of the screen. The in-PC camera activated, displaying Elena's smirking face on the entire screen. She stepped back a little, opened the briefcase, and took out S. L. Babel's QR code painting. Taking a deep breath, Elena held the QR code in front of the PC's camera, adjusting the angles slightly. Within seconds, the PC finished scanning the QR code. Then, it emitted a melodious sound and displayed an instruction on the screen.

Please wait a minute…

A malicious, victorious smile flashed across Elena's face.

The next moment, the smile faded. The PC's screen turned black and displayed the next instruction. Laura, who was floating near the ceiling, jerked her head to read it.

Type how old you were when you took a hot air balloon ride with me for the first time. Also type the color of the balloon after a comma.

Elena frowned at the screen, scratching her head irritably. She typed "thirteen, red" and pressed the Enter key.

Access Denied.
Piss off, crooked thief!!!

Elena blushed, her fists shaking with anger.

"What a fucking surgeon!" she hollered, hitting the desk with her fist.

Suddenly, the heavy entry door of the laboratory with the biometric scanner outside the room beeped. Subsequently, footsteps echoed, approaching.

"What?" said Elena, looking pale.

She clutched the briefcase, packed the QR code painting inside, and opened the lid in the wall. After jumping into the hidden lift, she stretched out her arm and hung the calendar back on the wall. Then, she silently closed the lid.

A few minutes later, Laura and Alex appeared in the room.

"This is a VR gaming chair. Why is this here?" said Alex, striding toward the center of the room and turning back to her.

Suddenly, everything in her vision went dark, followed by a flood of dazzling light.

The LED screens welded to the VR chair's back were spreading out. As the chair slowly returned to its normal position, Laura's eyes opened to the room in reality. Alex Hubert still stood in front of her, his eyes anxiously resting on Laura's face, which had been hidden under the LED screens. She took in a mouthful of air. Her horror-struck eyes met Alex's.

Chapter Eighteen

"Alex Hubert must be inside this medical center. Some people saw the truck he'd stolen enter this building," Sampson Castor said to his fellow FBI agents as he slammed his car door shut.

"Why were you sure Alex was flying to St. Louis, Sampson?" asked the agent in the Hawaiian T-shirt, who had tried to arrest Alex at the coffee shop in Miami. Sampson's team had been heading to St. Louis before the priest Robert Porter called the local police from the church.

"I'll let you know later," said Sampson evasively.

"Terence Miller was found dead in the cemetery near Mackenzie Hills Park," said the agent in the Hawaiian T-shirt. "You thought Hubert would chase Miller to St. Louis, didn't you? How did you know Terence Miller was heading to St. Louis, Sampson?"

"I have a special network to gather any sort of information," responded Sampson in a thick, frightening voice. "Nobody against our network can survive in America. We gotta arrest Hubert now!"

The other FBI agents surrounding Sampson looked at his face in awe and fear.

Standing on the sidewalk, Sampson Castor silently gazed up at St. Louis Innovative Medical Center. More than fifty police cars, all of which had intentionally turned off their sirens, swarmed the street, circling the building. A bearded cop lit a blue searchlight, circling it around the seventh floor. It was the only floor with lit windows.

Once we frame Alex as a criminal who killed James Brown, Sampson silently thought with his arms crossed, *we'll get his phone, check IP addresses, and identify S. L. Babel, who sent him emails. We must kill S. L. Babel for humanity until we accomplish the mission for eternal life.*

~ * ~

"Now I know why my father took me to this laboratory to register my fingerprint for the biometric sensor of the entry door so many years ago," said Laura in a quaky voice. "There must be data inside the desktop PC that he wanted me to see and prevent others from seeing. Babel's QR code is the key to unlocking his PC. There must be some tricks inside digital art itself. Elena could have taken a screenshot of the QR code in James Brown's mansion, but it wasn't enough. She needed the physical painting."

"Everything dawned on me now after learning what you saw in the VR video, Laura," said Alex, caressing his chest to calm himself down. "S. L. Babel blackmailed James Brown for years. That's why Brown, who used to purchase contemporary art pieces in Geneva Freeport for money laundering, paid exorbitant amounts for Babel's works. Elena killed Brown to stop him from financing the digital artist anymore. She probably killed Terence Miller too, then stole S. L. Babel's painting from him. Elena sneaked into this laboratory twenty minutes ago to log into your father's desktop PC using the QR code inside the digital art. If so, your father collaborated with S. L. Babel."

"Yes, I think so. My dad must've known who S. L. Babel is," replied Laura, ruffling her brown hair nervously. "But I'm very confused. If Elena killed James Brown, who is S. L. Babel? S. L. Babel's network predicted the deaths of James, Terence, and Peter. Elena is obviously not S. L. Babel since she's searching for Babel's artwork."

"Laura, do you remember whose node will be affected by the deadly virus in Babel's network?" said Alex shakily.

They pulled out their phones, opened their Internet browsers, and clicked the bookmarked link embedded in Babel's QR code. The red virus, which passed Peter Carli's node, was inching toward Elena Taylor's node across the skull and crossbones in the center of the network.

"Elena will be killed next, and then..." said Laura, her voice trailing off.

Laura's shivering finger pointed to the node of her name,

connected to Elena's node.

"No worries, Laura," said Alex reassuringly to Laura, who covered her mouth with trembling hands. "The edges bifurcate. We don't know if the 'deathly virus' will take the path to your node. It might go to Bella's node or somewhere else."

"Bella or I will be killed next, no doubt," said Laura shrilly.

"I don't think so. S. L. Babel is not a god. Nobody can predict the future," said Alex, anxiously raising the pitch of his voice. "Elena, who assassinated James and Terence, will be killed next. To be honest, this is a good thing. There'll be no more killers. Then, the 'deathly virus' will definitely die out."

"After Elena's node, the virus will go through the two edges, and both Bella and I will be killed," said Laura through gritted teeth.

"No, it won't happen, Laura," said Alex passionately. "Who can kill innocent people like you? Other victims, like James and Terence, were deeply involved in dirty business. Peter Carli bought illegal organs from James Brown and donated enormous funding to him through the Peter Carli Foundation. But you and Bella are…"

Alex stopped, gazing at the screen of his phone. Above the network, bloody letters emerged.

The deathly virus's infection rate is 50%.
It can fly through only one edge at a time, even when there is more than one edge connected to one node.

The same letters appeared on Laura's screen. Both Alex and Laura fell silent and stared at the screen for a while, hoping the letters would disappear.

Either Laura or Bella will be killed. Alex swallowed. *At least four people in this network—James, Terence, Elena, and Peter—were associated with the secret organization that trades organs. Either Laura or Bella must have also been involved in the organ trading business. Laura is the daughter of a surgeon who worked in this medical center. Should I really trust her? Should I protect her?* Alex raised his eyes, staring at Laura, whose gaze was riveted to the screen of her phone.

S. L. Babel will kill either me or Bella, Laura thought, a cold chill running through her spine. *But I have no reason to be killed. My friend Bella doesn't either. Why does this digital artist try to punish and threaten us?*

All of a sudden, a huge knocking noise reverberated outside the partitioned room.

Alex jerked his head up, gazing at the locked entry door of the laboratory.

"BILL! BILL! ARE YOU THERE? YOU MUST ESCAPE RIGHT NOW!"

That was Pablo's voice.

"It might be a trap, Alex!" said Laura as Alex strode to the entrance.

"I don't think so. He called me Bill. Pablo is the only person who recognizes me as Bill," said Alex, his voice echoing in the laboratory.

Laura didn't budge, watching Alex reach the entry door through the tanks of frozen dead bodies.

"Are you Pablo? Why are you here?" asked Alex in a hushed voice.

"YES, I'M PABLO, WHO MET YOU IN THE CHURCH. I WAS HIDING IN THE BACK OF THE TRUCK WHEN YOU DROVE OUT OF THE CHURCH TO THIS MEDICAL CENTER. YOU GOTTA ESCAPE NOW!"

The child's high-pitched voice resounded through the door.

Alex opened the door slightly.

Pablo stood in the corridor alone. An artificial light through the window illuminated his unkempt black hair.

Alex's heart raced. He squinted at the window in the corridor. The street was covered with at least fifty police cars.

"The cops are already blocking this building," said Pablo. "I saw cops with guns hiding outside the garage gate through the windows."

"Why did you come here, Pablo?" said Alex, raising his eyebrow. "You're also in serious trouble."

"I wanted to find my brother. He must be somewhere in this building," said Pablo enthusiastically.

"Don't push yourself too hard," said Alex. "You must take care of yourself first."

"You must take care of yourself first, too, Bill," replied Pablo slyly. "How can you get out of this building?"

"It's a good question," said Alex, biting his lip.

"You said the cops blocked all the exits?" said Laura in a level voice, walking toward them.

"Nice to see you again, ma'am," said Pablo, smiling.

"Nice to see you, Pablo. You saved us twice today," said Laura, hugging Pablo. "I know another secret exit."

"Where?" said Alex, looking surprised.

"I told you what I saw in the VR video, didn't I?" said Laura. "There's a secret lift in my dad's laboratory."

They ran back to the partitioned room where the VR emperor chair was perched. Jumping inside the room, Laura peeled the huge calendar with the Grand Canyon picture off the wall. A steel lid with two-barrel bolt locks and chains appeared.

"This is the second time we found a secret door," said Alex amusedly as Laura unlocked the bolts and untangled the chains.

"I hope the lift works properly!" Laura said, wrenching open the lid.

In front of their eyes was a vacant lift shaft. Cold air blew up from the bottom, pushing their bodies backward and ruffling their hair.

"There's a button," mouthed Pablo, pressing the down-arrow button inside the cavity.

In seconds, the rattling noise of the lift became audible, growing louder and louder.

"Alex, are you sure we should get on the lift?" said Laura, sounding anxious. "In the VR video, Elena said this lift is connected to Anthony's place. I don't know who Anthony is, but he must be an evil person Elena works for. Anthony is even more evil than James Brown. And also, we might encounter the serial killer Elena after taking the lift."

"We won't see her very soon," said Alex in a level voice, showing his iPhone's screen. The GPS location of S. L. Babel's QR code painting, which Elena must have with her, was now perched on a property one mile from the medical center.

"Where is that?" Laura squinted at his phone, tapping a Street View picture in Google Maps.

A gourd-shaped wading pool, featuring a glass panel in the center that reflected the mansion's gable and transom windows, popped up. Laura's finger rotated the 360-degree Street View picture. Across the aisle beside the wading pool, there was a huge, rectangular swimming pool encircled by white, reclining lounge chairs. As her finger rotated the picture by 45 degrees, a porch with Greek-style columns appeared. An initial A.R. was carved beside the gray main entrance door.

"The first initial 'A' must stand for Anthony. This must be Anthony's place," Laura snapped.

"This mansion looks so gorgeous. It smells like a filthy rich guy lives here," said Alex ironically.

"Anthony Ross!" shrieked Pablo. "A. R. stands for Anthony Ross!"

"Who is Anthony Ross? Why do you know him?" asked Laura, slightly raising her bow-shaped eyebrow.

"The priest called him Mr. Ross!" Pablo spluttered. "At night, I often sneaked up behind the wall of the meeting room in the church, placing my ear to overhear their conversation. A woman and a man were once in the meeting room. The woman called him Anthony, but the priest always called the same person Mr. Ross."

"The woman might be Elena," Alex interjected.

"Maybe," Laura nodded.

"After they discussed their deals of human trafficking, that guy, Anthony Ross, started to talk about research for obtaining eternal life using stolen human organs," said Pablo mysteriously. "I didn't understand most of the biochemistry vocabulary he used. But I remember he talked about gene-editing tools and the creation of immunized artificial organs. I also heard the jerk insult Jesus Christ depicted in paintings in the room. I cringed when he loudly said, 'We'll be gods, soon.' His long laughter was so creepy."

"Anthony Ross must be the guy who supports the dangerous scientific research behind the illegal trading of organs," said Alex darkly.

"I was wrong. James Brown wasn't the most powerful figure in this scheme. Anthony Ross must be the person who pulls the strings in this organ trade network."

With a huge bang, the black grilles of the lift popped up, glinting through the small hidden door in the wall. With a rattle, the grilles opened the door.

Laura and Alex got on the lift first.

"Pablo, you shouldn't come with us," said Alex, holding the door open for a while. "I think this lift will somehow lead to a very dangerous place. We must take this path because of the police blockage. But you don't have to. The police won't arrest you."

"No, I'll go downstairs, too," said Pablo hotly. "I have a hunch that I can find my brother downstairs. I ran through most floors in this medical center. There's nobody alive here. If I can find him, he should be somewhere beyond this lift."

"No, you can't come with us!" said Alex, pushing Pablo back and eyeing Laura.

As Laura pressed the close button, Pablo jumped through the small secret door and landed inside the lift.

The grille door shut. There were only three floor buttons: "-2," "3," and "7." Alex pressed the button "-2." The lift started to descend in the dark shaft.

Alex sighed. Pablo was smiling in the corner of the lift. Laura was so preoccupied with Babel's ominous prediction that she couldn't even think about Pablo's situation. S. L. Babel's ominous network occupied her mind. *Either Bella or I will be killed after Elena...*

There was no light through the long shaft.

After passing the third floor, a beam of blue light leaked through the gaps between the lift's floor and grilles.

Through the swish of the wind, soft voices in a foreign language started to dance. In the cold darkness, they stopped speaking and strained their ears.

Children's songs seeped through the lift's floor, enveloping their shivering legs.

Vamos a casa (Let's go home),
Vamos a casa (Let's go home),
La luz vence a la oscuridad (Light defeats darkness),
No existen fronteras entre nosotros (No borders exist between us).

Chapter Nineteen

As the lift's floor thumped on the ground, silver dust danced in the air, illuminated by the lights through the grilles.

Laura darted her eyes through the gaps of the grilles, her hand still clutching the handrail. Alex, standing in front of the lift button panel, looked back at her. As the lift stopped shaking, Pablo trotted to the door and signaled Alex to press the open button.

"No, Pablo. There's somebody outside," whispered Alex. "We heard strange songs."

"*Mis amigos*," Pablo said in a delighted tone, pressing his eyes between the gaps of the grilles. "All of them are my friends."

"Are you sure?" asked Alex skeptically, scratching his head.

Laura stepped toward the door, standing beside Pablo and pressing her forehead to the grille.

A long, concrete tunnel stretched outside the lift. Tiny blue lamps were installed at regular intervals on the ceiling, illuminating the steam leaking from piped conduits. The steam was drifting toward an alcove in the tunnel.

"My friends are there!" said Pablo enthusiastically, pointing to the alcove through the grille. "Their voices came from there."

"Alex, do you still have Internet access?" asked Laura.

"Yes," replied Alex quickly, turning on his iPhone.

The GPS location of S. L. Babel's QR code painting was still in Anthony Ross's mansion. The direction of the mansion was exactly where the tunnel was heading.

"Let's go," said Laura decisively. "But we have to be careful not to make any noise."

As Alex pressed the button and the grille rattled open, Pablo ran out of the lift.

"*Diego, ¿Estás ahí?* (Diego, are you there?)" Pablo's high-pitched voice echoed in the tunnel.

"Wait, Pablo!"

As Laura and Alex stepped out of the lift, the grille door rattled shut behind them. They turned back, casting a frightened look at the lift. With a creak, the lift climbed upward. The yellow, ominous letters painted on the wall of the shaft appeared in the darkness, seeming to dance in the air.

THIS IS THE BORDER BETWEEN LIFE AND DEATH
THE NETWORK OF ETERNAL LIFE GOVERNS HEAVEN
THE NETWORK OF ETERNAL DEATH GOVERNS HELL
YOU MUST CHOOSE EITHER OF THE NETWORKS

"What does this mean?" asked Laura in a trembling voice, frowning at the wall.

"We don't have the time to interpret this. Most scientists working here are nuts," said Alex, turning back and running toward the alcove where Pablo was shouting something in Spanish.

"I found my brother!" Pablo shouted, showing his yellow teeth as Alex and Laura reached the alcove.

In the alcove, separated from the main aisle of the tunnel by thick glass windows and a steel door, was a secret ward with rickety bunks. Through the glass window, they could see Mexican children lounging on their mattresses. A boy resembling Pablo stood on the floor, a blanket around his bare feet. His mouth fell open, his gaze riveted on Pablo through the window.

"Diego!" Pablo shouted, gripping the doorknob. Surprisingly, the steel door, which had been locked from the outside, smoothly opened as he twisted the knob.

"We gotta go, Laura," said Alex, eyeing the screen of his phone. Babel's QR code painting wasn't moving at all from Anthony Ross's mansion. "You need to find the QR code painting to access your father's database, right? That painting must be the key to unlocking his devices."

"Of course," said Laura sharply. "Pablo, we must go now!"

Pablo, who had stepped into the ward and hugged his brother, turned back and smiled at them. All the children swarmed out of their bunks, walking toward the open door with looks of disbelief on their faces.

"You guys shouldn't go toward the end of the tunnel," said Alex in a firm voice. "You should take the lift back to the medical center."

"Why? We don't want to go back to any experiment rooms!" Diego, Pablo's brother, shouted back. "Two of our friends were promised freedom after an experiment and taken to the third floor. They never came back."

"There's serious danger on the other side of the tunnel," said Laura in a soothing voice, thinking of Elena's malicious face that she'd seen in the VR video. "Take the lift to the seventh floor, which is completely safe. Pablo, you agree, don't you?"

Pablo nodded, eyeing the dark shaft of the lift.

"The police won't hurt any of you," added Laura. "Take the lift now."

"Let's go, Laura!" said Alex, gripping his phone and gazing at the location of the stolen painting.

As Alex and Laura walked toward the bottom of the tunnel, the air became colder and colder, prickling their skin.

In eight minutes, a shaft of light, flowing diagonally from the ceiling, loomed at the end of their eyesight.

Chapter Twenty

"Elena, can you move Babel's QR code a little to the right? I can't see it very well."

A coaxing female voice echoed from the screen mounted on the drawing room wall in cryptocurrency billionaire Anthony Ross's mansion. In the corner of the room, the four eyes of the bisected halves of a cow and her calf glinted, preserved in formaldehyde in huge glass tanks. They were a copy of Damien Hirst's sculpture, *Mother and Child, Divided*. Suddenly, the shadow of a slender female figure passed over the surface of the tanks.

"Of course, Congresswoman," Elena Taylor replied obsequiously, lifting S. L. Babel's QR code painting and bringing it several inches closer to the webcam at the end of the mahogany table.

"No! Move it back a bit so I can see the whole painting," the other female voice commanded.

Elena adjusted the painting, placing her chin on its edge and smiling at the webcam. She carefully tilted the QR code to capture the right angle. After a few seconds of silence, Elena's anxious eyes darted toward the screen.

Susanne Caldwell, a senator from Missouri, smiled gently, her eyes fixed on Babel's QR code painting through her computer screen. Susanne was sitting on a plush sofa by a window in a Grand Luxe King Room at the Plaza Hotel in New York City. The silky curtains were wide open, revealing skyscrapers glinting in the darkness like electronic cells. A helicopter hovered toward the crescent moon. Susanne, with her shiny blond hair reflecting the room's dazzling lamps, was preparing for a conference and party in New York the next day.

Every time Elena saw Susanne, she felt that the congresswoman resembled her official congressional headshot more than the headshot resembled her. Susanne didn't always seem like a real human being. Rather, she appeared as a construct created by some hidden organization. As Elena squinted at the screen, Susanne's smiling face looked petrified, as if she weren't breathing. Elena took her left hand off Babel's work and rubbed her eyes. Susanne moved slightly, then opened her mouth.

"Well done, Elena!" Susanne said jovially. "Let's get all the fingerprints on this work. I know many people have touched the painting, but one of the fingerprints must be S. L. Babel's. I'll ask an FBI agent to match it with their database. Once the FBI arrests Alex Hubert, I believe we'll be close to identifying S. L. Babel."

"It sounds like a plan," Elena responded evenly.

Susanne held her phone's camera up to her laptop screen and scanned the QR code on the painting.

"The QR code will display an ominous network," Elena said scathingly.

"Not really," Susanne replied curtly, frowning at her phone, which began to heat up. She threw it onto the table as the Safari browser turned blank.

"Did you manage to log into Steve Campbell's desktop PC using that QR code?" Susanne asked sternly.

"No, actually, Congresswoman," Elena said shakily. "There was another password after unlocking the system with Babel's QR code. But it was useful to bypass one of the security measures on Campbell's PC."

A fraught silence followed, with Susanne's cold eyes menacingly rotating on the screen.

"Well, it's only a matter of time before we log into Campbell's PC once we have the QR code," Susanne said icily. "Don't forget my order. We've already paid you, right? You must kill anyone who knows about our deals. Steve Campbell must've leaked our organ trade to S. L. Babel. We must log into his PC to track who he leaked the information to and what he leaked, AS SOON AS POSSIBLE."

"I know my mission, Congresswoman," Elena said stiffly. "And I know what I need to do now. His desktop PC prompted me to answer a question about how old someone was when they took a hot air balloon ride for the first time. Campbell had a daughter. I'm guessing Campbell set the password for his daughter to access the data. So, what I need to do now is," Elena smiled impishly, her eyes flashing maliciously, "to kidnap Campbell's daughter, Laura, and make her log into Campbell's PC. Then, I'll kill her and cover it up as an accident."

"Great plan," Susanne smiled on the screen. "But we might be able to get the FBI to arrest Laura easily. I'll contact Sampson later."

The door to the drawing room swung open behind Elena Taylor.

"Hi Elena, how are you doing?"

Anthony Ross, a fifty-year-old multibillionaire crypto currency investor who held 30% of the shares in James Brown's pharmaceutical company and served as a member of its Board of Directors, stood before Elena with open arms. Elena let out a short cry of delight, hugging and kissing him.

As Elena pulled away from him, Anthony glanced at his favorite piece in his art collection, a copy of Damien Hirst's sculpture *Mother and Child, Divided*. Anthony always enjoyed the sensation of observing the completely different world that the bisected cow and her calf, preserved in formaldehyde, inhabited. They lived in an eternally silent realm of death, existing outside the order of time. Placing his elbow on the edge of the cold glass and leaning against it, Anthony examined the crystal eyes of the cow and her calf. Unlike Damien Hirst's original, Anthony had asked a professional artist, proficient in art forgeries, to replace their eyes with actual crystals. *I'll control the world of death very soon*, Anthony said to himself, a smug smile flowering on his face. Every time he saw the bisected cow and calf locked in this work, multibillionaire Anthony felt he was getting close to being a god, capable of altering anyone's destiny.

"Anthony, the congresswoman is waiting for you on Zoom," said Elena.

"I see," said Anthony casually, striding to the table and sitting in an armchair. He adjusted his position so the webcam on the table could capture his craggy face, etched with lines from years of cunning and ruthless machinations. His half-gray, half-dark hair curled on the right side of his forehead, falling over the end of his teardrop-shaped eye. His eyes flickered from Elena's flushed face beside the table, to the red light glinting from the webcam, and then to the screen on the wall showing Congresswoman Susanne Caldwell.

"Great to see you, Mr. Ross," Susanne said meekly. "We were discussing a plan to unlock Steve Campbell's PC. It seems we need to either kidnap or arrest his daughter."

"Yeah, I heard about it from Elena," Anthony replied in a ringing voice, crossing his legs and gazing at the painting on the table. "It was so lucky that we managed to retrieve S. L. Babel's QR code painting. I was really upset when I heard Terence stole the painting."

"Money really changes people, Anthony," Elena said scornfully. "Not many can resist the temptation to steal a thirty-million-dollar painting."

"How did you retrieve the painting, Elena?" Susanne asked from the screen.

"It was easy. I texted Terence, saying I'd pay thirty million dollars in crypto using Anthony's funding," Elena replied with a malicious smile. "Although Terence stole the painting, he didn't know how to sell it. That gullible surgeon showed up in a cemetery with the painting, expecting to receive the money. He didn't expect to be killed right in front of a chapel. He thought the presence of a priest guaranteed safety. I shot him in front of the tomb of the boy Terence had killed many years ago."

Elena gave a tinkling laugh, her blond hair swaying around her shoulders.

"Well done, Elena," Anthony said in a thick voice.

"So, what shall we discuss today, Mr. Ross?" Susanne asked in a servile tone.

"Susanne, S. L. Babel invited me to a private auction of his works in New York," Anthony said, rubbing his beardless chin. "It'll take place in real estate mogul Michael Perry's penthouse."

"What?" both Caldwell and Elena shouted, their eyes widening.

"I've been keeping a low profile for years. I even asked *Forbes* not to list my name in the billionaire ranking," Anthony said in a silky voice. "But some people know I'm the largest shareholder of James Brown's company. S. L. Babel knew I was rich enough to participate in the auction for his artwork. I don't know who else will participate in the upcoming auction, but we have to purchase and destroy Babel's new works if they reveal our secret network."

"S. L. Babel may not know you're controlling our group yet, Anthony," Elena said softly, sitting on the armrest of Anthony Ross's chair and caressing his chest. "Did S. L. Babel blackmail you like he did to James Brown?"

"No," Anthony replied, his eyes nervously darting around. "But in his email, Babel wrote his pieces of artwork would reveal some secrets I don't want exposed."

"That is what you call blackmail," Susanne frowned on the screen.

"I'll fly to New York tonight in my private jet," Anthony said, a note of excitement and anger in his voice. "Do you know Michael Perry, Susanne?"

"Yes, he's one of my best friends," Susanne smiled impishly. "And I plan to meet him at a fundraising party for his green city plan tomorrow."

"Can you come to the private auction in Michael Perry's penthouse, Susanne?" Anthony asked, a faint smile flickering across his sallow face. "S. L. Babel wrote to me that I am only allowed to attend the auction only if I bring you. Otherwise, I can't even attend."

"Sure. But that's strange," Caldwell said, sounding surprised but leveling her eyes at her laptop camera. "I never thought S. L. Babel would be interested in me. Why does S. L. Babel know the connection between you and me?"

"I donated millions of dollars to you, Susanne," Anthony said dryly. "The public record is available online."

"Which art dealer will bring Babel's new works to Perry's penthouse?" Elena interjected, her eyes riveted on Anthony's face.

"I don't know yet," Anthony replied, grabbing Elena's hand on his chest.

"I want to fly to New York to kill the next art dealer," Elena said hotly, her eyes glinting violently. "Just like we did to the art dealer who sold Babel's work to Hoyt Pence."

"No, you should stay here to oversee St. Louis Innovative Medical Center," Anthony snapped, tapping Elena's shoulder. "We don't need to assassinate anyone unless the secret of S. L. Babel's digital art is revealed. In Michael Perry's penthouse, Susanne and I will observe whether Babel's new works reveal information harmful to us. Once the FBI arrests Alex Hubert, it's only a matter of time before we can identify who S. L. Babel is. In the meantime, we should hide Babel's works from the public."

Elena stood up, crossing her arms over her chest. She was mulling over *Your Clone Will Live After Your Death,* the digital artwork that the deceased multibillionaire Hoyt Pence had purchased. The digital screen with the AI-camera didn't just display a clone version of a viewer; it also showed the secret laboratory of St. Louis Innovative Medical Center filled with tanks of frozen corpses in the background. When the same viewer stood in front of the camera ten times in a row, the digital screen even revealed the location of the medical center. *S. L. Babel knows too much about our business*, Elena thought, clenching her fists. Babel had struck a deal with Hoyt Pence that gave him control over the resale rights of his work. Upon Pence's death, the digital art *Your Clone Will Live After Your Death* was sent back to Geneva Freeport, the Swiss warehouse in the tax haven. This digital art was awaiting the next private auction scheduled by S. L. Babel himself.

"If Babel's works sold in the upcoming auction in Michael's penthouse contain any information related to our organ trades, we must destroy them," said Anthony in a menacing tone. "Or we must compromise the buyer in some way."

"Anthony and Elena," Susanne said in an anxious voice, frowning at the corner of her PC screen, "I saw two people's heads moving above the hedge in the garden from the window behind you."

"Housemaids?" Elena asked, narrowing her eyebrows.

"No, my housemaids went home," Anthony mouthed.

As both Anthony and Elena turned back, the sound of footsteps jumping into the wading pool reverberated across the windows.

~ * ~

Nine minutes earlier, Alex and Laura reached the end of the tunnel illuminated by a shaft of light through the ceiling. A long steel ladder was welded to the wall. Alex and Laura looked up at the ceiling where the ladder led. Through the circular glass window in the ceiling, the crescent moon floated. Suddenly, streaks of white smoke enveloped the moon. Laura turned on her phone light, illuminating the smoke.

"They look like splashes of water," Alex mouthed.

"When we looked at Anthony Ross's mansion on Google Maps and Street View, I remember there was a glass window in the wading pool," said Laura breathlessly. "We're probably below the wading pool. I can hear trickling water."

Alex strained his ears. Indeed, a slight sound of water trickling through the pipes seeped through the walls.

"Let's go," said Laura, jumping onto the ladder and climbing it.

Alex followed her.

Reaching the glass window, Laura rotated an L-shaped knob welded to it. The window swung open.

"Be careful," said Alex in a hushed voice, climbing the ladder right beneath Laura's toes.

Laura stuck her head out of the window gingerly, looking around. Stars shone on the rippling surface of the wading pool. She felt droplets of water on her cheeks. Sprinkler nozzles embedded around the glass window created a dome of water over her head. Craning her neck, Laura saw a hedge lit by garden lights at regular intervals. Across the hedge, Anthony Ross's drawing room was illuminated. The curtains were completely open. Laura could see two people's heads in the room.

Stepping onto the wading pool, Laura felt her feet in white leather loafers freeze. The water was extremely cold, as if designed to trap intruders. Alex stuck his head out of the opened window, looking around.

"This way," said Laura in a low voice, pointing to the drawing room across the hedge.

They trotted across the wading pool through the water from the nozzles, reaching the hedge and crouching down. While trying to calm their pulses, they darted their eyes to the windows of the drawing room.

Elena stood in the room, clutching a painting. Before showing it directly to the webcam on the table, she rotated it. Alex caught a glimpse of the painting's surface and swallowed. It was S. K. Babel's QR code painting that Terence had stolen.

The screen on the wall displayed a female face.

"I feel like I saw that face on TV before," Alex puffed.

"She's senator Susanne Caldwell," answered Laura huffily. "We saw her represented as a marionette puppet in a painting in the atrium of James Brown's mansion."

"Yeah, I remember. Why is she speaking to Elena on Zoom?" said Alex, raising his brow.

"Interesting," said Laura, licking the end of her lips. "I know Susanne Caldwell represents Missouri and serves on the Senate Committee on Health. Last year, she bought five million dollars' worth of stock in James Brown's company. Several months later, the US government released a plan for research collaboration with Brown's company, and the stock price skyrocketed by 70%."

"It's a textbook example of insider trading," said Alex indignantly.

"Exactly," said Laura scornfully. "Caldwell also sold all the stocks before the murder of James Brown."

A tall man entered the drawing room from the door and kissed Elena.

"That's probably Anthony Ross," said Alex, lowering his voice. "Elena is his lover."

"No doubt," said Laura, clenching her fists. Rage boiled inside her, crawling up to her throat. *That guy must be the evilest person who pulls the strings behind the organ trade network.*

"Look at the glass tank in the corner of the room. It contains a severed cow and calf preserved in formaldehyde," whispered Alex. "That looks like Damien Hirst's work. It's probably not authentic, though."

"Oh, are they actual dead bodies of animals?" spluttered Laura, shuddering. "Anthony Ross must be an art collector with bad taste, too."

"I wish we could overhear their conversation," said Alex, biting his lip. "S. L. Babel's QR code is there. We've got to retrieve it."

"You need to retrieve it for money, right?" said Laura snidely. "I need to retrieve it to log into my father's PC and access his data. Can you promise to lend the painting to me until I unlock his PC?"

"Sure," said Alex quickly. "However, the first thing we need to think about is how to get the painting back. We don't have any weapons, but Elena is likely carrying a gun."

"Good question," said Laura with a slight sigh. "We don't have to storm into the drawing room right now. Since Elena brought the painting here, I guess she'll leave it inside. We can wait for hours if needed. When Anthony and Elena go to bed, we can sneak into the mansion to steal Babel's work."

"I can't agree with that plan, Laura," said Alex in a hushed voice. "They should be cautious about the security of the thirty-million-dollar painting. Anthony Ross will probably store it in a safe. It'll be difficult to steal it later. Now is our chance."

"Then, shall we throw one of the deck chairs at the window of the drawing room?" said Laura snidely, pointing to a deck chair along the swimming pool near the wading pool.

"Are you serious?" said Alex, squinting at Laura's face.

"Yes, I am," answered Laura, a cocky smile twisting her lips.

Alex looked around the dark garden, the wading and swimming pools, and the drawing room. There was nobody else outside. He measured the distance to the swimming pool from the hedge with his eyes. After picking up the deck chair, it would be difficult to bring it to the outside of the drawing room without being noticed. They would need to rush to the room's window and throw the chair to crash it apart. Then, they would storm into the room through the broken window, snatch the QR painting, and run away quickly.

"We've got to do it right now, Alex," said Laura decisively. "We've got to run to the deck chair first."

All of a sudden, their phones vibrated in their pockets. Laura ignored it, but Alex took his phone out of the back pocket of his jeans. As he turned on his iPhone, a screen of S. L. Babel's network popped up. The deadly virus reached Elena's node.

A puppet resembling Elena appeared in her node. The puppet looked shocked and suddenly dropped an ignited bomb at its feet. The bomb exploded, tearing the puppet apart.

Alex cast a fearful glance at the drawing room. Elena was still clutching S. L. Babel's QR code. For the first time, Alex noticed the painting was unusually thick. It seemed to him that the QR code painting on the table in the drawing room was different from the one Alex had brought to James Brown's mansion. He gasped, his heart pounding hard.

"We need to get back to the tunnel right away!" Alex shouted, pulling Laura's hand.

"What? Are you scared?" Laura turned away from the hedge, frowning at Alex.

"We gotta return to the tunnel, or we'll die!" Alex roared. "THAT QR CODE PAINTING IS A BOMB!"

Alex jumped into the wading pool, the sound of water splashing loudly.

"Stop, you lousy intruders!" Elena shouted from inside the drawing room as she opened the window and aimed her gun at the dark garden beyond the hedge.

"Alex, you're so stupid!" Laura rushed to the wading pool.

Gunshots echoed behind her, piercing through the hedge and sending powdered leaves into the air. As Laura jumped into the hole under the glass panel in the center of the wading pool, another gunshot hit one of the sprinkler nozzles, causing water to cascade upwards in a large fan.

"Hurry up, Laura!"

Alex, who had reached the middle of the ladder, jumped down to the tunnel floor and shouted. Laura slipped her foot off one of the ladder rungs, falling toward the tunnel bottom. Alex caught her body and they both fell onto their buttocks.

As he got up, Alex tasted blood. He looked at Laura, examining her body.

"Thanks, Alex. I'm alright," said Laura, getting to her feet and anxiously checking on Alex, who was bleeding from a cut on his cheek.

"We need to get away from that painting," said Alex, running toward the opposite end of the tunnel.

"Why, Alex?" Laura's voice echoed loudly. "We were so close to retrieving S. L. Babel's work!"

As her voice faded in the long tunnel, an explosion roared above them. The glass panel in the tunnel ceiling was bathed in sparks and light for a moment. As the explosion's roar subsided, flaming debris flew over the glass ceiling. Both Alex and Laura covered their ears and moved away from the tunnel's end, expecting the explosion to shatter the glass panel. However, the explosion above ground only rocked the glass panel. Once the fire subsided, the sprinkler in the wading pool extinguished the flames. Alex and Laura clutched the ladder rungs again, staring at the silent stars swimming above the glass panel.

"Alex, you brought a bomb into the US," Laura said in a trembling voice.

"I'm not sure if Elena brought the same QR code painting to Anthony Ross's mansion," Alex replied breathlessly, his shocked eyes uncontrollably darting around. "We need to escape before the police arrive."

~ * ~

In the dimly lit single room on the thirteenth floor of the Plaza Hotel in New York City, Senator Susanne Caldwell stared irritably at the black screen of her PC, which had suddenly gone blank. The Zoom application informed her that the meeting organizer had abruptly ended the session. However, the last scene Susanne saw was unsettling. It was very unnatural that both Elena and Anthony had shifted their attention from the intruders in the garden to S. L. Babel's work. Elena shouted at Babel's QR code painting, which emitted an unnatural noise. While Elena strode toward the QR code painting with her gun aimed at it, Anthony jumped up from his armchair and ran toward the swimming pool outside.

"Don't worry, Anthony," Elena shouted before the Zoom meeting abruptly ended. "I never brought anything suspicious into your mansion. Don't run away, Anthony. I'll do anything because I love you the most."

Before the Zoom meeting ended, a sparkling light erupted on the screen.

"What happened?" Susanne blurted out alone in the room, slumping onto the king-sized bed and scratching her head. *Did something happen to Andrew Ross and Elena Taylor? Were they killed?*

Lying on the bed, Susanne jerked her head to look at the dressing room mirror against the wall. Like a mechanical puppet, Susanne smiled in the mirror. This was a habit she'd learned from numerous TV interviews. Susanne felt as if the person in the mirror was someone else. The senator in the mirror opened her mouth and spoke eloquently.

"We must identify and kill S. L. Babel."

Susanne's bedside table phone rang. It was FBI agent Sampson Castor.

"Congresswoman, I have some bad news," Sampson's voice echoed thickly in the room. "There was a bomb explosion at Andrew Ross's mansion. The entire mansion collapsed. There's little hope that anyone inside survived."

Chapter Twenty-one

"Thanks. That was a great conversation. I didn't know such a great gooey butter cake shop had opened in this area," said Laura to the Uber driver as she got out of the silver Hyundai Elantra. "Have a good one, sir."

"No worries. You've got to try that cake at least once in your life. It's the best gooey butter cake on the planet," said the African American Uber driver, chewing gum and scratching his dreadlocked head. He turned around and smiled at her. "Oh, by the way, can you give me five stars, ma'am?"

"Sure," said Laura, tapping the Uber app on her phone.

Alex, hiding his face with Laura's red fedora and a black mask, followed her out of the Elantra and slammed the door. The Uber car quickly glided down the empty White Avenue, its taillights vanishing in the darkness.

"Thanks for chatting with the Uber driver," said Alex, taking off his surgical mask and breathing deeply. "I felt like I shouldn't speak at all. It's very lucky that the Uber driver is such a funny guy. He didn't recognize me at all."

"I think the public still doesn't know you're in St. Louis," said Laura sharply. "Everybody's attention is on the explosion at Anthony Ross's secret mansion."

"We've got to get our business done quickly. It's possible that the Uber driver will reach out to the police," said Alex, sounding anxious. "We picked up the Uber near Ross's mansion right after the explosion."

"Don't worry, Alex," replied Laura casually. "That Uber driver won't think criminals who set a bomb would take an Uber to a normal house right after blowing up a mansion. Let's go inside."

Laura and Alex stood in front of her father Steve Campbell's house, a Victorian-style two-story made of warm, earth-toned bricks. As they stepped up the stone staircase to the sleek, metallic entrance door, lights on the façade automatically turned on, illuminating their entire bodies. Feeling the glints of red lights on his eyelids, Alex gazed up at the roof. Security cameras tucked into the eaves glowered at them, capturing their motion. While Laura inserted a key into the entrance door and pulled the doorknob, Alex's eyes followed the security cameras, which slightly rotated to film their faces.

"Your father took very tight security measures," said Alex in a strained voice.

"He was a very cautious person," said Laura huffily. "There are many security cameras around this house—at least one for each window. Also, sophisticated alarms are equipped with every window. If somebody breaks a window, an alarm goes off and sends a signal to a private security company nearby."

"Why was he so cautious?" asked Alex as they stepped into the house. "Is there anything precious in this house?"

"There must be his laptop in his safe," said Laura, opening the door. "The data inside his desktop PC in his laboratory must be shared with his PC in this house through OneDrive. That's what my dad told me. He wanted to work from home, too. Let's get his laptop and quickly leave St. Louis."

As Laura stepped into the corridor inside the entrance door, she smelled her father's body wash, a slight lemon scent still floating in the air. Alex closed the door behind her. A sudden wind blew through their shoulders, and Steve's charcoal, duck-quilted jacket, hanging from a coat hook, swelled up. Laura touched the jacket and pressed her hand hard against the wall as if examining the body of its owner, who no longer existed. Pulling back her hand, Laura's face turned blue, a freezing chill running through her spine. Alex anxiously looked at her and pointed at the end of the corridor.

"Laura, we must go ahead, right?" Alex's sharp voice echoed in the air.

Laura nodded and shuffled down the corridor. The walls were adorned with family pictures. In one, Laura's mother, Linda Campbell, whom Laura had never seen before, was on a picnic with Steve in Forest Park, pointing to the hot air balloons flying in the blue sky. The next picture showed Steve and Laura fifteen years later, in the same place, riding in the wicker basket of a yellow hot air balloon. Who took this picture? Probably, Steve asked a friend to take it from the ground. Steve, with a thick beard, looked upward at the parachute valve, which he'd just closed, his hand turning on the burner. As the basket floated slightly, teenage Laura anxiously clutched the handrail, staring squarely at the camera. "Smile at the camera!" Steve's friend shouted, but the starting gun marking the annual hot air balloon race and the crowd's cheering drowned out his voice. Laura in the picture looked nervous, a bead of sweat slipping down her cheek.

As she roamed the corridor, Laura's heart raced, and her eyes went to each picture on the wall despite her effort to avoid them. *You'll never be able to go back to the past*, Laura heard the pictures speak to her in fuzzy, polyphonic voices. *You'll be an eternal slave to memory because you lost precious things you'll never get back. You tried to condemn your father through journalism. But your father did everything he needed to do to save your life...* Sharp pain erupted in her head, and her pulse throbbed in her forehead. Laura averted her eyes from the pictures, staring at the end of the corridor, which led to Steve's study.

"What?" Alex said hoarsely behind her, looking at the wall near the door at the end of the corridor.

Several picture frames, which had been hung on the wall, were now on the floor, stomped on by someone. Laura's eyes fell on one of the shattered pictures. Lightning-shaped fissures ran through the picture of a two-year-old Laura in a stroller, pointing to capybaras over a green fence in Saint Louis Zoo.

"Someone must've broken into this house," said Alex's low, alarmed voice behind Laura.

Laura pretended not to hear him for a while. It was impossible to break into this house. Her heart pounded so hard that she couldn't speak. *But my dad would never let any of these pictures drop on the floor. Who stomped on the pictures?*

With her lips bitten, Laura stepped forward, opened the door to

Steve's study, and turned on the light, letting out a scream. Alex straightened his back, looking into the room over Laura's shoulder.

The grey carpet was glinting with the shards of the window glass, among which a broken alarm sensor was emitting red lights. The monitor on the Ikea desk against the window had fallen over. The burglar must have tumbled it down when breaking in through the window. Muddy footprints led from the windowsill, across the desk, and to the floor. Opposite the desk was a mahogany bookshelf filled with thick biochemistry books. However, the burglar hadn't shown any interest in the bookshelf. The footprints circled around the desk. All the drawers were open, and the items inside, such as documents, pens, and file folders, were scattered on the floor. A leather-bound armchair close to the desk had been overturned. The burglar had seemingly suspected something hidden under the armchair.

The muddy footprints then headed toward the cabinet, emerging more clearly under the amber glow cast by the Tiffany-style lamp on it.

"Did you turn this lamp on?" asked Alex darkly.

"No," replied Laura in a trembling voice. "The lamp has been on since the burglar broke in. They must've left in a panic and forgot to turn it off."

All the drawers of the cabinet were also open, the items thrown out alike.

"Was anything stolen?" asked Alex.

"Probably not," snapped Laura, stepping toward the mahogany bookshelf. "I hope not. But I imagine the burglar from Anthony Ross's secret crime group came to steal my dad's laptop. I suddenly remembered where he was likely to hide it."

Laura took a very thick art catalogue titled *The Art of God: Bio Artist Apollo Barton and Cloning in Contemporary Art* out of the bookshelf. Then, as she removed a white napkin from the wall hidden behind the catalogue, a small, rectangular safe with a biometric scanner emerged.

"Interesting," said Alex breathlessly.

"It's fortunate the burglar didn't discover this," said Laura shrilly, pressing her index finger on the biometric scanner. "A decade ago, my dad told me about this safe. He said I should check it if something happened to him. I had completely forgotten about it after his death. I believe my dad registered my fingerprint for this safe, using the information for the locked door to his laboratory."

In five seconds, with a loud beep, the door of the safe swung open. Inside was a silver Dell Inspiron 16 laptop.

Laura's delighted eyes met Alex's.

"If we can unlock this PC, we can get all the data my dad had about the organ trade ring," said Laura, turning on the PC. Instead of a password entry, the laptop opened a camera application, prompting her to scan something. "We probably need S. L. Babel's QR code painting to unlock this PC. But it exploded in Ross's mansion," Laura sighed and shrugged.

"I guess Elena brought a fake QR code containing a bomb to Ross's mansion," said Alex in a strained voice. "And the real S. L. Babel painting must be somewhere else."

"I agree," Laura nodded. "If Elena killed Terence and stole the QR code painting from him, Terence might've replaced the real one with a fake one containing the bomb."

"No, it must be S. L. Babel who replaced the real one with the fake containing explosives," said Alex sharply. "Terence couldn't have had the time to prepare a counterfeit. You know, using *The Deathly Network*, S. L. Babel predicted Elena would be killed by a bomb."

"How and when did Babel replace it?" asked Laura, looking pale.

"I have no idea," said Alex, looking around the room blankly.

"I'll bring my dad's laptop with me," said Laura after ten seconds of silence, tucking the laptop into her tote bag.

"The data on the laptop must be helpful for us to prove the others in James Brown's mansion were criminals," said Alex crisply. "Oh, what's that? There's something else inside the safe."

As Alex cast an eye to the bottom of the safe, Laura quickly reached her hand in, snatching the item.

It was a 2.75-inch-barrel handgun.

Laura took her father's hidden gun, retreating several steps and aiming it at Alex.

"Yes, the data on my dad's PC will prove that people like Elena, Terence, and even James Brown were guilty of organ trading. They're all dead now," Laura said in a measured voice. "So, the data will help you in court only if you're not S. L. Babel."

"What are you talking about, Laura?" Alex froze, stepping forward with his trembling hand slightly raised.

"Don't move!" Laura shouted, aiming the gun precisely at Alex's chest. "I have to do this, Alex. You're wanted by the FBI. I can't cooperate with you unless you show me concrete evidence that you're not S. L. Babel."

"Are you kidding?" Alex snapped. "What makes you think I'm S. L. Babel? You're nuts!"

"If you're S. L. Babel, everything makes sense," Laura said, her finger on the gun's trigger. "What if the rising contemporary art star S. L. Babel didn't exist and an art dealer made up a fictitious digital artist? You said you brought his QR code painting out of Geneva Freeport. Did anyone witness it?"

"No," Alex replied, his hands raised, and his terrified eyes fixed on the gun. "The security at Geneva Freeport is very tight. I didn't take anyone inside to pick up Babel's work. You can't enter the warehouse without a valid reason. Any information about artwork trades there is completely secret, as you know."

"That sounds like an excuse," Laura said sharply, tapping the gun's barrel with her ring finger. "If you're S. L. Babel and organized the private auction at James Brown's mansion, it explains everything. I don't know if you killed Brown or not. I believe Elena shot him. But you might've conspired with her, you took Peter, Terence, and me on the yacht to set up Elena's murder of Brown. Although Bella stayed in the mansion because she was pregnant, it must've been easy for Elena to distract Bella so she could kill Brown. You abetted Elena, then made her bring the QR code painting to Anthony Ross's mansion, without her knowing about the bomb inside."

"Laura, stop spouting this nonsense!" Alex snarled, veins bulging in his forehead. Beads of sweat ran down between his blond eyebrows. "If I were S. L. Babel, why would I kill James Brown? He was one of the best clients, pouring millions into Babel's works."

"Because Brown was close to discovering Babel's identity," Laura said, her tone awash with fear and anger. "Not just Brown, but others involved in illegal organ trades wanted to unmask Babel, who blackmailed Brown into paying millions for his mediocre works. If it turns out that you, a leading art dealer in New York, are S. L. Babel, and you've been inflating the market value of this fictitious artist by blackmailing billionaire collectors, your business is over. That's why you killed Brown, Elena, and Anthony Ross. The mysterious deaths surrounding Babel's paintings will only increase their value."

As Laura finished, Alex recoiled several steps, his teeth chattering and his face pale. With his hands raised, he glanced around, his panic-stricken eyes darting between the door and the broken window.

"I'll never let you go," Laura said firmly.

"You want money, don't you?" Alex said scornfully, his eyes burning with anger. "If you pull the trigger, the FBI will award you a one hundred-thousand-dollar bounty. You'll be celebrated as a brave journalist who caught a serial killer."

"Are you admitting you're the serial killer now?" Laura said, adjusting her grip on the gun. "I know why you took me from Miami to St. Louis. You wanted to see how much I knew about the illegal organ trade network. You planned to kill me once you knew my book project would expose this crime ring. Once it becomes public, you can't blackmail them anymore."

Alex could no longer speak. His heart raced, seemingly shaking the air. In contrast to the heat in his chest, a cold, freezing sensation spread through his limbs. His trembling hands lowered as if to open a hidden, magic door to another world.

"You followed me here to steal and destroy my father's PC, didn't you?" Laura said firmly. "My father knew it would be important for someone to access his account after his death. I don't know why he used Babel's QR code painting as a login key, but he knew who Babel was. You never wanted me to discover Babel is you," Laura cut off her words, stepping forward, her fierce eyes locked on Alex's as she aimed the gun at his forehead. "If you're S. L. Babel, you know how to unlock my father's PC. You created the QR code, didn't you?"

"No, I didn't," Alex said shakily. "I'm not S. L. Babel."

"You are!" Laura roared, her finger tightening on the trigger. "You're the only one not depicted in *The Deathly Network* accessed through the QR code, among those who were at James Brown's mansion."

A cold silence fell over them. The whining blades of helicopters reverberated in the distant sky. The news media were dispatching helicopters to Anthony Ross's mansion, which had exploded. Alex's eyes, which had again drifted to the broken window, met Laura's. Their eyes locked for seconds as they tried to read each other's minds.

I shouldn't have trusted you at all, both Laura and Alex thought, biting their lips.

"I can prove I'm not S. L. Babel in seconds," Alex said calmly. "I can show you proof."

"What proof?" Laura asked, loosening her grip on the gun and stepping back slightly.

Suddenly, Alex's iPhone in the back pocket of his jeans beeped.

"Probably an email from S. L. Babel," Alex said breathlessly.

"You've got to be joking," Laura said scornfully, stretching out her arm with the gun again. "Turn around. I'll get your phone."

Alex turned to face the bookshelf. Laura took his phone out. The home screen showed a new email from "S. L. Babel."

"Unlock your phone," Laura said, handing it to Alex.

Pressing the Touch ID sensor with his thumb, Alex unlocked his iPhone and handed it back to Laura. Laura opened his email and began reading the latest message from S. L. Babel.

From: S. L. Babel
Subject: You Must Come To New York
Date: June 16, 2024, 8:11 PM
To: Alex Hubert

Hi Alex,

My real QR code painting is currently in Manhattan, New York.

During the chaos caused by James Brown's murder, someone replaced the real QR code painting with a fake one containing a bomb. It seems they took out the GPS tracker from the real one and inserted it into the fake one. Dumbass Terence Miller stole the fake painting with the bomb, and then Elena stole it from Terence, I guess. There were so many crimes happening during James Brown's assassination.

But now I know where my QR code painting is. Jack Bazin, an art dealer in New York—you pretend to be friends with him but secretly badmouth him on your anonymous social media accounts—somehow got my painting from an unknown source. He confirmed it is my real work and plans to sell it along with my new work at a secret auction in Michael Perry's penthouse in Manhattan. While I reported this to the Art Loss Register, the public still doesn't know this painting was stolen from James Brown's mansion. Art blogger Bella published an article about the theft, but the FBI denied her claim and even pressured her into deleting the post. As you know, the FBI controls corporate media and never lets them report this news.

As I promised, I'll send you thirty million dollars via Bitcoin if you get back my QR code painting from that lousy thief Jack Bazin. I believe the price of this work will skyrocket once all the truth behind James Brown's murder is revealed.

Go to New York right now, get my QR code painting, and return it to Geneva Freeport.

All the best,
S. L. Babel

"As I said, I'm not S. L. Babel. If I were him, how could I receive an email from him?" Alex said in a low voice, his hand still raised. "Can I read the email?"

Laura silently handed his phone to Alex, still aiming the gun at him, though her grip had loosened slightly.

Why does Babel know I am circulating bad rumors about Jack Bazin on social media? Alex wondered as he read the email. *Perhaps Babel has been hacking my phone and PC?*

"This is good news for us. We can get back the QR code painting in New York City," Alex said, turning to face Laura.

"Don't move," Laura shouted, putting her finger on the trigger again. "I don't understand one thing in the email. How does S. L. Babel know that art dealer Jack Bazin got the stolen QR code painting and plans to sell it at a private auction in a billionaire's penthouse? Bazin wouldn't let him know about this."

"I have no idea," Alex shrugged.

"Ask him!" Laura said in a high-pitched voice. "Reply to S. L. Babel and ask how he knows his QR code painting will be sold at the upcoming secret auction!"

Alex silently started to type an email on his iPhone with trembling fingers.

From: Alex Hubert
Subject: Re: You Must Come To New York
Date: June 16, 2024, 8:16 PM
To: S. L. Babel

Dear S. L. Babel,

Can I ask how you know Jack Bazin got your QR code painting and plans to sell it at a secret auction in Michael Perry's penthouse?

Sincerely,
Alex

In twenty seconds, a reply from S. L. Babel popped up on Alex's phone. Laura snatched it from his hand.

From: S. L. Babel
Subject: Re: You Must Come To New York
Date: June 16, 2024, 8:17 PM
To: Alex Hubert

Hi Alex,

It's because I can hack anyone's phone that scanned the QR code in my painting. I know where you are, what you think, and where you're heading.

By the way, I forgot to mention one thing. I just had an interview with Bella Saba in New York. She already published this interview on her blog.

Best,
S. L. Babel

"S. L. Babel has been hacking our phones!" shrieked Laura, raising an eyebrow. "Babel is a genius. Everyone in James Brown's mansion scanned the QR code with their phones. That's how S. L. Babel tracked everyone. He knew where Terence was going with the stolen painting and where Elena was running after stealing it from Terence."

"And probably, Babel read all the emails and text messages on my phone. I need to delete any viruses from my phone right away," Alex said, sounding shocked. "But everything makes sense now. Babel's QR code painting is a secret tool to hack art collectors' phones and collect information to blackmail them. He probably got information about the hidden organ trade by hacking James Brown's phone years ago using another digital art."

Laura's confused eyes switched between Alex's phone and his face. Her disbelief ebbed away as she lowered her gun.

"So, you're not S. L. Babel?" Laura asked breathlessly.

"That's what I've been saying," replied Alex in a slightly irritated voice. "Babel says he had an interview with Bella just now in New York. Let's read it. Is Bella in New York now?"

Laura clicked the hyperlink in Babel's email. As the browser opened on Alex's phone, Laura double-checked the URL of Bella's blog. It was undoubtedly Bella's authentic website, which Laura had visited many times to collect information about S. L. Babel and his works. If Bella indeed had an interview with S. L. Babel in New York, Alex Hubert couldn't be Babel himself.

The New Wave of Digital Art: Bella Saba's Art Blog
June 16th, 2024

Digital Art as a Mirror Reflecting Human Sin and Desire
Interview with S. L. Babel

Foreword

I left Miami this afternoon and arrived at John F. Kennedy International Airport just half an hour ago. Taking an Uber, I reached the Champagne Bar in the Plaza Hotel without much delay. Soon, I caught sight of his figure through the pallid glass door that separated the hotel's lobby from the bar. At first, I wasn't entirely certain it was S. L. Babel. However, as his tall, broad-shouldered form loomed larger behind the glass, my conviction solidified. He swung open the door, giving me a wave. I thought, *there's the arm that crafted digital art worth millions.*

I couldn't believe the unidentified digital artist had contacted me through my website. Initially, I suspected it was a prank from a casual reader. Yet, the details provided left no doubt that the person reaching out was indeed S. L. Babel himself. Intrigued by my art blog, S. L. Babel agreed to a brief interview in New York, and without hesitation, I flew in from Miami.

No formal introduction was needed. The rising star of contemporary art, S. L. Babel sat before me, ordering a bellini cocktail. Although he had prohibited me from describing his appearance, I felt it appropriate to offer a brief impression. He appeared younger and more handsome than I had imagined: smart, ambitious, meticulously groomed. Having interviewed various artists for my blog before (check out my previous interviews with contemporary artists), I found that most artists rarely looked better than their Wikipedia profile pictures. They were passionate about their art but indifferent to their appearance. In contrast, the enigmatic S. L. Babel wore subtle makeup, his complexion flawless. With our interview time limited, I wasted no time in asking my questions.

Bella: When did you first decide to become an artist?

S. L. Babel: To be honest, I never decided to become an artist (*Babel shrugged*). I simply wanted to create objects that would shock the world, using cutting-edge information technologies like artificial intelligence. I began selling my works in art galleries. An art agent labeled them "digital art," and that's how I inadvertently became an artist.

Bella: Your debut work, *Stolen Heart*, which featured a bloody heart alongside viewer faces on an LED screen, made headlines four years ago. The art dealer attempting to auction it at Christie's was murdered, and his heart extracted. The killer remains at large. This initial murder tied to your work propelled you to stardom. Why do you think he was killed?

S. L. Babel: I have no idea. However, I suspect the art dealer who sold my first work had ties to the mafia, facilitating money laundering through artwork purchases at Geneva Freeport. When you buy artwork secretly stored in Geneva warehouses, you can convert illicit funds into valuable art pieces. There were likely conflicts of interest between the art dealer and the mafia. Frankly, I'm distressed by the deaths associated with my works.

Bella: It seems themes of organ trafficking and bodily exchange feature prominently in your art. For instance, your work *Fusion* (2023) captures viewers' bodies via AI-integrated cameras, depicting a cyborg using their bodies. Do you intend to continue exploring similar themes in your future work?

S. L. Babel: Absolutely. The imagery of the "stolen heart"— not just figuratively, but physically—has been a central inspiration for my creations. I'll share some exciting news with you; my next artwork will delve deeper into this "stolen heart" theme. However, I won't be unveiling this work to the public anytime soon. The art business is complex. I can't afford to rush the release of my new work.

Bella: Thank you for the insight into your upcoming work. I look forward to seeing it with hopes that this time, there won't be any fatalities (*S. L. Babel chuckled softly at my remark***). Are you currently involved in any projects? How many works do you plan to release this year?**

S. L. Babel: None.

Bella: None?

S. L. Babel: I'm retiring from art. Achieving dominance in this industry has been too easy (*Babel raised his chin slightly and ran a hand through his hair*). Creating art has become monotonous; there are no worthy competitors. I've grown weary of the superficial critiques from clueless art critics. As I mentioned earlier, I created my works solely to shock the world.

Bella: So, you no longer seek to shock the world with groundbreaking artwork? Is it because you've already attained fame and fortune?

S. L. Babel: No, you misunderstand me (*Babel gulped his bellini, set the glass down, and straightened up*). I never pursued money or fame. Once you suddenly acquire wealth, you're likely to lose it. I don't trust art dealers, gallery owners, auction houses, or financial advisors who seek to exploit me. That's why I've operated anonymously under the name S. L. Babel, working covertly. Allow me to reiterate the purpose behind my creative endeavors. My true satisfaction in the art business lies in shocking the world. However, perpetually shocking the world risks becoming mere mannerism. I intend to astound the world once more, like a grand firework in the sky, before concluding my career as an artist.

Bella: What kind of shock are you planning?

S. L. Babel emitted a long, humorless laugh, drawing suspicious glances from other bar patrons.

S. L. Babel: I won't divulge that. However, my next digital artwork will expose the most significant organized crime ring in America. The public knows little about how billionaires and powerful people operate with impunity. They've been captivated by my work and funded my digital art projects. My objective is to hold them accountable.

Bella: Can you share more details? Who are these billionaires and powerful people operating with impunity?

S. L. Babel: We're out of time, my friend. I must take my leave.

S. L. Babel rose, donned a wool cashmere blend overcoat, and headed toward the exit.

Having read Bella's blog post, Laura handed his phone to Alex with trembling hands. Alex's confused eyes fixed on the screen. After finishing reading, he looked up, his eyes reflecting a mix of triumphant relief and anxiety.

"Can you lower the gun?" Alex spoke in a shaky voice, sweat glistening on his face. "This interview proves I'm not S. L. Babel. It's surprising that S. L. Babel agreed to such an interview while keeping his face hidden. Trust me, I'm not S. L. Babel, the mastermind behind the murders predicted by *The Deathly Network*. I have no reason to harbor animosity toward everyone involved in that network."

Laura hesitated, staring into Alex's dark eyes. She felt her mouth go dry, the echo of her saliva seemingly filling her father's study. Her grip on the gun slackened. Finally, after a long moment, Laura lowered the gun. She had decided to trust him.

"We need to go to New York City, Laura," Alex declared firmly, wiping his face with his sleeve. "We have to recover the genuine QR code painting."

"Absolutely," Laura nodded. "And we must meet Bella. She's met S. L. Babel—she now knows the identity of the digital artist."

"I agree. Bella should be in Manhattan too," Alex croaked, sinking into a nearby armchair. In his distraction, he inadvertently knocked an elbow against a remote control lying on the desk.

Suddenly, a panel in the ceiling swung open, and a TV monitor descended, hanging in mid-air.

"What's this?" Alex exclaimed.

"It's a monitoring system my dad liked," Laura explained, seizing the remote and pressing a button. "He enjoyed watching TV when he was tired."

The TV screen lit up with NBC News. At the bottom of the screen, the caption "BREAKING NEWS" flashed. In the newsroom, a black-haired anchorwoman began reporting the latest update.

"The FBI has issued a warrant for *Washington Post* journalist Laura Campbell," the anchorwoman announced in a composed voice, displaying Laura's LinkedIn profile picture on screen. She continued, "The FBI alleges that Laura Campbell is aiding in the escape of Alex Hubert, wanted for the murder of James Brown, CEO of a pharmaceutical company, in his Miami mansion."

Laura trembled for a moment, then swiftly stowed the gun in her tote bag containing Steve's laptop and pulled out her phone instead.

"What are you doing?" Alex asked.

"Now we not only have to trust each other, but also provide support," Laura stammered, unlocking her WhatsApp account. "I'm calling the pilot of Peter Carli's private jet. Peter instructed him to protect us, no matter what happens."

Chapter Twenty-two

"Wonderful. Thank you so much," said senator Susanne Caldwell in a delighted tone, holding the door frame of the Grand Luxe King Room on the thirteenth floor of the Plaza Hotel.

A suave room service server in a white uniform with the Plaza emblem smiled, holding out a tray to her.

"You're very welcome, Congresswoman," said the server in a humble voice. "Is this everything you need?"

Before receiving the tray, Susanne's shining eyes quickly scanned each dish on the tray: a mozzarella pizza with peppers, olives, shrimp, and lobster; a mini-Caesar salad with salmon and pineapples; an empty wine glass along with a red wine bottle. For a moment, Susanne imagined severed human organs scattered in the salad and the wine glass overflowing with blood. *I'll always be the winner, drinking the most exquisite wine at the end of the day.*

"That's all I ordered," Susanne smiled, drooling a little and taking the tray. "I appreciate it."

"Have a great evening, Ms. Caldwell," said the server.

"The pizza smells so good!" said a pregnant woman in an olive-green gown, walking down the corridor. As she passed the hotel server and Caldwell, who was wearing a bathrobe and craning her head out of the door, the pregnant woman's eyes met Caldwell's.

As if to hide her makeup-free face and her actions from the public and paparazzi's cameras, Susanne Caldwell averted her eyes and quickly shut the door. Caldwell didn't want to be recognized by anyone during this trip, though she knew it would be difficult.

The hotel server stood in the corridor, dumbfounded. *Did I do anything rude?*

The pregnant woman's footsteps echoed down the hallway.

"Can I order a bottle of wine?" the pregnant woman asked mischievously after walking ten steps ahead of the server.

"Of course, ma'am. What's your room number?" the server asked, smiling like an automatic robot.

"Oh, my room is here," said the pregnant woman, inserting her card key into the Grand Luxe King Room next to Susanne Caldwell's room.

"I got it, ma'am," said the server. "What kind of red wine would you like?"

"The same red wine that Susanne Caldwell ordered," said the pregnant woman, curling her lips. "I liked the red wine's color. It looked like blood."

Before the server could reply, she closed the door of her room.

After locking the door from the inside, Bella Saba glanced at her luggage, which a hotel employee had brought from the lobby and placed on the mosaic floor between a luxurious wood-paneled closet and the king-sized bed.

Bella closed all the curtains around the windows and jumped onto the bed. Taking a deep breath, Bella glowered at her own body reflected in the mirror hung on the wall along the headboard. *I'm still young. And I know I'll be eternally young,* Bella thought, caressing her swollen stomach. *But I don't live only for myself.* She gazed at the mirror again to see the entire room reflected in it. Nobody else was in the room. Bella strained her ears. Classical music of a tragic tone—Richard Strauss's *Also sprach Zarathustra,* Op. thirty—seeped through the wall. Susanne Caldwell, who was having dinner in the next room, must have started playing this music from her phone. *This world is so hot. Hatred. Trauma. Desire for money and power. All of these negative emotions were swirling everywhere, igniting the passion for crime.* As the music dropped an octave and cymbals roared, Bella started to take off all her clothes, her sweat falling onto the bed. Throwing her white shirt and navy bra on the floor, she stroked her stiff belly with her fingers. The classical music suddenly stopped. Bella gazed up at the mirror in front of her. A naked girl with a fake pregnancy belly bodysuit stood there, her eyes burning with vengeful shine. Bella tapped her belly. The girl in the mirror copied her motion, tapping the fake pregnancy belly. As Bella shifted the position of the shoulder straps, long, red marks made by these straps appeared on her shoulder blades. Cold, silent laughter erupted from the mouth of the girl in the mirror. Taking off the bodysuit, the girl was taking out something from her fake belly. *This girl, who tricked the whole world by wearing a fake pregnant stomach, is you.* Bella said to herself, but her body didn't feel like her own. Her hands were moving without her intention and control. It seemed that the girl in the mirror moved first, and Bella's body was imitating her motion. Bella felt that the girl in the mirror was real, and she in reality was fake.

Bella turned around to avoid seeing the mirror. She found herself holding a pair of huge Nike basketball shoes and S. L. Babel's QR code painting, both of which had been stored in her fake pregnancy belly for more than a day. Small pieces of soil and grass from James Brown's mansion were attached to the bottom of the Nike shoes. Throwing the shoes on the floor, Bella hugged the QR code painting while completely naked. Then, she raised the painting in the air and faced the wall adjacent to the other Grand Luxe King Room where Susanne was staying.

"You want this painting, lousy corrupt politician," Bella said maliciously in a low voice. "I promise you, Caldwell. When you get this, you'll lose your life."

Bella's phone beeped. She jumped off the bed, snatching up her phone from the bedside table. A text message from art dealer Jack Bazin, who had just arrived at the lobby of the Plaza Hotel, popped up. Jack Bazin was her friend who had once been featured on her contemporary art blog. Bella had struck a deal to sell S. L. Babel's real QR code painting to Bazin for five million dollars. For Bazin, who could sell this work on the dark market, this was an incredibly lucrative deal. Moreover, Bazin wouldn't need to pay Babel after selling his work because he'd secretly traded the stolen painting.

Bella dressed and tucked Babel's QR code painting into a large Whole Foods Market shopping bag. Going out of the room, Bella felt the air in the corridor flowing into her throat. When she closed the door of her room with a bang, Jack Bazin sent her another text message: "*I'm sitting on a white sofa close to the peace lily vase. Let me know when you arrive."*

"*I'm coming, Jack.*"

Bella quickly typed a reply while striding to the elevator with the Whole Foods Market shopping bag. As she pressed the elevator button to the first floor, Bella said to herself:

Jack Bazin, S. L. Babel will kill you, too. Babel will never forgive anyone who betrays him.

When Susanne Caldwell heard the door of the adjacent room close, she trotted to her door and pressed her eye to the peephole. Bella, holding a Whole Foods Market shopping bag and her phone, was walking toward the elevator. Surprisingly, her belly looked slim.

"Wasn't she pregnant?" Caldwell whispered, rubbing her eyes. Caldwell didn't want to attract any attention from the paparazzi. Especially, her visit to Michael Perry's penthouse tomorrow and her interest in S. L. Babel, whose works had been tied to numerous mysterious murders, must remain secret. After Bella entered the elevator, another footstep echoed in the corridor.

"Leave the wine in front of the door!" Bella's voice echoed as the elevator doors closed.

Eight seconds later, through the peephole, Caldwell saw the hotel server bring an empty wine glass and a red wine bottle on a tray to Bella's room.

"That woman doesn't look like a journalist, anyway," Caldwell said to herself reassuringly while striding back to the center of the Grand Luxe King Room. "If she's a journalist following me, she wouldn't take a room next to mine. It's too risky for an undercover journalist."

Susanne Caldwell took her phone from the bedside table and dove onto the king-sized bed. After staring at the immaculately clean ceiling sluggishly for ten seconds, she took a deep breath, turned on her phone, and opened her email inbox. There were 159 unread emails sent to her primary email address. Caldwell skimmed through some of them. Among the messages, her lawyer and secretary had sent her a barrage of emails about the defamation lawsuit against a news media outlet that had linked her to a child-trafficking group operating on the US-Mexico border. Also, her ghostwriter had sent Caldwell's ongoing book manuscript titled *Iron*

Woman Fighting For Global Health and speech drafts, seeking approval. Caldwell rarely read any books after graduating from college and didn't even want to read the 200-page manuscript entirely written by the ghostwriter, who was an award-winning nonfiction author. She sighed and skipped these emails. Scrolling for a minute, she finally landed on the email she was looking for. It was from her billionaire friend Michael Perry: *"See you tomorrow at noon in my penthouse in Upper East Side. I honestly don't know who else will join the secret auction to buy S. L. Babel's works. Only the digital artist knows about it. I'm sorry about Anthony Ross and his lover. My condolences to our friends. I believe S. L. Babel will still allow you to join the private auction even without Anthony."*

Caldwell replied: *"Thank you, Michael. I'm looking forward to seeing you and Babel's works, then."*

After sending her reply, Susanne Caldwell threw her phone onto the bedside table and turned off the antique lamps around her. Complete darkness reigned in the room.

Anthony Ross was killed in the bomb explosion. Who killed him? S. L. Babel?

The FBI still hadn't located the explosives that had demolished Anthony Ross's mansion. However, Caldwell knew it had been the QR code painting that had exploded. As she closed her eyes, snaky flames whirled around her. Caldwell started to remember Anthony Ross's cold, snarky voice echoing in the blazing winds. As a dragon-shaped fire engulfed him, Elena Taylor let out a shriek, chasing him. The fire metamorphosed into an anaconda, spitting powdery fire on Elena's body and burning her down.

Feeling beads of sweat on her eyelids, Caldwell opened her eyes. Nobody else was around her. James Brown, Terence Miller, Elena Taylor, and Anthony Ross. All of them were killed. Who else would continue to carry out their mission? Susanne Caldwell was the only main figure of their secret group who was still alive.

As a ripple of fear ran through her spine, Caldwell took out a sleeping pill from a bottle. She swallowed the pill with a glass of sparkling water. Then, Caldwell lay on the bed, wrapping herself in a blanket. In twenty seconds, she started to snore.

~ * ~

Another private auction of S. L. Babel's works will take place tomorrow in New York City. S. L. Babel is in Manhattan now.

Bella, who had handed S. L. Babel's QR code painting in the Whole Foods Market shopping bag to art dealer Jack Bazin in the lobby, thought in the elevator ascending to the thirteenth floor of the Plaza Hotel.

The elevator beeped. It arrived on the thirteenth floor.

As the elevator door opened, Bella saw a tray with an empty wine glass and a red wine bottle left in front of the door of her room in the corridor. Feeling thirsty, she stuck out her tongue, licking the edge of her lips painted pink.

Stepping out of the elevator, Bella started to walk to her room slowly, suppressing the sound of her footsteps. Passing Caldwell's room, Bella ruffled her hair as if to mock her. As Bella strained her ears, Caldwell's snores seeped through the door. *I shouldn't wake up the congresswoman. This will be her last peaceful moment. Have a nice dream.*

Chapter Twenty-three

The imposing door of the Senate Chamber swung open. Caldwell's secretaries, who had been patiently waiting for her, visibly relaxed and dispersed in various directions on the blue carpet adorned with a gold star pattern.

As Senator Susanne Caldwell stepped up to the podium, a silence filled with anticipation fell over the room. Taking a deep breath, Caldwell stared at the coffered ceiling for a few seconds. When the flashlights of cameras engulfed her, she smiled at the crowd in the chamber, the cameras, and the people watching on TV.

"Today, I stand before you not just as a senator but as a voice for the millions of Americans who find themselves at the crossroads of health and uncertainty," Caldwell said in a sharp voice into the microphone. "The state of our nation's healthcare demands our attention and dedication. As a member of the Senate Committee on Health, I've had the privilege of hearing the stories of Americans—narratives of people who urgently need organ donations and accounts of children who require more affordable medication. It's our duty, as representatives of the people, to translate these stories into decisive and urgent action, right now!"

There was a short pause as Senator Caldwell took in a mouthful of air, her breath echoing through the microphone, while the room erupted in applause and jeering. Caldwell remained calm, the same coquettish smile still floating on her face.

All of a sudden, Caldwell and the flashlights surrounding her froze. Everything became a still image as Alex tapped the screen of his iPhone, stopping the YouTube video.

"This is disgusting! This congresswoman is the textbook definition of a phony, hypocritical politician!" Alex Hubert said impishly, turning off the YouTube application. The battery of his iPhone was below

15% and he needed to charge it.

"She has control over policy decisions regarding US healthcare," Alex continued scathingly, looking back at Laura. "When making this speech, Caldwell was only worried about the money she could get from deals with James Brown and Anthony Ross—both are dead today."

Alex and Laura were in Peter Carli's private jet, leaving St. Louis and heading to John F. Kennedy International Airport in New York City.

"Who do you think Susanne Caldwell is working for now?" asked Laura conspiratorially, as she took off her loafers and lay supine on three seats.

"I have no idea," Alex shrugged. "Anthony Ross was probably killed in the bomb explosion. I still don't know much about Anthony Ross, but he seemed like the guy who was pulling the strings."

"Peter was gone too," said Laura, sipping a can of Sprite. Her sad eyes suddenly fell on the painting on the cabin's ceiling. It was a portrait of Peter Carli's wife—the young, blond Swiss woman wearing a diamond necklace was smiling without knowing what had happened to Peter or what he was planning.

"Alex, you said Peter was planning to buy Babel's work to reduce his divorce settlement?" asked Laura, her eyes still fixed on the portrait of Peter's wife on the ceiling.

"Well, generally, yes," Alex mumbled between bites of Pringles potato chips. "Converting his cash into expensive pieces of art and keeping them abroad has been his strategy to reduce his divorce settlement. But when it comes to his interest in S. L. Babel's works, Peter was probably blackmailed by Babel as well."

"I agree," said Laura, shifting her body on the seats and wrapping herself in several blankets. "Those compromised billionaires have made exorbitant bids on Babel's works at auctions."

It became colder and colder in the cabin as the airplane flew north. The moon outside the windows shone like a forgotten toy in a dark park. Alex pulled down the plastic curtain.

"I brought Peter's flash drive containing the VR video," said Laura, taking it out from her tote bag. "This will prove your, or technically, *our* innocence. Elena must've killed James Brown."

"That's great!" said Alex, his eyes shining slightly with confidence. "But we must run away from the FBI for a while to get more evidence about the organ trade network to prove our innocence."

Alex eyed the collage of Leonardo da Vinci's drawings of human organs hung on the cabin's wall. The room's lamps illuminated each organ painted in grotesque colors. Peter must've known a lot about the crime deals behind S. L. Babel's art business.

"What Elena said in this VR video taken from the bug in my dad's laboratory gave us a lot of clues," said Laura pensively, putting her hand on her chin. "James Brown purchased so many expensive pieces of art over the years for money laundering. He needed to wash the money he'd obtained from his illegal organ trade business. But at some point, S. L. Babel, who somehow discovered his secret business, started to blackmail him. That's why Brown poured millions of dollars into Babel's digital art."

"Not just blackmail," said Alex hotly. "Do you remember James Brown attempted to break the QR code painting with an axe right before being killed? I guess S. L. Babel might've embedded hidden messages revealing James Brown and others' illegal organ trading in his works. That's why Brown needed to collect them and secretly destroy everything created by Babel. At first, the website accessed through the QR code said the deadly virus killed the apparent head of human organ stealers. Then, Brown was killed."

"It makes a lot of sense," said Laura, licking her dry lips. "Actually, Bella told me Babel's digital art piece in the atrium of Brown's mansion, the one combining AI and digital panels, was fake. Probably, Brown destroyed the real one, which contained information related to his crime deals in organ trades."

"Is that *Fusion*, the one showing a cyborg using viewers' bodies?" asked Alex, raising his brow.

"Yes," said Laura, crossing her legs under the blanket. "I still don't understand one thing. If Elena killed James Brown, who is S. L. Babel? Elena was killed by the bomb inside the fake QR code painting. S. L. Babel, who predicted the murder of James Brown in the QR code painting, is still alive, sending you emails. Obviously, Elena isn't S. L.

Babel. Did Babel hire her to kill Brown?"

"Although it was evident that Elena intended to kill James Brown, somebody else might've done it," said Alex darkly. "Someone who wasn't invited to the secret auction broke into his mansion. The footprints didn't match any shoes we wore."

"It's plausible," nodded Laura.

As the airplane shook violently due to turbulent winds, red *fasten seatbelt* signs turned on across the ceiling of the cabin. Laura straightened up in her seat, fastening the buckles of the seatbelt. Alex, who ignored the fasten seatbelt signs, placed both arms on the armrests, staring at the flight map on the screen in front of his seat. Their flight was crossing the boundary between West Virginia and Pennsylvania. The estimated time to their destination, New York City, was one hour and a half.

"Ladies and gentlemen, this is your captain speaking," the pilot's hoarse voice reverberated over the aircraft's intercom system. "We've encountered some turbulence ahead, so for your safety, please return to your seats and fasten your seatbelts immediately."

"Alex, we must meet Bella," said Laura passionately. "Bella is in Manhattan. She met S. L. Babel. We can ask her who Babel is."

"I'm sure Bella signed a non-disclosure agreement with Babel," said Alex. "But it's not a bad idea to meet her. She's the only person who met S. L. Babel on the planet."

"And I want to know who is in the circle of collectors trying to get Babel's works," said Laura decisively. "In his email, S. L. Babel said art dealer Jack Bazin will sell his works in a secret auction in real estate mogul Michael Perry's penthouse. Folks who will appear at the auction are likely to be associated with the organ trade business."

"It might be inevitable that the FBI will end up capturing us," said Alex darkly. "But we'll do our best to keep escaping and gathering more evidence to prove our innocence."

"This is not about getting 30 million dollars back from the psychopath digital artist, Alex," said Laura ominously. "This is about life or death. We can't stop escaping! Florida has capital punishment."

A cold silence hung between them. Laura and Alex were both looking out of the windows, peering downward at the night cityscape of

Pittsburgh. What if this was the last time they saw the outside world? All of a sudden, the city, cracked with spidery webs of buildings' lights and wrapped by the snaky Allegheny and Monongahela Rivers, looked ethereally beautiful. Straining their eyes, they could see cars crossing a bridge between the rivers, under which a small boat was silently inching along. This landscape represented a world to which they no longer belonged.

"How can we set up a meeting with Bella?" said Alex in an anxious tone. "I mean, can we really trust Bella? She might call the police."

"Bella is my friend," said Laura firmly. "She won't turn us in to the police."

"You never know," replied Alex in an uncouth voice. "She may not be able to resist a one hundred-thousand-dollar bounty."

"Bella knows we're innocent," said Laura irritably. "She knows we were sailing the Lamborghini yacht when Brown was shot."

Alex shrugged and rubbed his chin.

"Okay, I won't disagree with meeting Bella," said Alex gruffly. "It seems Bella is the only person who has met S. L. Babel. Asking her who this digital artist is would be the quickest way for us to solve all the mysteries. I hope Babel won't try to kill us if we reach out to her. Did you run an antivirus scan on your phone?"

"Oh, yes, of course. I deleted one fishy app the phone downloaded when I'd scanned the QR code in Babel's work," said Laura, clutching the armrest as the airplane shook in the turbulence. "Otherwise, Babel could have listened in on our conversation just now."

"That's so true," Alex trembled.

"I'll send a message to Bella via Instagram. We follow each other on Instagram," said Laura crisply, connecting her phone to the airplane's Wi-Fi. "Let's pretend to ask for her help to clear the FBI's prosecution against us. We should hide our intention to learn S. L. Babel's identity in order to meet Bella."

"Sounds good," replied Alex, his anxious eyes watching the flight icon inching across the map on the screen.

Bella replied to Laura's message in two minutes:

Hi Laura, I'm so sorry about your situation. But I'm glad to hear both of you managed to escape the lousy FBI. Shall we meet in front of Babel's artwork exhibited at noon in MoMA??

"MoMA? It's too risky for us to enter the Museum of Modern Art," said Alex huffily. "There are thousands of visitors every day,"

"Indeed. We wanna avoid crowds," said Laura, typing her reply to Bella.

Why MoMA?

Bella immediately read her reply and answered.

Haven't you heard of S. L. Babel's new VR art titled "Who Killed James Brown?", Laura? It's a headset that shows only 'chosen' visitors the truth behind the murder of James Brown. I have a hunch that Babel would show you and Alex a piece of VR art that is secret to other visitors. I'm sure you'll be able to prove your innocence once you see the VR art.

"What if this is a trap set by S. L. Babel," said Laura dubiously.

"That's what I'm thinking," replied Alex.

"But our enemy is the FBI. S. L. Babel himself has never attempted to let the FBI capture us," said Laura in a high-pitched voice. "S. L. Babel is simply punishing people associated with the secret organ trade organization."

"I agree. The information about Babel's VR art exhibited in MoMA looks public," said Alex, googling Babel's new VR art titled *Who Killed James Brown?* and reading online news articles about it. "Actually, MoMA might be a safe place to see S. L. Babel work. I mean, his work can't contain any bombs given the museum's safety protocols."

"Let's visit MoMA at noon," said Laura decisively. "We should cover our faces with masks and caps when entering the museum."

Laura typed a reply:

I see, we'll be there at noon. See you tomorrow, Bella

In seconds, Bella replied to Laura along with a screenshot of *The Deathly Network.*

Btw, Laura, did you see the latest network accessed through Babel's QR code painting? Only two people are left in the network.
Either you or I will be killed next.

Chapter Twenty-four

"That's Senator Susanne Caldwell," whispered a college student, wearing a gray hoodie with the New York University logo, as he walked out of the "Special Exhibition: Digital Art" on the sixth floor of the Museum of Modern Art, to his girlfriend.

"Really?" said his girlfriend, striding toward Terrace Café on the western end. She turned back, following her boyfriend's line of sight.

An elderly, blond woman in a black suit was slipping through the automatic glass entrance doors with a somewhat practiced gait. Her features were completely obscured by the dark lenses of oversized sunglasses and a black surgical mask. As the glass door shut behind her, she looked around at the other visitors, appearing like a burglar about to steal expensive artworks.

"I'm 100% sure," said the college student confidently as the woman's figure grew smaller in the distance. "She's Susanne Caldwell, who might become the U.S. president in the future."

"I don't think so," replied his girlfriend snidely. "If that were really Susanne Caldwell, she would never wear sunglasses and a mask. She's always pompous and showy. The real Caldwell would smile at all the visitors and try to shake hands with them to gain more votes."

"I don't doubt that was Caldwell," said the college student hotly, screwing up his face and rolling up the floor map in his fist. "Politicians often pretend to be knowledgeable about art and culture. I wouldn't be surprised if Caldwell were interested in S. L. Babel's digital art, which billionaires around the world have collected. Anyway, politicians and artists are kind of similar. They're all fake."

"I agree," said his girlfriend, pulling open the entrance door of Terrace Café.

As the couple entered the café, Susanne Caldwell, weaving

through the throngs of visitors and skipping most works in the exhibition rooms, reached the small room displaying S. L. Babel's new digital artwork, *Who Killed James Brown?* In the center of the vacant, white room was a VR headset on a Corinthian column pedestal. There was nothing else in the room. On the wall in front of the pedestal, a graffiti-like message was painted in red spray:

ONLY THOSE WHO ARE CHOSEN CAN SEE THE TRUTH

With a deep sigh, mid-forties art dealer Jack Bazin, who wore a blue double-breasted wool gabardine suit and a Rolex watch, placed the VR headset back on the pedestal. He seemed unimpressed by the VR art. His face, etched with years of experience in the art business, was flushed. Caldwell even thought his grizzled hair had turned red.

"Holy shit! This is a scam," Jack Bazin said gruffly, scratching his head. Noticing another visitor, he turned to Susanne Caldwell, still wearing her mask and glasses. "The latest Babel work in this exhibition is hyped up! Only people chosen by Babel can see the truth behind the murder of James Brown in this VR art—I never doubted I was one of the chosen since I'm the best art dealer in New York City after Alex Hubert went out of business. I wanted to find out who killed James Brown because…" Bazin clenched his fist, the golden band of his Rolex clicking. Clearing his throat, he continued, his voice echoing in the room. "I'll never forgive the scumbag who murdered James. James Brown was one of the greatest art collectors of all time and I greatly benefited from him. If only that legendary biotech entrepreneur had survived and kept pouring millions into the contemporary art market…" Bazin rubbed his eyes with thick fingers. "I'll wait outside this room, hoping a chosen visitor will find clues to James Brown's murder. I hope you can see something important in this VR art, ma'am."

Jack Bazin irritably banged on his chest and briskly left the room.

Once the exit door closed and Bazin was out of sight, Susanne Caldwell stepped toward the pedestal, taking off her sunglasses. She looked around. No other visitors were present. The security camera in the corner of the ceiling glinted red, capturing her and the pedestal. Suddenly, she noticed the noises from the other rooms were completely shut out. Taking a deep breath, Caldwell put on the VR headset.

~ * ~

Half an hour after Caldwell left the exhibition room of Babel's VR artwork, Alex and Laura arrived, both hiding their faces with fedoras and black surgical masks. They checked the time on their phones, which were set to airplane mode to avoid FBI tracking. It was precisely noon.

"Bella hasn't arrived yet," Laura whispered to Alex, looking around the corridor.

"Let's see Babel's artwork in the meantime," Alex replied enthusiastically, lowering his voice. "One of us needs to oversee the entire floor, including the exhibition room and corridor. Hopefully, Bella will arrive soon. We don't want to get stuck in the crowd here. We need to run quickly if cops come."

There were other visitors in the exhibition room. As Alex opened the entry door, they heard a male voice mumbling near the exit door at the opposite end of the corridor.

"Oh no, I have to go soon. The folks chosen by S. L. Babel haven't come yet to solve the mystery of his VR art…"

Laura and Alex glanced at a man in his mid-forties, wearing a blue suit and nervously checking his Rolex. *That's art dealer Jack Bazin, my enemy number one! Isn't he holding a secret auction to sell Babel's QR code today?* Alex thought, averting his eyes. Laura noticed a wave of shock run through Alex's face but didn't say anything.

As they entered the exhibition room for Babel's VR art, the high-pitched voices of children resounded. A white kid wore Babel's VR headset, glaring and shouting at his brother against the wall. When Alex and Laura stepped in, their mother sternly said, "Stop!" and made her son return the VR headset to the Corinthian column pedestal.

"This looks more like an amusement park than an art exhibition," whispered Laura sarcastically as the mother and her two children left.

"Babel's work must've boosted ticket sales," replied Alex slyly, glancing at the entrance door. "Bella hasn't come yet. We were supposed to meet her here, right?"

"Yeah, but I think she'll be here soon," said Laura, pointing to a security camera on the ceiling. "I don't like that camera."

"They installed it to protect the artwork, not to catch us," said Alex, adjusting his black surgical mask to cover his nose completely. "Let's avoid showing our faces to it."

Noticing the ominous red letters "ONLY THOSE WHO ARE CHOSEN CAN SEE THE TRUTH" on the wall, Alex stood in front of the VR headset on the pedestal and turned his back to the camera. He saw a biometric scanner, requiring visitors to press their fingers to activate the VR art. This scanner must be identifying if each visitor is "chosen" to see the "truth" of James Brown's death.

"I'll try this VR art first," said Alex firmly, taking off his sunglasses. "Can you watch the entrance and exit doors?"

"Sure," said Laura, her eyes darting toward the exit door. She noticed the man in the blue suit peering into the room from the corridor.

Is that Alex? When Alex took off his sunglasses and put on Babel's VR headset, Jack Bazin's heart leapt into his throat. Jack pressed his forehead against the glass window of the exit door, gawking at Alex, whose face was now covered by the VR headset and mask. Suddenly, Jack noticed Bella's reproachful gaze. He winced and turned to face the wall.

"Alex, did you find something interesting?" asked Laura, still cautiously watching the doors.

Alex didn't reply. He couldn't hear Laura. He'd already pressed his finger on the biometric scanner and donned the VR headset, covering his ears with its headphones. If this device was connected to the Internet, the creator S. L. Babel would know Alex, the suspect in James Brown's murder, was at MoMA in New York City. Since Babel had hacked Alex's iPhone and Touch ID, he must have Alex's fingerprint. This VR art could be a trap, and the police might already be on their way. Despite these suspicions, Alex didn't stop wearing Babel's VR headset. *This VR art will choose me.* Heart racing, he began to swivel with the headset on.

Gradually, the white walls of the exhibition room faded away, and the sound of ocean waves filled his ears. He turned to locate the source of the waves and saw a shattered window and footprints on the soil outside. Sunlight shone through palm trees in a garden. Alex shifted his gaze to the contemporary paintings and sculptures covering the walls: Tracey Emin's depictions of naked women and graffiti-like poems, Jeff Koons' blue balloon dog worth two million dollars. He was in the atrium of James Brown's mansion on Star Island, Miami.

Laura stood in front of Koons' sculpture, her feet rooted to the floor, gazing at a digital art piece on the wall. Feeling dizzy, Alex shambled towards her.

"Are you also in Brown's mansion, Laura?" Alex asked shakily.

"Somebody is looking at us from outside," Laura said nervously, pointing to the digital art on the wall.

"Who is looking at us?" Alex frowned, examining the piece.

It was an AI-incorporated monitor entitled *Fusion*, part of S. L. Babel's 'Transplant' series. Alex recognized the piece James Brown had bought for millions. It was supposed to show a cyborg using the latest viewers' bodies. Scratching his head, Alex remembered the killer who had murdered James Brown had shot this work because the monitor had shown the killer's face. Alex froze as the fuzzy monitor gradually became clear, revealing a cyborg with James's chubby belly in a white T-shirt and Laura's slim, long legs in a skirt. A wind blew, unveiling the cyborg's face.

It was Josh Stevenson, a medical student who had worked for Terence Miller's medical center and had been killed by him. Josh smiled viciously, caressing his stomach.

Alex shouted at the top of his lungs, "JOSH STEVENSON KILLED JAMES BROWN. JOSH IS ALIVE. JOSH STEVENSON IS S. L. BABEL."

"What are you saying, Alex?" asked Laura, raising her brow. "Josh Stevenson was killed years ago. We visited his tomb, remember?"

"Josh Stevenson is taking revenge on everyone involved in the organ trade," Alex said, trembling. "He was killed because he had information that could ruin them. He became a ghost, killing the key figures of the secret business."

Suddenly, the entrance door to Brown's mansion atrium opened.

"Bella!" Laura turned towards the door and said in a delighted tone.

Bella Saba, her stomach swelling under her floral dress with a deep V-neck, stood in the atrium, smiling at them.

"Hi, how are you both?" said Bella casually.

"YOU MUST LEAVE RIGHT NOW, LAURA AND BELLA!" Alex screamed.

"What are you saying, Alex?" said Laura irritably. "Take off the VR headset. Bella finally came."

Alex's shocked eyes were still fixed on the digital art *Fusion*. The cyborg with Josh Stevenson's face stretched its robotic arms out of the monitor. Alex swallowed. The cyborg planted its legs, resembling Laura's, on the frame of the digital art, craning its head out of the monitor. The cyborg was about to emerge. Its fingers, now visible, were made of sharp daggers, dripping with blood.

"JOSH STEVENSON IS COMING TO KILL EITHER OF YOU!" Alex screamed at the top of his lungs.

"Stop, Alex!" Laura suddenly strode to Alex, peeling the VR headset off his head.

Alex was back in the exhibition room at MoMA, New York City. Laura and Bella stood beside him. Cold wind from the air conditioner touched Alex's head.

"It seems you were one of the people chosen to see the truth about James Brown's death," said Bella snidely, her hand on her swollen stomach.

"What did you see, Alex?" Laura, who had taken off her sunglasses and surgical mask, anxiously asked.

"Josh Stevenson is S. L. Babel. He killed James Brown and everyone else," said Alex, out of breath, wiping the sweat from his forehead with his sleeve. "In this VR art, I saw the atrium of James Brown's mansion. Josh's face appeared in Babel's *Fusion* as part of a cyborg."

"It's impossible," said Laura in a husky voice. "Josh is dead."

"It might be possible," said Bella conspiratorially. "Josh may be alive."

They fell silent.

"If you saw the cyborg with Josh Stevenson's face in the VR art, it might be a prank S. L. Babel cooked up," said Laura jerkily. "You know, we saw another work of Babel at Art Basel Miami Beach, which features Josh Stevenson."

Alex rubbed his right eye, looking at the VR headset in his hands. *S. L. Babel is waging psychological warfare against us*. Taking a deep breath, Alex returned the VR headset to the pedestal.

"So, why did you want to meet me?" asked Bella nonchalantly. "I'm happy to assist you in proving your innocence."

"Who is S. L. Babel?" asked Laura firmly, staring squarely at Bella. "You interviewed him, right?"

"Yes, I did," said Bella, a smug smile spreading across her face. "I can't tell you who he is. I signed a non-disclosure agreement. If I breach it, I'll have to pay a million dollars."

"Please, Bella," said Alex beseechingly. "If you reveal who S. L. Babel is, we'll be able to prove our innocence and sue the FBI for defamation. Babel is likely the person pulling the strings behind the serial murders."

"No, I can't tell you," said Bella sharply, twisting her lips.

"Please, Bella. Otherwise, the FBI will arrest us, and we'll probably receive capital sentences," said Laura passionately, grabbing Bella's hands. "S. L. Babel predicted all of the murders through the QR code. He is the mastermind."

"I said no," snapped Bella, retracting her hands. "I can't breach the agreement. It's not just about the NDA. I don't want him to hurt you. Most people who got to know Babel's identity have been killed."

"Is that why some art dealers who sold his works have been killed?" asked Alex darkly.

"I believe so," said Bella, deadpan.

Laura glanced at the exit door and froze. The man in the blue suit, who had been peering into the exhibition room through the glass window, hung up his phone and tucked his iPhone into the pocket of his black pants.

"We must escape as early as possible," said Laura, trembling, eyeing the exit door. "The guy in the corridor has been observing us. He must've called the police."

"I actually know him, Laura," said Alex bitterly, putting on his sunglasses again. "He's art dealer Jack Bazin, my primary competitor in the contemporary art market."

"Jack Bazin? Is he the dealer organizing the secret auction to sell Babel's work today?" said Laura in a low voice.

"Yes," croaked Alex. "I'm sure Bazin was delighted when the FBI placed me on the wanted list. And I won't be surprised if he called the police. He can get an enormous bounty... He likes money just like I do."

"We gotta run away right now," spluttered Laura.

"No, I won't let you go," Bella suddenly shouted as Alex and Laura rushed toward the entrance door and bumped into other visitors entering the exhibition room.

"THEY ARE ALEX HUBERT AND LAURA CAMPBELL, WHO MURDERED JAMES BROWN!"

Bella shouted at the top of her lungs, galloping out of the exhibition room and continuing to scream.

"ARREST THEM NOW! THEY ARE THE MURDERERS WANTED BY THE FBI!"

As Bella shouted, other visitors in the museum pointed at Alex and Laura, who were running toward the emergency staircase.

"That's Hubert and Campbell!" shouted the college student in the gray hoodie with New York University's logo, who was leaving the Terrace Café. His girlfriend followed his pointing finger and screamed. "They look like the pictures I saw on the Internet!"

"They are the murderers who killed James Brown!" another visitor shouted.

A panicked museum staff member picked up her phone, calling the security team as Alex and Laura swung open the emergency staircase door and rushed down the stairs, their footsteps thundering across the floor.

"Hey Alex, wait! What did you see in Babel's VR art?" Jack Bazin started to run toward the emergency staircase but suddenly stopped and ran back toward the elevator.

The elevator beeped and the door opened. As all the visitors inside the elevator left, he jumped in, pressing the button to close the door without waiting for others trying to catch the elevator. "I can help you run away, Alex," said Jack, out of breath, as the elevator started to descend. "I'll need your help to tell if the QR code painting I got is real or not."

"*Attention all visitors at the Museum of Modern Art,*" a female voice announced through the PA system on all floors. "*For your safety, we kindly request that all visitors evacuate the museum immediately. To ensure a smooth and orderly evacuation process, we ask visitors on the first floor to proceed to the nearest exit point right now. If you're on the second floor or above, please wait for further instructions. Once outside, please move away from the building and await further instructions. Thank you for your cooperation and understanding.*"

"That's why I said we shouldn't trust Bella!" said Alex huffily to Laura when they reached the landing between the first and second floors. They stopped for a moment along the window. "It's too risky to go to the first floor through this emergency staircase," added Alex. "The museum's security team might be blocking the exit."

"I still have the gun I took from my dad's safe," smirked Laura, taking out the gun from her tote bag.

"How did you pass the metal detectors at the entrance?" Alex raised his brow.

"I wrapped the gun in aluminum foil and concealed it in my large makeup bag," said Laura smugly.

"You can't beat a bunch of armed security guys, though," said Alex gloomily. "There should be cops coming, too."

They heard the sirens of police cars approaching. With trembling hands, Alex unlocked the crescent locks and opened the windows on the staircase landing. Dazzling red lights of police cars were heading to the museum at high speed.

"We'll never quit, Alex," said Laura firmly. "We must go now. Otherwise, the cops will block the street."

"HEY, ALEX!" a vibrant male voice shouted at them from outside the window. "JUMP DOWN FROM THE WINDOW, NOW!"

Alex craned his head out of the window.

Art dealer Jack Bazin parked his Volkswagen Atlas along the street, waving at them.

"Jack! Are you serious?" Alex shouted back. Onlookers cast curious glances at them.

"JUMP ONTO THE TRUCK!"

Jack Bazin pointed to a truck parked nearby. Dozens of museum staff were around the truck, starting to bring out a huge piece of contemporary art, shaped like a massive castle made entirely of pink marshmallows, from the truck's bed. They lowered the cargo bed, making a huge cart closer to it.

"Can we really trust him?" asked Laura nervously. "He might've called the police."

"No, he didn't call the police. If so, he wouldn't say we should jump onto the truck. Trusting him is our only choice now," said Alex bitterly, planting his foot on the windowsill and taking Laura's hand.

Laura nodded, eyes wide, and planted her foot on the windowsill as well. Together, they leapt into the air filled with heat, wind, and sirens. As they fell toward the sculpture made of marshmallows on the truck, both Alex's and Laura's minds raced, feeling their bodies pierced by the gazes of onlookers. In seconds, with a huge thud, they landed on the marshmallows, enveloped by the sweet, fragrant smell. As they got up and jumped out of the truck's cargo, they felt their arms sticky with fragments of marshmallow. They dashed toward Jack Bazin's Volkswagen Atlas, swarming into its backseat.

Jack kickstarted the car, weaving through the police cars approaching MoMA.

Laura heaved a sigh of relief, settling herself in the backseat next to Alex and tasting a fragment of marshmallow.

"Thanks, Jack!" said Alex, out of breath. "Where are you going now?"

"I'm going to Michael Perry's penthouse in the Upper East Side," said Jack Bazin. "I'll hold a private auction of S. L. Babel's works there."

"That's perfect! We wanted to see his new works, too," said Laura breathlessly. "But why did you save us?"

"Because I don't think you guys killed James Brown," said Jack, rotating the steering wheel to cross the street. "I know your profession very well, Alex. You wouldn't kill such a great patron of art. Besides, I believe you guys will help me determine if Babel's QR code painting I got is real or not."

"You got the QR code painting? How did you get it?" asked Laura, her chin shooting up.

"I can't tell you now," said Jack, his gaze swimming across the crowded street ahead.

"Where are Babel's works now, if you're holding the auction?" asked Alex.

"They're in the trunk of this car," replied Jack blankly, pointing to the trunk of his car with his thumb. Then, he picked up his phone and added, "We're already close to Michael Perry's penthouse. I'll call Michael to ask him to let us in."

Soon, the white thirty-five-story high-rise condo, standing like a giant's severed leg, appeared before their eyes. White, wispy clouds in the sky were reflected in the windows of each story, slowly floating eastward. It was the highest building in the area. Both Alex and Laura slightly lowered their sunglasses, gazing at the tower's top. The penthouse balcony jutted out from the towering edifice, shaping a mysterious palace in the skyline. They strained their eyes. Among the pine trees and their swaying shadows on the balcony stood a man, clutching the handrail with his left hand and picking up his phone with his right.

~ * ~

"Good job, Jack. I really wanted to invite Alex Hubert to the secret auction. I'll let you guys enter the garage," said multibillionaire real estate mogul Michael Perry on the balcony of his penthouse and hung up his phone.

A sudden breeze blew across the balcony, casting a huge shadow of pine trees onto Michael's swarthy face, darkening his thick, gray beard for a moment. As he stepped out of the pine tree's shadow, he touched his nose, the fragrant scent of orchids and bromeliads planted in vases invading his nostrils.

"This is an oasis where greedy travelers who hunt for treasures are bound to reach," said Michael Perry arrogantly, standing beside the swimming pool reflecting the blue sky with wispy clouds. He crouched down, staring at his wrinkled face reflected in the water and scooped up a handful of water. Michael's face flashed with a malicious smile. "And then they end up drinking delicious water filled with poison."

Chapter Twenty-five

In the contemporary art market, collectors don't fly to artworks. Artworks fly to the collectors, Alex silently thought as Jack Bazin's Volkswagen Atlas trundled into the underground garage of real estate billionaire Michael Perry's penthouse. The sirens of police cars were completely shut out as the thick entrance door to the garage closed. *And then artworks create money, dreams, and desires for murders around the world.*

Having parked his car in the corner of the garage where luxurious cars such as Ferraris, Lamborghinis, and Rolls-Royces were lined up like gems, Jack got out of his Volkswagen Atlas. Alex and Laura followed. There was nobody else in the garage.

"Let's go to the penthouse by taking the elevator," said Jack, pointing to the gold-hued elevator at the western end of the skyscraper.

"Are you serious?" said Laura in a doubtful tone. "If you take us to Michael Perry's penthouse to protect us, the FBI will consider you an accomplice. Also, other participants will probably turn us in."

I can't trust this guy. Laura's anxious eyes met Alex's.

"You can't leave this building anytime soon, no matter what. The police are searching for you right now," said Jack, opening the trunk of his car and bringing out Babel's QR code painting in a Whole Foods Market shopping bag and a square, wooden box containing Babel's new work for the upcoming auction.

On the lid of the box were drawings of Cleopatra wearing a golden, beaded headpiece and a huge Egyptian cobra curled up around her feet, its forked tongue flicking out. "As I said, I need your help to determine whether the QR code painting is authentic or not. Don't worry about the other guests at the auction. Both of you will wait in a secret room, isolated from others. I already discussed this with Michael Perry."

"So, Michael Perry knows we're coming to his penthouse?" asked Alex, his voice echoing in the underground garage.

"Yeah, Alex," replied Jack airily. "It's a great opportunity for you to connect with a wealthy collector like him."

Jack Bazin had already started walking toward the elevator, holding S. L. Babel's works in both hands.

"If we dally in this tower," Laura quietly said to Alex, her voice unexpectedly echoing in the garage, "we'll lose our chance to leave New York City and escape from the FBI."

"Don't worry, Ms. Campbell," Jack turned back, catching Laura's voice. "Michael Perry will dispatch a helicopter for both of you to escape the city—or the USA—if necessary. There's a helipad in this tower."

"Let's go," said Alex firmly.

Laura nodded in the darkness.

"Can you press the button?" asked Jack Bazin, who stood in front of the gold-hued elevator door with his hands full of Babel's works.

"Sure," said Alex, pressing the button with his elbow.

The upper arrow sign lit above their heads. As the elevator rattled down to the underground floor, a sharp, dry sound beeped like the final song of a choked bird.

~ * ~

"Oh my god!" Senator Susanne Caldwell shrieked as she entered Michael Perry's penthouse, stretching out her arms to a tall man standing by the floor-to-ceiling windows. "You're alive, Anthony!"

Caldwell and Anthony Ross hugged briefly. *I'm not alone,* Caldwell thought as Anthony pulled away, his face filled with a sinister smile.

"How did you survive?" Caldwell asked in a shrill voice. "Sampson told me your St. Louis mansion completely collapsed."

"I jumped into a swimming pool before the fake QR code painting exploded," Anthony said drily. "I dove to the bottom. The swimming pool is connected to one of the tunnels around my mansion. Priest Robert Porter picked me up and drove me to the airport. I took my private jet to

Manhattan."

"What about Elena?" Caldwell sat down in an armchair by a table and asked in a shaky voice. "Is she okay?"

"She's dead," replied Anthony tartly.

A cold silence hung between them.

"I'm sorry for her," Caldwell said sadly, crossing her arms and gazing at Anthony. A malicious smile still floated on his face.

"Don't you miss Elena?" Caldwell asked, a slight note of irritation in her voice. "Didn't you love her?"

Anthony didn't immediately reply. He sat down in an armchair across the table, picked up a cup, and sipped tea. As he put the cup back on the saucer, he spoke in a monotone.

"No, not at all. Since James Brown was killed, Elena became useless."

"She loved you, Anthony," said Caldwell testily.

"She loved me because I didn't love her," said Anthony, his eyes flashing. "She knew I'm more powerful and ruthless than James Brown. She knew I don't love anyone. Susanne, why would you frown on me? We've sacrificed many individuals to achieve our mission, which hasn't been completed."

"I don't frown on you. I was just curious about your reaction," Caldwell said, suddenly changing her tone to casual. "I agree with you. We must complete our missions."

A shaft of sunlight poured through the floor-to-ceiling windows, lighting up the luxurious furniture in the Greco-Roman-style drawing room of Michael Perry's penthouse. The green forest of Central Park lay outside the windows, rippling under sudden gusts. Rubbing his chin covered with a thick brown beard, Anthony Ross gazed upward at the gold glass chandelier above his head. Susanne Caldwell's head was reflected in the crystal cube embedded in the chandelier. Anthony strained his eyes. He could see Caldwell's undyed hair at the top of her head, looking gray like an old object with gold plating peeling off. *This congresswoman is a textbook example of a fake individual*, Anthony thought, sinking back into the armchair and darting his eyes to the walls covered with contemporary cubism paintings.

Susanne Caldwell, on the other hand, silently peered at the mirror hung on the wall behind Anthony Ross. *I hope Jack Bazin will bring S. L. Babel's works safely. We shouldn't let others outside our circle get his artwork.* Susanne licked her dry palate, slightly tasting blood. *I must keep track of who will buy Babel's works. Anthony and Michael, the biggest donors to our political party, are fortunately on our side.* Caldwell's eyes suddenly contracted as she saw something like a dark veil twirling over her face reflected in the mirror. *Is it really a mirror? Is there a ghost inside the mirror, observing us?* Rubbing her eyes, Caldwell silently observed the mirror again over Anthony's shoulders. The dark veil covered her face completely for a second, then suddenly retreated to the bottom of the mirror, vanishing. *This isn't a mirror. Michael Perry installed this to scare us.* Caldwell stood up, striding shakily to the mirror. Anthony turned his head and looked at her suspiciously. Caldwell knocked on the mirror with her fist as if to shake off a hidden creature inside.

"What are you doing, Susanne?" asked Anthony jerkily.

"There's a dark ghost hidden inside the mirror," said Caldwell in a quavering voice.

"Dark ghost?" replied Anthony, raising his eyebrow and looking at the mirror. "It's just a mirror reflecting the two of us."

"There must be something shady in this mirror, Anthony," said Susanne, lowering her voice a notch. "I saw my own face wrapped by a ghost. Michael Perry set this weird mirror to scare us."

"Are you nuts? I don't think Michael would do that," replied Anthony in a low voice, shrugging. "This is just a normal mirror, Susanne."

"JACK BAZIN ARRIVED AT THE GARAGE WITH BABEL'S NEW WORKS!"

Michael Perry's thick voice reverberated from the balcony. The real estate tycoon came into the drawing room through the sliding door to the balcony. Behind Michael, the leaves of huge pine trees on the balcony were dancing like fans blowing cool winds for him. "He is probably in the elevator, heading to this penthouse."

"Who else will come to this auction, Michael?" asked Anthony

Ross.

"Nobody else will come," said Michael, slouching in the armchair next to Anthony's. "It's S. L. Babel who chooses the potential buyers. He designated you, Susanne, and me as invitees to this auction."

"Why did Babel invite her?" Anthony whispered to Michael, eyeing Susanne Caldwell.

Caldwell was still gazing at the mirror. With a slight cough, she touched her own face in the mirror. *Something is hidden in this mirror. Or is it hidden in my face?*

"She's not as wealthy as us. But she's still one of the richest politicians in the U.S. Congress," Michael replied in a low voice. They were still within earshot of Caldwell, who was absorbed in the mirror. "The public frowns on politicians' stock trades. But investment in artworks won't attract their attention."

"Susanne, does the FBI know about this auction?" asked Anthony loudly, shooting a stern look at Caldwell's back.

"I only told Sampson Castor to come to New York City," Caldwell turned back and said curtly. "But I didn't tell him the exact address of this auction."

"Michael, the FBI is worried that other murders might happen," said Anthony edgily. "You know, many people involved in S. L. Babel's works have been killed. We might be killed today, too."

"How come?" said Michael arrogantly. "We're in our penthouse. How can a killer enter this building and climb to this floor?"

"I have a hunch that S. L. Babel is now in Manhattan, secretly observing us," said Caldwell in a trembling voice. "It's better to be cautious and ask the FBI to stick around in Manhattan. I can call Sampson Castor anytime."

"Nobody can stop us," said Anthony smugly.

"I have a question for both of you," said Susanne Caldwell, stepping back to the armchair by the floor-to-ceiling window. Her blond hair shone under the sunshine, overlapping the lake in Forest Park through the window. "Why do billionaires like you want to buy expensive pieces of art?"

Michael Perry and Anthony Ross met eyes and then burst into

laughter, clutching their stomachs and throwing their legs out in front of them.

Caldwell bit her lip, enraged by their laughter, and slammed her cup back onto its saucer.

"I know why James Brown desperately collected Babel's works," Caldwell said sulkily. "Why do you want to buy Babel's work as an investment, Michael?"

A silence hung among the three. Michael and Anthony exchanged sneaky glances.

"Congresswoman, you'll never understand our feelings," Anthony said sarcastically.

"It's not enough to buy a penthouse to look down on the public, Susanne," Michael said, standing and prancing toward the floor-to-ceiling window. "We'll never run out of money, no matter what we purchase. We don't have any materialistic desire like the public. We don't want a Ferrari, a Rolex, or even a yacht because the values of these commodities are bound to decline."

"Exactly, Michael," Anthony said in a ringing voice. "Why do we buy expensive pieces of artwork? We know the value of art lasts forever. For example, the *Mona Lisa*, the only painting we probably can't buy, will outlive any tourists visiting the Louvre Museum and gawking at it."

"Last time, I bought a Picasso and lent it to MoMA," Michael said, swirling around and gazing at the cubist paintings next to the mirror on the wall. "I felt the genius of art flowing through my veins."

"I felt the same when I purchased Jackson Pollock's paintings at Christie's auction last fall," Anthony said in a silky voice. "I felt like I'm part of art history and have surpassed all the conditions of a normal human being. You'll never understand us, Susanne, unless you become as rich as we are."

"Eternity, that's what I want," Michael Perry said in a thick voice. "I do my best to invest in eternal art and life. Life isn't usually eternal, but James Brown worked on developing life-extending technology. That's why Anthony and I have been investing in James Brown's company. James was killed, but nothing will stop Brown's company as long as Anthony serves on its Board of Directors."

"Exactly, Michael," Anthony nodded, an impish smile spreading across his face. "Eternal life is no longer a far-fetched sci-fi idea. Once we extend someone's life by five years, the next biotech innovation during those five years will extend it further. This way, we'll achieve eternal life. We never hesitate to sacrifice others to achieve our mission."

Michael Perry doesn't know about the human organ trades we're undertaking. Anthony's smug eyes met Susanne's. *To achieve life-extending technology, we need an enormous amount of live human organs for research on the effects of drugs and hormones.*

Someone knocked on the door twice.

Michael Perry strode to the door and opened it.

Art dealer Jack Bazin, holding a Whole Foods Market shopping bag and a wooden box, entered the drawing room.

~ * ~

Five minutes ago, the elevator arrived at Michael Perry's penthouse. A long corridor adorned with antique lamps stretched in front of the elevator doors. Jack Bazin stepped ahead of the elevator and whispered to Alex and Laura.

"Walk quietly. Don't utter a single word in the corridor. Other guests have already arrived at this auction."

Jack swiftly walked to the middle of the corridor, stopping in front of an S. L. Babel MoMA exhibition poster hanging on the wall. Alex and Laura stared at the poster, which showed a VR headset on a Corinthian column pedestal shining in a vacant, white room.

S. L. Babel's VR headset was a trap, Alex thought. *The moment I touched the biometric sensor on the VR headset, Babel knew I had come to New York.*

Jack Bazin slid the picture frame sideways, revealing a hidden door. He pushed it open. The candelabras on the blond-wood table in the back of the room automatically lit up, illuminating the simple interior of the small, oblong room. A round cocktail table stood in the center, surrounded by three stools. A huge mirror hung on the wall, reflecting the candelabras.

What if this was also a trap? Laura shot an anxious glance at the elevator door, which had closed. With a rattle, the elevator started to descend.

Alex had already stepped into the hidden room. As Laura shuffled in, Jack closed the secret door.

"This is a hidden room where Michael often brings me when he strikes an art deal in the drawing room," Jack said with a sinister smile, pressing a button on the wall and pointing to the huge mirror.

Laura and Alex gasped, seeing their faces drowned in a sudden mist covering the mirror. Laura stepped forward, touching the mirror. As the mist gradually dissipated, Susanne Caldwell's anxious, wrinkled face materialized in the center, glowering at them. As Laura recoiled and withdrew her hand, a wave of shock rippled through Caldwell.

"Don't worry, Ms. Campbell," Jack said in a low voice. "It's a one-way mirror. Caldwell can't see us."

Caldwell rubbed her horror-struck eyes and sighed.

Laura retreated to the cocktail table in the center of the room. Alex was gazing at the other figures in the one-way mirror, which now showed the adjoining drawing room entirely.

"Why was this one-way mirror installed here?" Alex asked in a low voice.

"People usually detect a secret camera because they think they're important enough to be bugged," Jack replied snidely. "But they never discover that the mirror is one-way. When they look at mirrors, their faces are the most important."

"Anthony Ross is alive," Alex and Laura gasped simultaneously, seeing Anthony sitting on an armchair through the one-way mirror. Anthony was speaking with Nancy Caldwell, whose back was visible to Alex and Laura.

"JACK BAZIN ARRIVED AT THE GARAGE WITH BABEL'S NEW WORKS!"

A thick male voice reverberated from the drawing room. Alex and Laura exchanged glances. From the left side of the one-way mirror, Michael Perry suddenly appeared, galumphing toward the table and smiling at both Anthony and Caldwell. Michael's voice echoed again:

"He is probably in the elevator, heading to this penthouse."

"He's real estate mogul Michael Perry," Alex whispered to Laura. "I remember everyone on the *Forbes* list. His net worth is around ten billion dollars."

"I saw him exchange words with Caldwell about abortion issues on X," Laura said quietly. "Perry has donated millions of dollars to Caldwell in the past."

"Hey, I didn't bring you guys to this room to showcase high-profile figures like goldfish in a water tank," Jack said sarcastically, taking S. L. Babel's QR code painting out of the Whole Foods Market shopping bag and placing it vertically on the cocktail table. "Alex, look at this carefully. Is this the real Babel's work you brought out of Geneva Freeport?"

Alex didn't reply. He gasped, his eyes transfixed on Babel's autograph, "*Artist a.k.a. S. L. Babel,*" at the edge of the painting.

"How did you get the painting?" Laura asked quietly.

"I can't tell you, Ms. Campbell," Jack replied tartly, shooting a sharp glance at Laura. Then he stared at Alex's face again, raising the QR code painting slightly in the air. "Alex, is this real?"

Stepping toward the painting, Alex touched Babel's autograph to examine the thickness of the paint and whispered, "Yes, this is Babel's real work. This is the one I got at Geneva Freeport and brought to James Brown's mansion."

Victorious laughter flashed across Jack Bazin's face. He sneaked a glance at Michael Perry and Anthony Ross through the one-way mirror, then returned S. L. Babel's QR code painting to the Whole Foods Market shopping bag. Retreating to the entrance door of the secret room, Jack Bazin pointed to the one-way mirror and said quickly, "Look at that!"

Both Alex and Laura turned to the one-way mirror on the wall, following Jack's finger. Simultaneously, the explosive laughter of Michael Perry and Anthony Ross reverberated through the one-way mirror. Susanne Caldwell, who sat on an armchair across the table, frowned and slammed her coffee cup back onto the saucer. Michael and Anthony couldn't stifle their laughter for a while, twisting in their armchairs.

"I've never seen that pompous Caldwell mocked and humiliated like that," Laura whispered to Alex joyfully.

"Indeed," Alex mumbled, turning to Jack Bazin, and froze.

Jack Bazin aimed his gun at Laura, who was still peering into the one-way mirror. He clutched the wooden box containing Babel's new work, holding the QR code painting in the Whole Foods Market shopping bag under his arm.

"Don't move!" Jack said in a menacing tone, retreating to the door.

"What?" mouthed Laura, looking sideways at Alex.

"Don't turn around, Laura. He has a gun aimed at you," Alex said scathingly, his eyes furiously burning at Jack Bazin.

"Don't move, Alex. Otherwise, I'll shoot the lady," Jack said maliciously, kicking the door open behind him with his toe. With his gun aimed at the back of Laura's head, Jack stepped back into the corridor and closed the door. As Alex rushed toward the door, its lock clicked from the outside.

"You fucking betrayed me!" Alex spat, banging on the locked door.

"Betrayed? Nobody on the planet trusts you now, Alex. I decided to wear a gun as an additional precaution to meet the suspects who murdered James Brown," Jack's vicious voice echoed outside the door. "I'm happy to sell Babel's new, authentic QR code painting. You're of no use anymore. I'll turn you in and get the bounty from the FBI later. There's no way to escape this room for you."

Jack Bazin's malicious voice trailed away. Alex pressed his ear to the door, listening to the sound of footsteps gradually fading.

~ * ~

As he stepped into the drawing room of Michael Perry's penthouse, Jack Bazin placed the Whole Foods Market shopping bag and wooden box on the table. Susanne Caldwell instantly moved the coffee cup and saucer to the side. While Michael and Anthony's eyes were riveted on the bag and box, Susanne's nervous gaze fell on the pocket of

Jack Bazin's pin-striped jacket, which looked unnaturally swollen. Jack had tucked his gun into the pocket.

"It's so funny, Jack," said Anthony sarcastically. "Are you bringing a multi-million-dollar S. L. Babel work in a Whole Foods Market shopping bag?"

"Yeah, nobody thinks I'm carrying an expensive painting," said Jack slyly, taking the QR code painting out of the shopping bag and placing it on the table.

Michael and Anthony simultaneously stood up and stared at Babel's QR code painting, on which the shade of the gold glass chandelier on the ceiling was silently dancing. They didn't take their eyes off the painting, as if they were in a trance.

Meanwhile, Caldwell felt her heart pounding, holding her chest with her sweaty hand. As she closed her eyes, a dark room in Anthony Ross's St. Louis mansion materialized in her mind. The scene under her eyelids looked somewhat similar to the drawing room in Michael Perry's penthouse, where Caldwell currently sat. There was an oblong table. Elena Taylor clutched Babel's QR code painting, tilting it at the right angle for Caldwell, who was peering into the room through Zoom. Anthony Ross shifted in the armchair to face the camera on the table. As Caldwell tried to read his face, the painting on the table exploded, and an orange flash bathed Elena's body. Total darkness reigned under her eyelids. Caldwell opened her eyes to see the two billionaires, Michael and Anthony, standing along the table and observing every corner of the QR code painting.

"Isn't this QR code painting a bomb, gentlemen?" asked Caldwell shakily, retreating to the floor-to-ceiling window behind Central Park.

"Are you kidding?" said Jack in a ringing voice. "This painting is so light."

"I don't think this is a bomb this time," Anthony piped up, scanning every corner of the QR code painting.

"Can you turn the QR painting to the other side?" shrieked Caldwell, shuffling toward the floor-to-ceiling window overlooking Central Park. "The painting is my trauma."

"Okay," Jack said, putting S. L. Babel's QR code painting upright on the table.

Just like iron attracted to a magnet, Michael and Anthony started to walk to the edge of the table on the side of the one-way mirror on the wall.

~ * ~

"Great timing," whispered Laura, who stood on the other side of the one-way mirror in the adjoining locked room. She took her father's laptop from her tote bag and turned it on.

Alex, standing next to her in the one-way mirror, felt his heart race, hoping that Michael and Anthony wouldn't obscure the QR code painting. Fortunately, Michael and Anthony slouched in the armchairs with thuds, the painting remaining visible between their heads. As if waking up from anesthesia, Michael took his phone from the pocket of his pants. Anthony did the same. Both simultaneously started to scan the QR code.

"This is exactly what S. L. Babel planned," Alex whispered to Laura. "Babel sent this QR code to the wealthiest people on the planet, hacking into their phones."

"Soon, Babel will discover that the QR code is in Michael Perry's penthouse through their phones' GPS," said Laura scathingly. "But the QR code must also be the key to unlock my dad's PC."

Laura held Steve's PC up to the one-way mirror, scanning the QR code to unlock its Windows system.

The PC pinged and started to whir.

Chapter Twenty-six

From: S. L. Babel
Subject: Follow My Order Or Your Career Is Over
Date: June 16th, 2024, 9:52 PM
To: Jack Bazin

Hi Jack,

The QR code in the painting is my eye. I can see who stole my painting and who is attempting to sell it illegally. I can even see the future of those traitors; I know who will be killed and who will survive.

You're a crooked art dealer. I know what you're thinking right now. You want to sell the QR code painting along with my new work in the wooden box to the guests at the upcoming auction in Michael Perry's penthouse, right? As long as the creator, in other words, me, doesn't know about the transaction, you don't have to pay anything to the artist. But I know where my artwork, which is my soul, is always going.

I can sue you or even turn you into the police. Then, Jack Bazin, your career as an art dealer will be over.

But I can give you a chance. If you showcase my QR code and make all the guests at the auction scan it with their phones, I will not turn you into the police. Make them scan the QR code, which is my eye.

Also, this QR code will lead to another piece of art. You'll be able to sell three of my works at the upcoming auction. I'll let you know about this tomorrow.

All the best,
S. L. Babel

While the two multibillionaires, Michael Perry and Anthony Ross, stared at the QR code painting, Jack Bazin turned on his phone under the oblong table, rereading S. L. Babel's email sent to him last night. After receiving the QR code painting from Bella, he brought it back to his apartment on the Upper West Side yesterday. Taking it out of the Whole Foods Market shopping bag, he scanned the QR code with his phone. Suddenly, his phone started to heat up, and he threw it onto the floor. S. L. Babel's blackmail-like email popped up on the screen. Babel somehow knew Jack Bazin was aiming to sell his stolen QR code painting.

This QR code is S. L. Babel's eye, Jack Bazin silently thought, gazing at the two multibillionaires whose eyes were riveted on the QR code. *Once you scan the QR code, Babel hacks your device, reading everything in your mind and life.*

Michael Perry and Anthony Ross simultaneously took out their phones, scanning the QR code in the painting from different angles. Hearing the sound of the cameras, Susanne Caldwell turned around and looked at the painting. She couldn't resist the temptation to scan the QR code. Exploring S. L. Babel's million-dollar digital art was a privilege reserved for the exclusive guests at the auctions.

"Before starting the auction, I'm giving you a tip," said Jack jovially. "There are three of S. L. Babel's works in this room."

"Three?" said Michael and Anthony huffily, peeling their eyes away from the QR code painting and raising their heads.

"Are there two Babel works in the box?" asked Michael, flicking his chin at the wooden box on the oblong table.

"Open the box now, Jack!" shrilled Anthony, scratching his half-black, half-gray head impatiently.

"No, I can't do that," said Jack Bazin in a measured voice. "In his email, S. L. Babel told me not to open the wooden box by myself. He said the wooden box will automatically open at the right time."

"It'll automatically open," Michael growled, folding his arms.

"Interesting."

"Something disastrous will happen when the wooden box opens," said Caldwell ominously. "S. L. Babel is the worst killer in history."

"Why does S. L. Babel want to kill us, Susanne?" said Michael, his lips curling impishly. "Artists will never surpass patrons. You know, we're the modern Medici Family that financed Leonardo Da Vinci and Michelangelo."

"Exactly, Michael," said Anthony croakily, his eyes once again falling onto the QR code painting on the table. "In that sense, we created S. L. Babel, the greatest artist of our time."

It doesn't matter how these condescending multibillionaires think about S. L. Babel. Susanne Caldwell twisted her body in the armchair, crossing her legs. *I'll learn which of them will win the auction to buy this crappy QR code. Then, I'll ask the winner to lend the painting to me for a while to log into Steve Campbell's desktop PC in his laboratory.*

"Jack, where's the third work of S. L. Babel in this room, if it's not in the wooden box?" asked Michael in a thick voice.

"Did you get anything interesting after scanning the QR code in the painting?" replied Jack tartly.

"Yeah," said Michael, a note of annoyance in his voice. "I found a network with my name indicated in it."

A network had appeared on the two multibillionaires' phones several seconds ago.

THE LAST VICTIMS

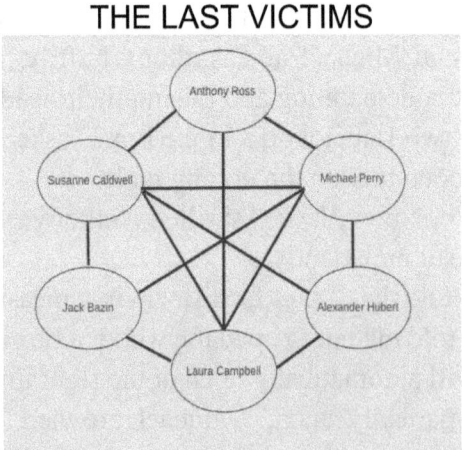

Jack Bazin stepped behind the two multibillionaires and peered at their phones. Observing the names in each node, he froze. All the people named in the network were currently in Michael Perry's penthouse. *Does S. L. Babel know I brought Alex Hubert and Laura Campbell here? How does he know?*

"Why are Alex Hubert and Laura Campbell on this network?" spluttered Anthony, straightening up.

"They're the suspects who murdered James Brown, right?" said Michael tartly, turning to Jack Bazin and motioning him to the balcony. "Jack, can I speak with you alone?"

Michael led Jack out to the balcony, closing the sliding glass door behind them. They walked beside the swimming pool, reaching the handrail under the shade of pine trees. As Michael turned to the sliding door, Susanne Caldwell and Anthony Ross, who had been observing them closely from inside, averted their eyes.

"Susanne and Anthony can't hear us anymore," said Michael, his voice muffled by the rustle of pine trees in the wind. "Did you bring Alex Hubert and Laura Campbell to my penthouse as I asked?"

"Yes, I did," said Jack snidely. "I locked them up in the secret room next to the drawing room as you told me. I confirmed with Alex that the QR code painting is real."

"Good job, Jack," replied Michael drily, his gaze wandering toward Central Park. His eyes followed the wispy clouds drifting over the Lake toward the east. "Alex is useful. Before turning him into the FBI, let's glean any information he has about S. L. Babel and the contemporary art market. But now, the problem is this network."

Michael turned on his phone, leaning against the handrail. His thumb scratched each node as if he wanted to erase the names in the network.

"Why does this network show the names of all the people currently in my penthouse?" Michael said gruffly. "It can't be a coincidence. Does S. L. Babel know who is here now? Is he showing these names to scare us?"

"I have no idea," replied Jack, his voice tense, his eyes surveying the wooden box on the table inside the penthouse. Jack was anxious that Babel's works might be stolen.

"Are you S. L. Babel, Jack?" said Michael, glaring menacingly. "Only you and I know Alex and his accomplice are here."

"What a joke," Jack gasped, gazing at Michael, whose phone now displayed an emergency number. With one touch, Michael's security team would rush to the penthouse.

"If you're S. L. Babel, everything makes sense," said Michael. "You created the QR code and another work in the wooden box, right?"

"If I were Babel, I wouldn't risk indicating the names of everyone in the penthouse," said Jack huffily. "I communicated with S. L. Babel this morning via email. I can show you his email if you want."

"Show me the email now," growled Michael.

From: S. L. Babel
Subject: Private Auction Today
Date: June 17th, 2024, 12:05 PM
To: Jack Bazin

Hi Jack,
I'm just double-checking with you. Don't reveal the existence of the third artwork until Michael and Anthony scan the QR code in the painting.
Make them scan the QR code, no matter what.

Best,
S. L. Babel

Michael snatched Jack's phone and read the short email carefully. Handing it back, he sighed and turned to see the penthouse through the sliding door. Anthony, who was chatting with Susanne Caldwell, sank his head into his palms on the armchair's backrest. Despite their casual pretense, both Anthony and Caldwell sat equidistant from the QR code painting and wooden box, regularly checking their positions.

"It's possible you sent this email to yourself," said Michael drily.

"But it's unlikely. I trust you, then."

"What if S. L. Babel hacked the security cameras?" said Jack anxiously. "You know, he's a digital artist. He might be a hacker."

"If so, that's a huge issue. If S. L. Babel knows you brought Alex to my penthouse and I helped, he could blackmail me," said Michael indignantly. "We have to find out who S. L. Babel is and kill him."

Jack flinched at Michael's furious tone and nearly stepped into the swimming pool.

"Stay with me after the auction, Jack," said Michael, scratching his chin and looking at his reflection in the water. "If you know Babel's email address and regularly communicate with him, we can send him a virus-loaded email to hack his PC."

"If I do that and Babel discovers the virus, he'll kill me," shrilled Jack.

Anthony and Caldwell turned to look at Jack and Michael. In fact, they strained to catch their conversation outside the sliding door.

"Calm down," said Michael, gazing at Jack reproachfully. "I'll hire bodyguards for you. Don't worry. Let's go back inside. I'll outbid Anthony and Susanne to buy Babel's works, no matter what."

Michael and Jack walked along the swimming pool. A pine branch shaped like an arrow floated on the water. With a whistle of wind, a wave brought the branch toward their steps.

"By the way, what is the third work?" asked Michael in a whisper.

"I can't say now. I have to abide by the contract," said Jack, smiling impishly. "I'll let you all know inside."

As Michael and Jack stepped into the penthouse, Anthony and Caldwell shifted in their armchairs, eyeing the QR code painting and the mysterious box on the table.

"While you were outside, I discussed the meaning of this network with Susanne. We feel something crazy is going to happen," said Anthony, a mix of excitement and anxiety in his voice. He placed his phone on the table, still displaying the network. "I don't feel comfortable that my name is included with the suspects who killed James Brown. But if this QR code painting becomes one of the greatest pieces in digital art history, our names will be recorded forever."

"That's a good point," Michael nodded as he slouched in the armchair. He turned on his phone and checked his name featured in the network. "Our names will be recorded forever if this QR code is a milestone in contemporary art. Imagine, Anthony, one of us purchasing this painting and lending it to MoMA. Tourists from all over the world would scan this QR code, seeing our names as supporters of the greatest contemporary artist, S. L. Babel."

"Exactly, Michael," said Anthony, his eyes riveted on the network shown on his phone. "I made a fortune from my business in the dark online market using Bitcoin. Most people don't know how I built my wealth. As a result, I haven't established a great reputation. The world will know I support the noble cause of art. And in the future, we'll be part of art history."

"If both of you feature this network as supporters of contemporary art," interjected Susanne Caldwell sarcastically, "why are Jack and I included in the network? What about Hubert and Campbell, who allegedly killed James Brown?"

"This network depicts the most important moment in contemporary art we're experiencing," said Jack, still standing, tapping the table with his fist and looking at each multibillionaire's face. "Four people in this room will see who wins this auction. Alex Hubert and Laura Campbell are running from the police in Manhattan. This network symbolically records the moment when this QR code is sold."

"It doesn't matter what the network means," said Anthony testily. "Why don't we start the auction?"

"Sure," Jack Bazin put the QR code painting vertically on the floor. "Let's begin with this painting."

"Wait, tell me what the third work is first," said Michael hoarsely. "Otherwise, I won't know which work I want to buy."

"The second work is in the box, right?" said Anthony, pointing to the box on the table. "Jack, can you open the box now?"

"No," said Jack firmly. "S. L. Babel told me the box will open automatically at the right time. I'm not allowed to open it for you. But there must be a piece of artwork inside."

Michael and Anthony exchanged irritated glances.

"What's the third work?" they asked arrogantly.

A short, mysterious silence hung among the four. The gold glass chandelier cast light on their phones on the table. While the two multibillionaires and art dealer peered at each other, Susanne Caldwell glanced out the floor-to-ceiling window, casually staring at the blue, cloudless sky over Central Park. In the corner of the sky, a gray stain grew larger, inching toward their penthouse.

"Okay, I'll let you know," said Jack in a strained voice. "S. L. Babel told me to reveal this after you scanned the QR code. Now is the right time."

Jack turned, striding toward the window as if looking for a way to escape. Caldwell saw the stain transform into a helicopter approaching Central Park. Heaving a deep breath, Jack swiveled around and pointed to Anthony Ross's phone.

"The network is the third S. L. Babel work."

Chapter Twenty-seven

"Is this network the third work?" asked Anthony, his gray eyes widening. "How is that possible? Can you sell this network at an auction?"

"A piece of artwork must be exchangeable for money. That's the definition of art in the age of capitalism," said Michael grumpily. "A piece of art mustn't be reproducible—the more identical works there are, the cheaper their prices will be. That's why normal photographs won't sell in the contemporary art market. This network isn't art."

"It is art," said Jack sharply, spreading his arms in the air. "This network is NFT art."

Michael and Anthony gasped audibly, flinching in their armchairs.

"What's NFT art?" asked Caldwell in a slightly shaky voice.

"Non-fungible token," snapped Anthony, gripping his phone with a trembling hand.

"What does it mean?" said Caldwell, glancing at the network shown on Anthony's phone.

"NFT art is digital art traded on a blockchain platform," explained Jack Bazin in a silky voice. "The key aspect is that this JPEG picture has a digital provenance. Put simply, it allows us to distinguish S. L. Babel's authentic network picture from all the other copies. As Michael mentioned, when multiple identical works by the same artist exist, their values are likely to decrease. However, thanks to blockchain technology, much like the singular *Mona Lisa* by Da Vinci in the Louvre Museum among numerous counterfeits, this JPEG portraying the network stands as the sole authentic creation by S. L. Babel."

"Exactly, Jack," said Michael Perry. "We don't need to worry about counterfeits when purchasing NFT art."

"I know American artist Beeple's NFT art was sold for seventy million dollars at Christie's," said Anthony snappishly, wiping sweat off his hooked nose with his finger. "When was that?"

"It was in 2021," said Jack quickly, his eyes drifting outside the floor-to-ceiling window as if to stare at the misty past scene. "I was in the auction house when Beeple's NFT work was sold. I still remember the crazy uproar among the art collectors when the auctioneer hit the gavel. Somebody in front of my seat jumped up and shouted, 'Contemporary art finally enters the Metaverse Era!' Subsequently, an artist named Pak made a series of NFTs to fund the legal defense fees for Julian Assange, the founder of WikiLeaks. NFT art has been one of the biggest trends in digital art."

"Have you ever bought NFT art, Anthony?" asked Michael, rubbing his bearded chin.

"No, I haven't," replied Anthony, throwing his phone onto the table and heaving a deep sigh. "I've never thought of buying NFT art. I've mainly bought paintings to decorate the walls in my secret mansion in St. Louis. You know, we can't hang NFT art on the wall. But I don't want to miss out on the burgeoning NFT art trends." Anthony's eyes switched between the QR code painting, and the network NFT art shown on his phone, calculating the risks and rewards of his potential investment in these artworks.

"I haven't thought of buying NFT art at all, either," Michael said in a hoarse voice and stomped on the floor as he crossed his legs. He turned on his phone, re-accessing the link embedded in Babel's QR code painting. His eyes took in every corner of the network in which their names appeared in the nodes. "My name is in this node," said Michael, his trembling thumb rubbing the node containing his name. "What if this network was the greatest NFT art? Why can't I miss this beautiful network?"

"Jack, if I buy this NFT art," asked Anthony huffily. "Can I resell this NFT art at Christie's or Sotheby's auction later?"

"Upon purchasing this piece today," replied Jack quickly in a monotone voice. "You must sign a contract that prevents you from selling it to other parties within a year. But you can sell it in a year."

"That's perfect," said Anthony, eyeing Michael who sat across the table. "I feel like I should pass up the QR code painting and focus on this NFT art instead."

"Me, too," said Michael in a thoughtful voice. "The trend of NFT art has just begun. S. L. Babel is already a bigger name than Beeple and Pak. This network as a JPEG picture will be worth an eight-figure sum in the future. What do you think, Jack?"

"No doubt about it," said Jack crisply, opening his fists which he'd nervously clenched. "Several years later, this NFT art will sell for fifty million dollars at worst at a huge, public auction. But I'd recommend you consider buying the QR code painting as a set. You know, it's a good strategy to buy both right now and sell them together."

Susanne Caldwell, who had no chance to participate in the auction between the two multibillionaires, stood up and roamed to the floor-to-ceiling window along Central Park. Her eyes were chasing the gray, pill-bug-like stain in the blue. It was a helicopter, slightly tilting its cockpit downward. As she strained her ears, the whining blades of the helicopter started to echo through the window.

"I disagree with that," said Anthony hotly, gripping his phone tightly as if his phone itself was a precious piece of art. "This QR code is nothing, but a QR code signed by S. L. Babel. Nothing more than that."

"But that's what contemporary artists do, my friend," replied Jack in an anxious voice. "Think about ready-made art. For example, Marcel Duchamp's *Fountain*. He only signed a urinal."

"Oh, my boy, are you invoking such an old art example," spat Michael sarcastically, knocking the table with his fist. "This QR code painting has no more value than S. L. Babel's autograph. Probably, his fingerprints might be found somewhere on the painting, which will be a lead to his identity. I can't see any other value in this."

"You're making a serious mistake, Michael and Anthony," said Jack in a quaky voice. "This QR code is the entry to S. L. Babel's Metaverse. I don't doubt Babel will create and display more Metaverse-themed works through this QR code. If you don't purchase this today, I have to return this QR code to Geneva Freeport, the warehouse under high security in the Swiss tax haven."

"It doesn't matter," said Anthony, shrugging mockingly. "I saved the URL embedded in this QR code."

"I saved the URL too," said Michael, checking his phone. "I'm already satisfied with the experience of scanning the QR code in S. L. Babel's painting, to be honest. I'll pass on this QR code painting."

"I don't need this QR code painting, either," said Anthony in a thick voice, licking the tip of his lip. "I gotta sell some Bitcoins to purchase this QR code painting. But I don't want to pay capital gain taxes this year. Let's discuss how much either of us will pay for the NFT art."

Susanne Caldwell turned around to face the table. *Michael Perry and Anthony Ross won't try to buy S. L. Babel's QR code painting?* She felt a cold chill ripple down her back. The chill turned into anger, then into sweat and steam seeping from the pores under her dyed blond hair. *This isn't the plan. Anthony, you're forgetting your role due to the crazy attraction of the NFT art. You need to buy the QR code painting so that I can borrow it and log into Steve Campbell's desktop PC in his laboratory.* Caldwell heard her heart pound, tucking her hand into the pocket of her navy jacket. Her finger examined the position of the gun she'd concealed. Suddenly, Caldwell flinched as her eyes saw a shade twirling inside the mirror on the wall as if a ghost was observing her. She rubbed her eyes with her left hand while her right was clutching her gun in the pocket. The shade vanished from the mirror.

"I'm not an art connoisseur, but I can tell you this," said Caldwell eloquently while her own eyes were still observing herself in the mirror, where she looked like an emotionless humanoid. "You've got to buy Babel's QR code painting, too. Otherwise, you'll fail to sell Babel's NFT art in the future."

In the following cold silence, the four in the room didn't budge at all, their eyes riveted on different objects. Caldwell stared at her face in the mirror, hoping a ghostly shade would never appear to engulf her reflection. *Nobody saw us from inside the mirror.* Her voiceless words moved her lips in the mirror. Michael, Anthony, and Jack were still watching the NFT picture displayed on their phones. Anthony apparently forgot his objective to participate in this auction. He was supposed to buy Babel's works to protect the secret of his organ trade association. At least, he needed to buy the QR code to unlock the desktop PC of Steve Campbell, who was likely to leak secret information. However, Anthony's bloodshot eyes were absorbed in the screen of his phone, the sense of excitement flowing up to his head and shaking the veins in his forehead. This NFT art, which simply depicted a network, would inscribe his name in an art history book in the future.

"SUSANNE, YOU ARE NOT OUR BOSS!" Anthony suddenly roared and threw his phone onto the table irritably. "YOU'RE NOT WORTH MORE THAN US. WE'RE RICHER THAN YOU. WHY WOULD I LISTEN TO YOU?"

"Ten million dollars," said Michael, his voice cracking with greed and excitement. "I can pay ten million dollars for this NFT picture."

A mix of delight, anxiety, and confusion crossed Jack's face.

The box, which contained another piece by S. L. Babel, was still on the table. It started to vibrate slightly from inside, but nobody in the room noticed it.

"FIFTEEN MILLION!" Anthony barked, getting to his feet. "You can't beat me, Michael."

Susanne Caldwell stepped back and leaned against the floor-to-ceiling window. She hid her hands behind her back, putting on a pair of white cotton gloves. Then, she tucked her hand into the pocket of her jacket, clutching her gun's barrel.

~ * ~

"I saw Caldwell grabbing a gun," Laura whispered to Alex. They crouched down in the room adjacent to the drawing room, peeping into the weird auction scene through the one-way mirror.

"Are you sure?" asked Alex in a low voice.

"Yes, the pocket of her jacket swelled unnaturally," said Laura anxiously. "She must have a gun."

"We should stay away from the mirror, then," replied Alex in a whisper. "Jack has a gun, too. He might shoot back at Caldwell if she really shoots one of them."

Alex stepped back to the blank wall on the opposite side while

Laura roamed to the cocktail table in the center of the room. Steve's laptop, which had been unlocked with the QR code, started to whine, emitting heat on the table. Laura located a folder on this laptop, which contained hundreds of CSV and JSON files compiling data about surgical operations at St. Louis Innovative Medical Center. Feeling her heart race, Laura searched for her mother's name, Linda Campbell, in this folder. Only one CSV file named "071995_groupE.csv" popped up. With her shivering fingers, she clicked the file. Its size was more than 600,000 KB. It took more than fifteen seconds to open it.

"Laura, look at that!" said Alex in a quaky voice, tapping her shoulder.

Laura instantly touched the pocket of her black, high-waisted pants, where she'd tucked Steve's gun. As she gazed at the one-way mirror, she saw the two multibillionaires stand up alarmingly, staying several inches away from the table, and staring at the vibrating box on the table in the drawing room. Susanne Caldwell still stood by the window, her eyes traveling over the box on the table and then to the pocket of Jack's jacket, which also contained a gun.

Through the floor-to-ceiling window over Caldwell's shoulder in the drawing room, Alex saw a helicopter with gray and black stripes flying in the sky, approaching the penthouse. Its whining blades gradually became raucous and seemed to shake the air inside the penthouse. But none of the guests at the secret auction were paying attention to the helicopter.

"What's this?"

Art dealer Jack Bazin's shout echoed through the one-way mirror to the adjacent room where Alex and Laura were locked up.

Dark blood seeped through tiny cracks from the mysterious wooden box on the table, resembling the cobra on its lid spitting venom. Cleopatra's emerald eyes gleamed, as though amused by the scene of her slaves being struck down by the serpent. The crimson fluid flowed towards S. L. Babel's QR code painting. Jack Bazin lunged for the painting, cradling it in his arms, staining his jacket sleeves with the viscous liquid. He gently placed the painting on an armchair and removed his blood-stained jacket, draping it over the chair's backrest. Caldwell's gaze darted to the sagging pocket of Jack's jacket, her hand gripping her gun inside her own jacket pocket.

"Open the box now, Jack," Michael snarled, glaring at Cleopatra's image on the lid.

"Wait," Anthony interjected nervously. "Are you sure it's safe to open?"

Jack hesitated at the box's lid, his eyes flicking anxiously between the multibillionaires.

"No worries," Michael insisted gruffly. "S. L. Babel's provocations are just part of his promotional strategy."

"It's not just provocations," Anthony added darkly. "Murders linked to his artworks have made him infamous. What if the box holds something deadly?"

"Ridiculous! There's no reason for him to want us dead," Michael scoffed, a vein pulsing in his temple. "We're funding his projects. Open it, Jack!"

As Jack peeled back the lid, two silenced gunshots echoed through the room, the sound muted like the click of unlocking bolts.

A wave of air shook the gold glass chandelier on the ceiling, its lights swaying like pendulums reflected in the wall mirror. As Susanne Caldwell lowered her silenced gun, she saw a mid-fifties woman in the mirror, her eyes glinting viciously. It took several seconds for Caldwell to realize it was her own reflection. Tearing her eyes away from the mirror, Caldwell glanced at the table. Art dealer Jack Bazin lay motionless, sprawling across it with his arms outstretched. A gunshot had pierced his head and the armchair behind him. Blood flowed from his head, mingling with the crimson liquid leaking from the wooden box on the table. It felt as if she could hear another fallen man gasping for breath. Suddenly, a surge of fear coursed through her, causing her to aim the gun at Anthony, who lay slumped in the armchair, shot in the heart. The gunshot had left a spiderweb crack in the wall beneath the mirror. Caldwell moved toward Anthony with her gun raised, her legs trembling. As she pressed the gun's muzzle against his pale forehead, Caldwell's legs kicked involuntarily against the chair's leg. Anthony's head and shoulders slumped to the side, lifeless. His blood flowed from his heart, dripping onto the floor through the armchair's fabric. A cold chill ran down Caldwell's spine. She'd never killed anyone before, never fired a gun. Yet, with chilling efficiency, she'd eliminated the art dealer and the cryptocurrency billionaire with minimal shots. *I must win, no matter the cost*, Caldwell thought, glancing briefly at her reflection in the mirror. *In this world, it's kill or be killed. Anthony, I never liked your power. Now, I'm the queen of the organ trade network.*

Suddenly, movement in the mirror caught her eye—a lone survivor in the drawing room. She aimed her gun.

Real estate mogul Michael Perry staggered to his feet, retreating against the wall, horror etched on his face. His trembling hand reached for his phone, but it slipped from his grasp to the plush carpet.

"Don't shoot," he pleaded. "You won't get out of my penthouse without my help."

"If the public thinks I'm the killer," Caldwell sneered, advancing toward Jack's body and the armchair. She retrieved a gun from Jack's jacket pocket. "This gun has Jack's fingerprints. Who would suspect me?" Caldwell raised her chin arrogantly, yet her voice carried a high note of panic and anxiety as she aimed Jack's gun at Michael with trembling hands clad in white cotton gloves.

Michael pressed against the wall, eyes wide with terror. Outside, a helicopter's blades whined. *Did Susanne call somebody to escape from my penthouse secretly?*

"Jack's prints are on this gun," Caldwell warned, voice shaky. Her hand, clutching the gun, trembled. "After you die, I'll press your fingers onto my gun and make it look like Jack shot Anthony first, then you and Jack shot each other. I'm sure the FBI will believe me and conclude as such." Caldwell placed her finger on the trigger of Jack's gun, tapping the barrel with another finger to mock Michael.

"Don't shoot me, Susanne!" Michael cried, dropping to his knees and casting a beseeching gaze at Caldwell. The multibillionaire lay prone on the floor, rubbing his head and hands against Caldwell's black leather shoes. "I'll donate more money for your next run in the US presidential election. I'll do everything to make you the next US president, Susanne. You'll be the first female leader of the Free World."

Caldwell kicked Michael's face and aimed Jack's gun at his forehead.

"Did you call anyone? What's with the helicopter?" Caldwell demanded furiously, eyeing the vibrant shade of the helicopter's blades slicing through the room's wall-to-ceiling window.

"I didn't call anyone," Michael said, wiping blood from his nose.

"Don't lie!" Caldwell thrust Jack's gun toward Michael. "Who did you call?"

"I didn't call anyone! It's probably the FBI," Michael huffed, looking pale. "They came to arrest Alex Hubert and Laura Campbell!"

"What? Are they in this penthouse?" Caldwell frowned. "Where are they?"

Michael's eyes silently darted toward the one-way mirror on the wall. He pointed to the center of the mirror with his shaking hand.

As she followed Michael's gesture, the helicopter's skid thudded onto the helipad. The ceiling of the drawing room trembled slightly, and a speck of dust drifted down onto Caldwell's nose like a spider's thread. Caldwell aimed her gun at the one-way mirror, advancing toward it.

"I knew someone was behind that mirror," Caldwell said scornfully, glaring at her reflection. "Hubert and Campbell are hiding there."

~ * ~

When Caldwell aimed her gun at the one-way mirror, Alex, who had covered Laura's mouth to stifle her scream, withdrew his hand as Laura pushed him away. They trembled, gripping the edge of the cocktail table for support, unable to believe what they had witnessed through the mirror. One of the most prominent politicians—potentially a future US president—had just killed two men, including Anthony Ross, who had amassed billions through dark web operations, facilitating illegal trades and leading a clandestine organ trade network. Caldwell had targeted Anthony to assume leadership of the network and advance life-extending technology.

Jack Bazin's blood splashed, reaching even the one-way mirror on the wall. Alex and Laura rubbed their eyes simultaneously with trembling hands. For a moment, it felt like watching a thriller movie through a cracked screen. Their throats tightened as they saw Jack's blood dripping down to the floor.

Steve's laptop fan hummed on the cocktail table, emitting heat waves. The screen displayed a CSV file compiling surgery data from St. Louis Innovative Medical Center, with thousands of scrolled rows. Laura had found her mother's name and clicked on a cell, sending a chill down her spine. Yet, her attention was now captured by the bloody scene reflected in the one-way mirror. She should have secured Steve's PC to protect her discovery, but her eyes remained fixed on the mirror.

Silently, Caldwell advanced toward the mirror, gun aimed at its center. Behind her, real estate mogul Michael Perry, who had collapsed but was now getting to his feet, calculated the right moment to strike Caldwell from behind. Caldwell caught Michael's movement through his reflection in the mirror.

"Don't move, Michael!" Caldwell barked, spinning around and aiming the gun at him. "I'll shoot your damn head if you disobey me."

Michael flinched, retreating to the wall with his hands raised.

"Are Alex Hubert and Laura Campbell hiding in that mirror? Answer me, Michael!" Caldwell roared, her face flushed with anger.

"Jack Bazin locked them in the adjoining room," Michael panted, his hefty belly heaving. "Why are you worried about them? They can't get out on their own."

"Did they see us through the mirror? Is this a regular mirror?" Caldwell demanded indignantly, banging her fists against it.

In the adjoining room, Alex and Laura recoiled. Caldwell mockingly struck the mirror again, the sound echoing violently in the room. Laura straightened up, drawing Steve's gun and aiming it at the back of Caldwell's head through the one-way mirror.

"Don't do it," Alex whispered, grabbing her hand. "If you shoot her, the FBI will add another charge against you."

Laura didn't respond. She pushed his hand away and stepped toward the mirror, gun steady.

As Laura's eyes met Caldwell's through the one-way mirror, a beeping sound emanated from the wooden box on the table in the drawing room. Tiles depicting Cleopatra on its surface rotated, her glassy eyes widening.

Then, the box's lid swung open.

Chapter Twenty-eight

As the tiles forming Cleopatra's waist swung from side to side, making her perform a belly dance, Caldwell swiveled around, approaching the open box on the table. A thin rubber conveyor belt, on which another Egyptian cobra was drawn, stretched out between the bottom of the box and the end of the lid. Caldwell aimed her gun at the box, straining her eyes. As the conveyor belt ran, S. L. Babel's new artwork started to move out of the box, dropping onto the table with a thud. At the sight of this, Caldwell screamed, feeling her spine turn glacial. It was a livid, still-throbbing human heart entangled with arteries. Inserted between the veins was a rectangular electronic panel displaying the letters "*Artist a.k.a. S. L. Babel*" in purple.

For a moment, Caldwell felt a dark veil envelop her eyes. Her limbs went numb. Biting her lips and taking in a mouthful of air, she regained her strength and straightened up. She stomped on the floor with her trembling foot to see if her senses had returned. All of a sudden, her eyesight blackened. A quick blow had hit her head from behind. She felt her gun fly out of her weak hands, skidding toward the wall against which Michael was leaning. Caldwell collapsed onto the floor, feeling a sweaty hand grabbing her neck and pushing her body downward. Turning her head toward the mirror on the floor, Caldwell saw Anthony Ross pushing her back with his knee and glowering at her scornfully.

"You played possum, you son of a bitch!" Caldwell mouthed bitterly.

"Did you think you managed to shoot two people at the same time, crooked Caldwell?" said Anthony, his eyes glinting victoriously. "I tainted my T-shirt with the blood from the wooden box to fake my death. You're a dumbass politician who can't achieve anything on your own. You're so overconfident that you thought you killed two people. That's how politicians make the country worse."

"Thanks, Anthony," said Michael, picking up Caldwell's gun from the floor and squinting at the human heart. "The blood was leaking from this human heart."

"They are fake blood and a fake human heart, aren't they?" said Anthony while pushing his knee hard against Caldwell's back.

"Of course, they're fake. If this was a real human heart, it'd smell bad," said Michael scathingly, touching the tip of the fake, throbbing human heart with his finger. His finger was smeared with red ink. "The surface is made of rubber. I won't buy this because I don't think this is art."

"It must be art because S. L. Babel created it," said Anthony, his hand grabbing the neck of Caldwell, who was moaning under his knee. Caldwell's dark eyes were swimming around the strange mirror hung on the wall. Her gaze perched on S. L. Babel's name displayed on the panel, which was shaking between vessels around the fake human heart.

"Jack must've known something about this artwork," said Anthony begrudgingly, shooting a glance at Jack's body lying nearby. "You know, anything that S. L. Babel has created has been quite successful in the market. This fake human heart must have enormous value. What makes it throb like a real human heart? Is there anything inside it?"

Michael held up the throbbing, fake human heart from the box and frowned.

"This is really heavy," said Michael in a strained voice as the throbbing object splashed fake blood on the cuffs of his shirt. "Something is inside!"

"Ahhhhhhh!"

Caldwell, who was wriggling under Anthony's knee, shouted and pointed to something reflected in the mirror on the wall.

"What?" said Anthony, frowning at the mirror. "Michael, you said Alex Hubert and Laura Campbell are across the mirror, right? Can they see us through the mirror?"

"No, absolutely not," lied Michael, averting his eyes from Anthony's and trying to maintain a calm voice. "They might've overheard our conversation, though."

"It doesn't matter," shrugged Anthony. "They'll go to jail and be sentenced to death."

"LOOK AT THE PANEL, SCUMBAGS!" Caldwell screamed, stretching out her wrinkled hand to the mirror. Her finger pointed to the electronic panel in the fake human heart in Michael's hands, which was reflected in the mirror. The panels were now blinking. "LOOK AT THE PANEL!"

"Are you crazy?" Anthony snarled. "You're trying to distract us, right? The panel only shows Babel's name."

"NO!" Caldwell shouted as Michael flipped the human heart artwork to see the electronic panel entangled in the fake vessels. "THE HUMAN HEART IS A BOMB! S. L. BABEL IS GONNA KILL ALL OF US!"

A frozen silence fell over the room.

Michael was staring at the panel, his face turning pale. S. L. Babel's name had disappeared from the panel.

"What is the panel showing now?" asked Anthony in a quaky voice.

"It's showing a timer," responded Michael hoarsely, his eyes following the timer as each second passed quickly. The remaining time was under ten minutes. Michael stepped forward and showed the panel to Anthony, who was still pushing Caldwell hard to the floor under his knee.

"Caldwell is lying," said Anthony scornfully, shifting his knee toward Caldwell's neck. "This is a timer, but it doesn't say this human heart will explode within ten minutes. Caldwell wants to escape us by making us believe this is a bomb."

"I agree," snorted Michael. "There's no reason S. L. Babel would want to kill us. Murdering us is equivalent to a stupid sheep killing a shepherd. We've been funding these artists."

"Exactly," said Anthony arrogantly. "How can Babel kill us?"

"IT'S A BOMB, YOU FOOL!" Caldwell screamed, scratching the floor. "ANTHONY, DON'T YOU REMEMBER THE BOMB EXPLOSION THAT SMASHED YOUR MANSION?"

"The QR code painting that Elena brought to my mansion was a counterfeit, Susanne," Anthony spat on Caldwell's face. "Somebody set a bomb inside the QR code painting and tried to kill me. But I believe it wasn't S. L. Babel who attempted to do that."

Suddenly, Anthony's and Michael's phones rang and beeped violently.

~ * ~

At first, Alex and Laura didn't notice their own phones also beeping. Across the one-way mirror, they saw Michael pick up his phone from the table. A wave of fear rippled through his face. Anthony, still pushing Caldwell onto the floor under his knee, motioned for Michael to show his phone. Michael shambled toward Anthony, displaying the screen. As Anthony's eyes captured the screen, Alex and Laura saw Anthony's entire body trembling through the one-way mirror. Laura stood up and tiptoed to the mirror, attempting to see what Michael's phone was showing. Alex got to his feet and moved sideways because Laura's body obstructed his view. Then, he noticed his phone beeping in the back pocket of his jeans. Laura turned around. Her phone was also beeping in her tote bag under the table.

As Alex and Laura unlocked their phones and stared at the screen, their insides became glacial. The Safari application popped up and opened the bookmarked URL embedded in the QR code painting they'd scanned at James Brown's mansion. The current network was the same as what Michael Perry and Anthony Ross had seen in the adjacent drawing room; it showed six nodes, indicating the names of all the people currently in the penthouse, including Alex and Laura. However, in the center of the circle depicted by the nodes was a bomb. Alex touched the bomb on the screen with his trembling thumb. It exploded on the screen, a snaky flame engulfing all the nodes.

"I remember your name wasn't in the original network when we scanned the QR code at James Brown's mansion," whispered Laura shakily. "This network now targets everybody in the penthouse, including you."

"S. L. Babel changed his mind... He no longer needs me,

probably," said Alex scathingly. "He promised to pay thirty million dollars if I brought the QR code painting back to Geneva Freeport. But it was a trap."

"Babel obviously tricked you," said Laura shakily. "Babel didn't include your name in the original network to avoid scaring you away. He took advantage of your greed."

"I see," mumbled Alex indignantly. "Our phones have still been hacked in some way. We set our phones to airplane mode, but S. L. Babel managed to send us the new network. He's been surveying us. He obviously knows we're in this penthouse."

"We shouldn't have scanned the QR code at James Brown's mansion in the first place," sighed Laura. "We gotta leave this penthouse as soon as possible. Everybody whose death was predicted in *The Deathly Network* has been killed so far."

"I agree," said Alex in a trembling voice. "But where is the bomb?"

"The bomb is inside this fake human heart art!" Michael's scream echoed through the one-way mirror. Michael gradually lowered the human heart artwork and returned it gently inside the box. Laura saw fake blood dripping from the artwork onto Cleopatra's smiling face painted on the lid.

"How many minutes left?" asked Anthony in a shrill voice.

"Eight and a half minutes," spat Michael, gazing at the panel inserted between the vessels inside the box.

"THROW THAT BOMB AWAY TO THE GROUND!" Caldwell shouted from beneath Anthony's knee, her face pale. "GO TO THE BALCONY, THROW IT AWAY! IT DOESN'T MATTER IF PEOPLE ON THE GROUND DIE. THEY CAN'T CHANGE THE WORLD LIKE US. OUR LIVES ARE MORE PRECIOUS THAN ANYBODY ELSE'S."

Congresswoman Caldwell twisted her head toward the one-way mirror, glowering at Michael's face reflected in the mirror.

Alex and Laura, observing the drawing room through the one-way mirror, flinched. They felt as though their eyes had met Caldwell's bloodshot eyes. Soon, Caldwell's head turned around to see Anthony's face. It was impossible for Caldwell to see Alex and Laura, no matter what. Knowing this, Alex and Laura silently stepped closer to the one-way mirror. Laura pressed her ears to the mirror, motioning for Alex to do the same. Feeling their hearts pounding, they heard a clock ticking away the cold moments of time. Laura and Alex peeled their ears away from the one-way mirror and darted their eyes around the drawing room. There was nothing like a clock. Laura and Alex followed where Michael's and Anthony's eyes were riveted. The mechanical click, sounding like a clock, was echoing from the throbbing human heart artwork. Michael was still clutching the edge of the box, shuddering.

"I have another idea," said Anthony snidely, grabbing Caldwell's neck. "I know you have helicopters at the helipad. We can lock this corrupt politician up with Alex Hubert and Laura Campbell in the room and leave the bomb there. We can escape to the sky in one of your helicopters."

"Great idea!" Michael clapped his hands, his jaw relaxing.

"TAKE ME WITH YOU!" Caldwell shouted and wriggled so hard that Anthony pushed his elbow against her neck. "I DON'T WANNA DIE HERE. I CAN HELP YOUR BUSINESS WHEN I BECOME PRESIDENT OF THE USA. TAKE ME WITH YOU, PLEASE!"

"By the way, somebody seemed to arrive at the helipad in a helicopter," said Michael in a crisp voice, ignoring Caldwell. "I haven't ordered any of my employees to fly a helicopter to the helipad. In any case, I can ask one of my pilots to fly the helicopter right now."

Michael's security team, including two helicopter pilots, were available to help him 24 hours a day. Michael called his pilot with his phone. The pilot responded quickly.

"My friend and I will go to the helipad in three minutes," Michael spluttered. "Prepare to fly the helicopter right now!"

"Where do you plan to go in a helicopter, sir?" the pilot replied in a confused tone. "I'm not sure if there's a helicopter with enough jet fuel loaded."

"It doesn't matter," Michael roared into his phone. "Take us out to the sky in three minutes! Come to the helipad right now!"

Michael hung up his phone, turning to Anthony and Caldwell.

"I wanna move away from this creepy human heart bomb as soon as possible," said Anthony scathingly, getting to his feet. He clutched Caldwell's armpits and made her get up, pinioning her from behind.

"Can you help me, Michael?" said Anthony as Caldwell wriggled like a drowning horse under his grip. "Let's lock her up in the next room."

"We probably don't have enough time to do that, Anthony," said Michael bitterly. "Let her go. We'll fly to the sky. It doesn't matter if Caldwell survives by taking an elevator to the ground. We'll turn her into the FBI for the murder of Jack Bazin later."

"No, Michael. If we don't have time to lock her up in the adjoining room," said Anthony coldly, his contemptuous eyes looking down at Caldwell's face. Caldwell was trembling, her teeth clattering and her bloodshot eyes staring at both multibillionaires beseechingly. Anthony continued. "Let this corrupt politician survive and become president of the USA in the next presidential election. We can blackmail her at any time, controlling US politics."

After mulling over Anthony's suggestion for a moment, Michael lowered his gun and barked, "Go away, Caldwell! Take the elevator and run away from this tower as fast as you can."

Caldwell gave a shriek, flinching and galloping toward the door to the corridor.

Before Caldwell grabbed the doorknob, the door swung open. Somebody stood in the corridor, aiming a gun at them. Caldwell fell on her buttocks on the floor.

"FBI! Drop your weapons!"

The female voice of the new visitor reverberated through the one-way mirror.

Alex and Laura couldn't see her from their position. They moved toward the edge of the one-way mirror, squinting toward the left end. They could only see the FBI agent's gun raised in the air.

"I feel like I know the voice," Laura whispered to Alex.

"Really?" said Alex, raising his brow.

Silence hung in the drawing room. Anthony and Caldwell retreated to the floor-to-ceiling windows.

"You'd better run away rather than investigate Jack Bazin's murder," said Michael jerkily, dropping his gun onto the floor.

"I'm not interested in Jack Bazin. I came here to arrest Alex Hubert and Laura Campbell."

The female FBI agent said coldly, stepping ahead into the room.

As she stood under the chandelier, Alex and Laura gasped.

It was Bella Saba, wearing a bullet-proof vest stenciled with the letters FBI and smiling victoriously.

"Wasn't she pregnant?" said Alex in a low voice, raising his eyebrow. Bella's stomach looked flat.

"Yes, she was pregnant. That's weird," Laura whispered.

Bella took the human heart from the table. Her finger pressed one of the vessels entangled with it. The timer disappeared from the electronic panel inserted among the vessels. Instead, the purple letters emerged.

Artist a.k.a. S. L. Babel

Bella's finger pressed one of the vessels one more time. Each of the purple letters started to move like ants. In ten seconds, the order of the letters changed, and they stopped moving. Then, the letters shone in a bloody color.

Artist Bella K. Saba

Alex and Laura saw the panel through the one-way mirror, flinching. Electric charge surged through their bodies. They winced and gasped together.

Bella Saba turned toward the one-way mirror as if to see through it and observe the presence of Alex and Laura in the next room.

Bella aimed her gun at the one-way mirror.

"That's just a normal mirror," said Michael huffily. "We don't have time to arrest anyone. We gotta evacuate now! S. L. Babel sent us a bomb shaped like a human heart."

"I know, Michael Perry," said Bella sharply, her eyes viciously glinting.

She turned around and aimed her gun at Michael.

Michael shivered and raised his hands. Anthony Ross and Susanne Caldwell flinched, gazing at Bella with fearful eyes.

"S. L. Babel is me," said Bella Saba coldly.

Chapter Twenty-nine

Michael and Anthony straightened up with a jerk, looking bewildered. Their bloodshot eyes scanned Bella's body from head to toe. *Is this woman S. L. Babel?* Michael and Anthony scratched their heads and exchanged glances. They still couldn't believe the woman wearing the FBI jacket in front of them was digital artist S. L. Babel.

Susanne Caldwell, who had collapsed onto the floor, didn't even pay attention to Bella. Caldwell's eyes darted from the gun Michael had dropped to the door, to the corridor, and to Bella's gun aimed at her forehead. With a screech, Caldwell retreated to the wall, her entire body shivering.

"WE GOTTA EVACUATE NOW! THE BOMB WILL EXPLODE!" Caldwell shouted, the memory of the flames that had enveloped Anthony Ross's mansion flashing in her mind.

"How did you enter my penthouse?" asked Michael, squinting at Bella's face. "The security is extremely tight here."

"I flew a helicopter to the helipad," replied Bella nonchalantly.

Michael and Anthony exchanged surprised glances.

"You can't be S. L. Babel," said Michael sarcastically, raising his chin arrogantly. "If so, why would you come here knowing the human heart artwork is a dangerous bomb?"

"I know her face," said Anthony flatly. "She's at least not an FBI agent. You're Bella Saba, the contemporary art blogger who recently interviewed S. L. Babel, right?"

Bella nodded, a vicious smile spreading across her face.

"If so," said Michael huffily. "Why can she be S. L. Babel? She interviewed the secret digital artist, didn't she?"

"You're fucking stupid," snapped Bella, raising her gun. "I interviewed *myself.*"

Gunshots erupted.

With moans, Michael and Anthony collapsed to the floor. Blood was flowing from their legs. Bella had shot them. She now aimed her gun at Caldwell, who was trembling along the wall.

"If I didn't come here, you guys would've let this lousy, corrupt politician survive," said Bella, her eyes flashing maliciously. "A murder is real art. I need to kill all three of you. Anthony Ross, you're the guy pulling the strings behind the organ trade network. Michael Perry, you've been investing in James Brown's empire and funding research on life-extending technology. And Caldwell, you're on the Senate Committee on Health—you've been actively assisting in Brown's illegal business circles and amassing millions of dollars from insider trading of biotech stocks."

Caldwell screeched as Bella put her finger on the trigger of her gun.

"Don't worry about the bomb. I can change the timing to explode it anytime," said Bella maliciously. "I'll detonate it after confirming all of you can't move out of this penthouse and after I fly away in the helicopter. Where is Laura Campbell? One of you must know where she is. She's the person I need to kill no matter what."

"Laura Campbell? The journalist who abetted Alex Hubert?" moaned Anthony, twisting his bloody leg on the floor. "Why do you need to kill her?"

"It's none of your business," replied Bella sharply, looking at the mirror on the wall.

~ * ~

Across the one-way mirror, Laura motioned Alex to the back of the room. Laura had taken Steve's gun out of her tote bag.

"Are you serious?" said Alex in a quaky voice.

"There's no other way for us to get out of this room," said Laura sharply, aiming the gun at Bella through the one-way mirror.

Taking in a mouthful of air, Laura pulled the trigger.

~ * ~

Bella saw her own face and body crumble in the shattered mirror. Within a second, a ghostly shadow enveloped her vision. Her severed body parts placed on a surgical table flashed in Bella's mind, floating and swirling in midair. Bella blinked and stepped back as roaring gunshots crashed into the mirror from the other side. Caldwell was screaming, hurt by the shards of the mirror. Gunshots from the adjoining room made random holes. Then, lightning-shaped cracks ran through the mirror. A female figure with brown hair materialized through the fissures, aiming a gun at Bella and stepping toward her. At first, Bella thought it was herself reflected in the mirror. In seconds, she realized another person stood in front of her, aiming the gun at her. All of a sudden, Bella felt the floor lurching. Her eyes caught the shining chandelier. Caldwell had tackled Bella, causing her gun to skid toward the edge of the room. Bella found herself lying supine on the floor. Caldwell turned to the broken mirror and shrieked.

Laura galumphed through the broken one-way mirror into the room; her gun aimed at Bella. Alex followed Laura and stepped in. His nervous eyes were riveted on the bomb shaped like a human heart on the table.

"Don't move, Bella!" barked Laura, aiming the gun at Bella's forehead as Bella was about to get up.

"You can't kill me, Laura," said Bella huskily, twisting her lips maliciously. "I'm controlling the bomb. If you kill me, nobody will be able to stop the explosion."

"Weren't you pregnant?" asked Alex behind Laura, glancing at Bella's flat stomach.

"My pregnancy from several days ago was fake, Alex. I wore a fake pregnancy bodysuit," said Bella slyly. "I hid the shoes inside the fake belly, which I used to camouflage the footprints of a fake murderer on the ground in James Brown's mansion."

"So, did you kill James Brown?" asked Laura sharply, frowning. "Tell me the truth, or I'll shoot you."

"Exactly, I killed James Brown," said Bella with hysterical

laughter, stretching out her arms to the ceiling.

Laura and Alex gasped, staring squarely at Bella's face.

"Did Elena assist you in killing Brown?" asked Alex in a strained voice. "Elena told the FBI that she'd heard James Brown say my name before his death. This wasn't true. I was on the yacht."

"No, I tricked Elena. When Elena went to the restroom, I had a chance to shoot James Brown in the drawing room of his mansion," said Bella impishly. "It was so easy to make it look like somebody else's crime. I pre-recorded an AI-generated voice impersonating James Brown on my phone. When I shot him, my phone played James's voice saying, 'STOP, ALEX, I CAN GIVE YOU ANYTHING YOU WANT. STOP, ALEX!!!,' which Elena certainly heard through the wall."

"Then, did you replace the QR code painting with a fake one?" asked Laura acidly, still aiming the gun at Bella's head.

"Exactly," smiled Bella maliciously. "I replaced the QR code painting with a fake one containing a bomb. I hid the real one inside my fake pregnant belly. I knew Elena and Terence would steal the artwork because I let them know the QR code would give access to Steve's PC in his laboratory. Surprisingly, idiot Terence stole it for money. Of course, he didn't notice it was a bomb. As I imagined, Elena killed Terence to get that fake QR code painting containing a bomb," Bella cut her words. Her mirthless laughter echoed in the room.

The digital art of S. L. Babel—or Bella Saba—in the drawing room of James Brown's mansion materialized in Alex's mind. It was an AI-integrated artwork which showed a weird cyborg, using the body parts of the three most recent viewers. The cyborg had James Brown's chubby stomach in a white T-shirt and Laura's legs, as they were the second and third most recent viewers of the art. The cyborg's face, which should have shown the face of the latest viewer, the killer who had entered the drawing room, was smashed by a bullet. With his trembling palm, Alex tapped his own cheek. It was Bella's face shown as the cyborg's face in the digital art painting.

Michael and Anthony, who were wriggling due to their bleeding legs, froze and looked at Bella. Alex bit his lips. *It wasn't Elena who killed James Brown. I should've realized Bella was the murderer much earlier.*

"WE GOTTA EVACUATE RIGHT NOW! THE BOMB IS GONNA EXPLODE!" Susanne Caldwell shouted.

"Shut up, fucking weasel!" Bella snorted. "I won't let it explode. I can control the bomb from my phone."

"Turn off the bomb, right now," said Laura testily, putting her finger on the trigger. "Or I'll shoot your head off."

"Okay," said Bella scathingly, pulling out her phone from the pocket of her fake FBI jacket. Alex stood beside Bella, looking at the screen of her phone. After unlocking her phone with her Touch ID, Bella opened an application. With her left finger, Bella touched a stop button under the tab named "Human Heart Bomb." All of a sudden, the human heart on the table in the drawing room stopped beating. A sigh of relief escaped from the mouths of Michael and Anthony. Susanne Caldwell gave a short shriek and leaned her numb body against the wall.

"Tell me why you killed James Brown now," said Laura jerkily, glowering at Bella and still aiming her gun at her forehead.

"We should evacuate now, Laura, no matter what," mumbled Alex, squinting at Laura. "Even though she turned it off, a bomb is a bomb. It can still explode."

Laura didn't reply. She wasn't willing to lower her gun at all, shouting at Bella. "Tell me why you killed Brown, now!"

"Okay, I'll tell you. But let me begin with the fake pregnancy," said Bella, her dreamy eyes absorbed in the crystal chandelier hung from the ceiling. "I did fake my pregnancy at the auction at Brown's mansion. But I was indeed pregnant several years ago. My baby wasn't born as I had a miscarriage. You know why? The loss of my boyfriend, the father of my baby, caused all the distress. It was Terence Miller who killed my boyfriend, who worked for St. Louis Innovative Medical Center as a research assistant."

"Is your boyfriend named Josh Stevenson?" asked Laura in a measured voice.

"Yes," said Bella, her lips trembling a little.

"You don't look surprised that Laura knew about Josh Stevenson," said Alex hoarsely.

"Because I knew Laura had once covered mysterious murders in St. Louis, including Josh's death," said Bella, her dark eyes glinting. "Before being killed, Josh left me some messages. He seized information about the illegal trading of human organs in Anthony Ross's medical center. Laura, it was me who sent a letter to your office at the *Washington Post*. The picture of a truck filled with cadavers and immigrant children included in the letter was taken by Josh; he secretly sent it to me via email."

Laura swallowed, widening her eyes.

"Josh also learned that Terence sold illegally harvested human organs to pharmaceutical companies owned by James Brown," continued Bella, her vein throbbing violently on her forehead. "Terence killed Josh because he stole secret organ trading data from his laboratory. The FBI did their best to cover this up. You know, this corrupt politician controls the FBI," spat Bella, pointing to Susanne Caldwell trembling in front of her. "I swore I'd take revenge on everybody in the crime ring. All the people in the network must die."

"Why did you choose to act as the digital artist S. L. Babel?" asked Laura in a resolute voice. "You could have chosen another path."

"Creating a successful contemporary artist persona was the easiest way to establish connections with billionaires like James Brown and Michael Perry," said Bella, twisting her lips maliciously. "In fact, years ago, I used a QR code in a painting. I exhibited a painting containing a QR code at Art Basel Miami Beach, which James Brown visited every year. Brown was a passionate art collector and keen on digital art trends. He scanned my work with his phone. I was present and witnessed the moment Brown scanned it, unwittingly downloading virus-loaded files. I managed to hack his phone and gather more evidence of his crimes, then started blackmailing him into paying millions for S. L. Babel's artworks. That's how S. L. Babel rose to fame. A few months later, I had another idea; it would be excellent if S. L. Babel, the most successful digital artist of our time, sent his QR code painting to multibillionaires associated with Brown's criminal dealings, hacking their phones and ultimately bringing them to justice."

"I didn't know anything about the illegal organ trades," moaned

Michael Perry, his face contorted with pain from his bleeding leg.

"It doesn't matter," said Bella coldly. "You invested in James Brown's company and his life-extending technology."

"Who killed Hoyt Pence and the art dealer who sold *Your Clone Will Live After Your Death?*" asked Alex, his voice tinged with anxiety.

"Elena killed them. Anthony Ross, you know all about it, right?" said Bella loudly, eyeing Anthony who writhed on the floor, his leg bleeding profusely. "James Brown failed to buy *Your Clone Will Live After Your Death* at the Christie's auction though this digital screen revealed secrets from Terence Miller's laboratory. Hoyt Pence undoubtedly learned these secrets afterwards. Elena, not only James Brown's secretary but also his hitwoman, assassinated Hoyt Pence and his art dealer. The FBI, under Caldwell's control, covered up these assassinations as accidents. *Your Clone Will Live After Your Death* was returned to Geneva Freeport, and no one dared to purchase this cursed work."

"Technically, Hoyt refused to sell the work when James and I later tried to buy it together," huffed Anthony, grimacing with pain. "There was no other option..."

"No matter what, you're all finished!" Bella roared, stretching her arms toward the ceiling. "S. L. Babel will bring justice to all of you because you financed Terence Miller and James Brown, who killed my sweetheart—the only person I ever truly loved. You know, love is a rare thing on this planet."

"Then why do you want to kill me?" said Laura sharply. "One network predicted that either you or I had to die, but I've never been involved in the human organ trade."

"Firstly, why did you invite Laura to the private auction at James Brown's mansion?" Alex interjected. His eyes scanned the floor-to-ceiling windows where the flashing red lights of police cars swarmed around Central Park, heading toward the penthouse. Alex asked without shifting his gaze. "S. L. Babel was you. So, you were the one who invited Laura, right?"

"Good question," said Bella, a mysterious smile playing on her lips. "Laura, I invited you to the private auction at James Brown's mansion for several reasons. Firstly, I wanted to test your investigative skills as a journalist. I gave you the opportunity to uncover all of James Brown's crimes. I gathered other criminals like Terence, Peter, and Elena for your benefit. Of course, my goal was to have everyone scan the QR code. I've been hacking your phone to track your location and to ensure your death. Do you know why?"

Bella rose to her feet, grabbing her phone from her chest. Cold silence filled the room. The sirens of police cars, the beep of Susanne Caldwell's phone in her jacket, and the rough breaths of the two bleeding billionaires. Laura aimed her gun at Bella, who didn't flinch at all. Licking her lips, Bella spoke in a resonant voice.

"Laura, I want to kill you because you are Steve Campbell's daughter."

Chapter Thirty

FBI agent Sampson Castor stood in front of Michael Perry's penthouse, calling Susanne Caldwell's phone. *We'll finally arrest Alex Hubert and Laura Campbell.* Sampson's delighted voice almost leaked from his throat. However, Caldwell never answered. He pressed his phone to his ear, only hearing an automatic message informing him that Caldwell wasn't available.

Gazing up at the top of the penthouse, Sampson felt his eyes pulsing and beating. The pine trees danced around the balcony outside Michael Perry's penthouse. The wind must be blowing hard around the top floor. He could see two helicopters perched on the helipads above the penthouse. The cockpits reflected the dazzling sun climbing the Manhattan sky. *Hubert and Campbell might escape in one of the helicopters.* Sampson felt his heart race as he swiveled around to face his team, who had emerged from a black FBI vehicle. All the entrances of Michael Perry's building were blocked by police cars, flooding the street with red beacon lights. Sampson pointed to the penthouse, and the other FBI agents gazed at it.

"Send a drone to the penthouse before raiding it," barked Sampson, grabbing his phone and striding toward the glass entrance door of Michael Perry's penthouse. "Send me the real-time video of the drone! I'll watch it from my phone."

"Where are you going, Sampson?" one FBI agent asked as Sampson showed his FBI badge to the doorman at the reception. Sampson never replied. The glass sliding door shut behind him as he ran to a gold-hued elevator door.

~ * ~

"You mean my father did something bad to you or your boyfriend?" asked Laura shrilly, still gripping the gun tightly and glowering at Bella. Beads of sweat trickled down Laura's forehead.

"He did," said Bella coldly, rubbing her eyes as if to dissipate a lingering nightmare. "It was your father who introduced Josh, who was a medical school student, to Terence Miller, the most hideous surgeon on the planet. Everything started from that point."

"My dad didn't know that your boyfriend would be killed," said Laura in a trembling voice. "Also, my dad was forced to work there to protect me."

"Your father surely didn't intend to kill Josh," said Bella, resentment, sadness, and madness in her voice. "In the first place, it was Steve who contacted me after Josh's murder. He felt responsible for letting me know about the truth behind Josh's death. I started planning revenge on James Brown and other cronies with Steve. I pretended to cooperate with him; once I achieved my goal to punish the key figures in the organ trade, I planned to kill Steve. It was actually Steve's idea to use a QR code in artwork to hack these evils' phones. Regarding the QR code painting that James Brown bought, Steve asked me to use a QR code he'd designed himself. He told me the QR code would be a key to solving some mysteries if something happened to him. But I didn't know the details. I linked the URL embedded in the QR code to a website where I would display *The Deathly Network*, printed it out on a canvas, and sent it to Geneva Freeport as a piece of artwork. A new work signed by digital art star S. L. Babel and kept in the tax haven. No art dealers or collectors would doubt its value and marketability."

"So, you used the Geneva Freeport only to make us believe in the value of the artwork," said Alex, biting his lip and feeling his temper rising. Soon, something at the corner of his eye attracted his attention. A black shade floated in the air outside the floor-to-ceiling window. It was a drone. Despite the whining sounds of its blades, nobody else in the penthouse paid attention to it. The drone's camera seemed fixed on Laura's face.

"While I collaborated with Steve, I never forgave him," spat Bella, her face flushing. "Without your father, Laura, Josh couldn't have been lured to Terence Miller's medical center and murdered. When Steve was killed by a hitman hired by James Brown's group, I felt like my prey was stolen. But now his daughter is in front of me."

For a moment, Bella closed her eyes, throwing her limb onto the floor. Her fingers stretched out, losing all strength. In a second, she got up and snatched her phone. When Laura aimed the gun again at her forehead, realizing Bella was playing possum, Bella's thumb touched the screen of her phone. The human-heart-shaped bomb on the table started to throb again. Caldwell screamed hysterically.

"Stop the bomb now!" Laura shouted at Bella, putting her gun to Bella's forehead.

"I can't stop the bomb, actually," said Bella slyly. "The explosion time of the bomb is fixed. I could only stop it for several minutes, but I can't change its explosion time."

"We gotta run away," said Alex, tapping Laura's shoulder. "But it looks like the police blocked all the entry points of this penthouse."

"Bella, you'll also die if the bomb explodes," said Laura flatly.

"I'm not afraid of death," smiled Bella. "Because I know my life is close to the end, no matter what."

"Because you got a heart transplant, right?" said Laura in a quavering voice. "You suffered from cardiomyopathy when you were a kid, right?"

Alex, Michael, and Anthony turned to Laura simultaneously, gazing at her face inquiringly.

"Why do you know that?" Bella frowned, her lips still trembling maliciously.

"One thing you don't know about my dad, Bella," said Laura, pressing her own heart to calm herself. "The QR code Steve provided for you was a key to sign into his Windows PCs. I brought his laptop from his house and managed to log into it, locating one CSV file, which compiled all the surgical data in the medical center. Steve did a heart transplant surgery for you to save your life."

"Then do you still hate Laura's father?" said Alex indignantly. "He saved your life."

"He saved my life once, but then he ended up stealing another life of mine," replied Bella scathingly. "The end comes. Everything has an ending. I know I'm gonna die due to the malfunction of the heart I got. This was a heart from an older woman and every doctor told me I won't survive long. Look at the human heart on the table. The bomb will explode. The world will end soon. It's gonna be the first massacre in Manhattan after 9/11. I can imagine the explosion, soaring flames, and dead corpses buried under the collapsed skyscrapers…"

"Steve didn't just save your life," said Laura emphatically. "He sacrificed the woman he loved to save you."

"What are you saying?" said Bella, her irritated hand tapping the floor. As she stood up, her dark eyes quickly searched for the bomb shaped like a human heart, which was still throbbing among the fake vessels. When her eyes captured the electronic panel displaying "*Artist Bella K. Saba*," a vicious smile flashed on her face. "No matter what, S. L. Babel's last work will explode soon! The explosion and mass murder are the greatest artwork of S. L. Babel! I'll be completing Babel's masterpiece!"

"You have my mother's heart," said Laura in a sharp voice.

A ripple of shock and fear ran through Bella's body. She swiveled around to face Laura, who had been lowering the gun.

"What?" said Bella throatily.

"The CSV file in my dad's laptop also contained information about whose heart was implanted into your body," said Laura in a shaky voice. "My mother left a will, choosing to donate her organs. Steve implanted her heart into your body. Your heart is my mother's. Steve respected the will of his loved one, cutting her body open and implanting her heart into you, who was still a small girl at that time."

The vicious smile faded from Bella's face. She flinched and gave a shuddering gasp. Her eyes rotated for seconds as if they were taken apart from her body and then rested on her own body reflected in the corner of the shattered mirror on the wall. Bella's hands caressed her stomach and climbed up to her chest. Heaving a deep breath, she turned around and strode to the table. The drone was floating in the air outside the floor-to-ceiling window, its camera tilting toward Bella's face. Bella didn't glance at the drone at all. She snatched up the human-heart-shaped device. Fake blood trickled down her arm to the floor. All the others in the room froze, gazing at Bella with frightened looks. Bella closed her eyes and kissed the human heart. The droplet of fake blood dyed her lips fiery red.

The FBI is coming, Alex thought, shooting a glance at the drone flying outside the windows. *Or the bomb may explode before they come.*

Bella turned around with the human heart artwork in her hands, silently roaming toward the corridor outside the drawing room.

"Where are you going?" asked Laura huffily. Her gun was completely lowered, facing the floor. She trotted to the corridor, following Bella.

Bella didn't reply. Reaching the end of the corridor, she pressed the button to open the elevator doors.

"Where are you going, Bella?" shouted Laura again, her voice echoing in the corridor.

"Don't chase her," Alex grabbed her arms, holding her back. "She has the bomb. We must stay away from her."

The elevator doors slammed shut. It climbed up toward the helipad.

~ * ~

FBI agent Sampson Castor stood in the shadow behind one of the helicopters on the helipad. He was staring at the screen of his phone, silently observing the live videos sent from the drone. Scratching his head, Sampson tried to understand what he'd seen in the video. Facial recognition systems had identified all the people in Michael Perry's penthouse. There was a dead body lying in the corner of the drawing room. He was Jack Bazin, a famous art dealer in New York City. Some art-related deal must've taken place. Alex Hubert occasionally glanced at the drone, noticing its presence. Nonetheless, he didn't attempt to run away. Laura Campbell lowered her gun after aiming it at the brunette woman in the fake FBI jacket in front of her for a long time. It was art blogger, Bella Saba. *Why is she there, disguised as an FBI agent? Wasn't she pregnant?* Lifting a human-heart-shaped object toward her head, Bella kissed it. The bleeding billionaires, Michael Perry and Anthony

Ross, were trembling near the wall, casting anxious eyes at her. Congresswoman Susanne Caldwell was shuddering in the shards of the mirrors. Caldwell should've told me the location of this auction much earlier. With the human heart object in her hands, Bella Saba disappeared into the corridor. Laura was about to chase her, but Alex held her back. Laura tried to break free from Alex's hold, but Alex stood to obstruct the door to the corridor. They started to argue. Laura slapped Alex's face, but Alex didn't budge and prevented her from leaving the drawing room. Laura Campbell dropped the gun onto the floor, covering her eyes filled with tears.

Taking out another phone from the back pocket of his pants, he called his colleague. "Raid the penthouse right now! Laura Campbell dropped her weapon," said Sampson quietly. "Make sure you don't shoot anybody. Congresswoman Susanne Caldwell is inside."

Sampson suddenly turned off his phone, looking around. The entrance door to the helipad opened. Somebody got off the elevator that had arrived at the helipad. Bella Saba in the FBI jacket, who had been in Michael Perry's penthouse, was walking toward the other helicopter with the bloody human heart object in her hands. Sampson stepped out of the shade under the helicopter, speaking to her in a crisp voice.

"How are you, Ms. Saba? Are you gonna fly the helicopter?"

Bella didn't reply. While she was walking to the helicopter, the human-heart-shaped bomb was throbbing in her hand. She planted her foot on the edge of the cockpit and slid open the door.

"What are you holding?" asked Sampson, frowning at the bloody, human-heart-like object in Bella's hand. Sampson was touching the holster around his waist.

"This is my piece of artwork, sir," said Bella sarcastically, putting the fake human heart on the copilot seat. "I asked an art dealer to bring this to Michael Perry and his friends. But nobody was willing to buy this human heart."

Bella started the engine. Pulling a lever, the blades of the helicopter started to rotate.

Sampson winced and averted his eyes from the helicopter. The window of the cockpit reflected the dazzling sun. Covering his bearded chin with his palm, he mulled over the situation for a moment. According to the video from the drone, the QR code painting was still in Michael Perry's penthouse. It was somewhat similar to—or maybe identical to— S. L. Babel's QR code painting, which Susanne Caldwell was searching for. *Did this brunette woman ask Jack Bazin to bring a human-heart-like artwork to the two multibillionaires? If the QR code painting in the drawing room was indeed S. L. Babel's, the human heart artwork must be as worthy as the QR code painting. Otherwise, it wouldn't make sense that the multibillionaires took the time to look at the artwork. Bella said that the human heart is her piece of artwork.* Feeling his heart race, Sampson looked at the cockpit. *What if this woman was S. L. Babel, bringing back her own artwork in the helicopter? She must've come to Michael Perry's penthouse in the helicopter to avoid the public's gaze.*

"Are you an artist?" Sampson shouted at the top of his lungs as the whining of the helicopter's blades erupted.

"Yes," answered Bella loudly, putting on the sunglasses. The helicopter started to float.

Sampson couldn't hear her voice but saw her nod.

"You're S. L. Babel, right?" Sampson Castor shouted back and unholstered his gun as the violent wind produced by the helicopter's blades pushed him back. "My mission is to identify and kill S. L. Babel."

"Yes, I am," Bella roared, flying the helicopter upward. But her voice was drowned out by the whining blades of the helicopter. "I'm gonna show you the masterpiece of S. L. Babel!"

Sampson started to shoot at the engine of the helicopter. However, the turbulent wind under the helicopter's blades made him stumble. The bullets only grazed the bottom of the helicopter. Bella's helicopter drew a huge curve in the air, flying toward Central Park.

~ * ~

When the FBI agents raided Michael Perry's penthouse, Alex Hubert and Laura Campbell stood beside the swimming pool on the balcony, gazing at the sky above the lake in Central Park. Despite the FBI agents' shouts and guns aimed at them, the two suspects wanted for the murder of James Brown didn't turn around. As the helicopter ascended vertically toward the sun, Laura Campbell strode to the handrail at the edge of the balcony, letting out a cry. Alex pulled her back just as a deafening explosion erupted in the sky, shaking all the buildings in Manhattan. Their ears rang, and the air around them grew uncomfortably warm.

Fire and sparks spiraled, engulfing the helicopter. Debris from the explosion rotated in the air, flames forming a red, heart-shaped cloud that pulsed several times. Like graffiti melting in rain, the burning wreckage of the helicopter slowly descended toward the lake.

Both Alex and Laura felt their phones vibrating. Laura, tears streaming down her face, covered her eyes with her hands and didn't answer. As the FBI agents reached the balcony, armed and kicking open the sliding door, Alex picked up his phone.

"Drop your weapon!"

At the FBI agent's command, Alex dropped his phone onto the floor. It hit the edge of a rose vase and bounced into the swimming pool on the balcony. Its screen was displaying the website embedded in the QR code painting. The entire network was obliterated by the explosive fire on screen. Alex's phone sank to the bottom of the pool, its screen gradually fading to black.

Chapter Thirty-one

"NYPD finally identified and revealed the identity of the mysterious digital artist S. L. Babel, who exploded a bomb in a helicopter above Central Park three days ago," said the Fox News anchorwoman smoothly. The video of the helicopter's explosion played next to her face. Red letter captions appeared at the bottom of the screen: ALEX HUBERT AND LAURA CAMPBELL ABSOLVED OF MURDER CHARGE.

"S. L. Babel was a female software engineer from St. Louis, Missouri, Bella Saba. This deceased woman is now the suspect for the murders of pharmaceutical titan James Brown and others. According to NYPD's press conference, billionaire Michael Perry saw Bella Saba admit her murder in front of them. We had an interview with the *Washington Post* journalist Laura Campbell, who was wrongly charged with the crime but courageously pursued the real murderer."

The screen switched to a recorded video. Laura Campbell, in a black suit, stood on the street near Michael Perry's penthouse. Although three days had passed, police cars still surrounded the building. The American flag installed at the entrance fluttered in the breeze. Laura's eyes were riveted to the top of the penthouse, her long, brown hair blowing in the wind. The same Fox News anchor held a mic to her mouth.

"Why did you visit Michael Perry's penthouse that day?" the anchor asked in a high-pitched voice.

"What the public doesn't know is," said Laura, a mischievous smile spreading across her face, "there are secret auctions of expensive artworks for billionaires. Artworks fly to the wealthiest people on the planet. But as a journalist who doesn't have billions of dollars, I couldn't wait until artworks flew to me. It's impossible. That's why I flew to the works of S. L. Babel—or Bella Saba—to solve all the mysteries."

The Fox News anchor frowned for a moment and then quickly

asked, "What kind of artwork did you see in Michael Perry's penthouse?"

"There were four pieces, including the explosion of the helicopter," said Laura, ruffling her hair with her finger. "I'll let you all know about them in my upcoming book."

"What do you think was Bella Saba's motive?" asked the anchor huffily.

"Revenge," said Laura tartly.

"Revenge on who?"

"An organized crime ring involved in illegal human organ trades," replied Laura, her eyes now staring squarely at the camera. "A famous and powerful politician, who could be the next president of the USA, controls this crime group. I know the FBI wants to sweep this under the rug. I'll never let them get away with this heinous crime. I will reveal all of it later in my upcoming book."

Laura's face, filled with a victorious smile, suddenly froze. Her hair, which had been dancing in the sky, seemed petrified. The wind around her died out. The American flag near the entrance of Michael Perry's penthouse stopped fluttering, looking as if wires inside the cloth made the artificial wrinkles. The Fox News anchor also froze, her mic still held up to Laura's chin.

Alex had touched the "Stop" button on his iPhone. Interrupting the interview video, he exited full screen mode. Fox News had posted the video of the interview with Laura Campbell this morning, along with the latest article about the helicopter explosion above Central Park in New York City. Scrolling down the news article, Alex saw the title of another section: SENATOR SUSANNE CALDWELL PRESENT IN THE MURDER SCENE OF ART DEALER JACK BAZIN. THE FBI HAS NEVER REVEALED WHY.

"Hi Alex," said Laura cheerfully, returning to their table from the restroom. Turning off his phone, Alex looked up at Laura. She gently smiled, pulled out her chair, and sat down.

Alex and Laura were on a dinner cruise, sitting at a table next to the floor-to-ceiling window. The sun was sinking, a red veil dancing in the sky. As the cruise made a graceful tack in the Upper New York Bay, the Statue of Liberty rotated across the window. Both Alex and Laura fell silent, looking at their empty wine glasses, which reflected the Statue of Liberty. Gradually, it became smaller and smaller. The cruise was heading back to the harbor. A waitress approached their table, pouring white wine into their glasses. Their dishes were completely empty.

When the cruise reached the Hudson River, Alex's foot touched Laura's under the table.

"Shall we go outside?" Laura crooned.

As they went out to the deck with wine glasses in their hands, the cool breeze surrounded them.

"What's this?" asked Laura, pointing to the briefcase Alex held with his free hand.

"S. L. Babel's QR code painting. NYPD returned it to me this morning," said Alex, opening the briefcase and taking out the painting. "I wanted to give this to you. This must be useful for your book project, right?"

"Do you think the QR code painting is still worth millions?" said Laura casually, gazing at the lit-up skyscrapers in Manhattan.

"Probably not," said Alex, clutching the handrail on the starboard. "The artist's identity is no longer a secret. Nobody can blackmail billionaires and force them to offer exorbitant bids for her works in auctions. This is nothing but a QR code."

Laura's eyes fell onto the QR code painting in Alex's hands.

"Are you giving this to me?" asked Laura.

"Yes," said Alex.

Laura received it, carefully scanning the QR code and S. L. Babel's sign at the bottom for a while. After taking a picture of the entire canvas, she threw it into the ocean.

Alex gasped.

"It's just a QR code, isn't it?" said Laura mischievously.

"It is," answered Alex, his hand lightly touching Laura's waist from behind. Laura didn't move, looking at the harbor where the cruise was heading back. Their shoulders overlapped closely. Their cruise was coming to an end.

"What's that gorgeous yacht?" asked Laura curiously, pointing to the huge yacht.

A two-hundred-sixty-foot yacht with a helipad and an oval swimming pool on the deck was moored at a pier.

"I know the yacht, Laura," said Alex softly. "I'll need to take the yacht to go to Europe."

"Why?" said Laura, raising her curvy eyebrow.

"It's my billionaire client's yacht," said Alex, staring into Laura's eyes. "The yacht is filled with his art collections. My client invites his wealthy art collector friends and gallerists from around the world to his cruise to showcase his artwork on the yacht."

"When will you come back to the US?" said Laura in an anxious tone.

"I don't know," Alex shrugged. "But you can come with me on the cruise. I can talk to my client to reserve another room for you. The yacht will arrive in Monaco in two weeks."

Laura fell silent, her eyes circling around the sky where sparse stars had started to shine.

"No, I can't," said Laura in a silky voice, smiling. "I gotta finish my book before discovering another crime ring on the next yacht. Good luck, Alex."

The bow of the cruise ship hit the tip of the wharf.

About the Author

Aiden Dufort is an author of mystery, thriller, and science fiction who currently resides in St. Louis, Missouri. A polyglot fluent in three languages, Aiden enjoys writing stories in English, exploring themes of contemporary art, capitalism, science, technology, and the American Dream.

Aiden's first book, *The Magic Tower* (a short story collection published by "Close To The Bone", explores the dark passions and crimes lurking in diverse fields, from art and jewelry dealing to sports, science, and technology.

The Deathly Network, published by Rogue Phoenix Press, is a plot-driven mystery featuring the enigmatic digital artist S. L. Babel and is his debut novel.

Aiden is now working on his second mystery and science fiction novel, *The Ark on the Map*. This work introduces a fictitious bio-artist, Apollo Barton, who incorporates cloning into contemporary art.